The Reprisal

Robert Cort

Published by Clink Street Publishing 2025

Copyright © 2025

First edition.

ISBN
paperback - 978-1-915785-73-2
ebook - 978-1-915785-74-9

To Robert and Sarah, out of my life
but not out of my thoughts.

ALSO WRITTEN BY ROBERT CORT

THE IAN CAXTON THRILLER SERIES
Volume 1 – The Opportunity
Volume 2 – The Challenge
Volume 3 – The Decision
Volume 4 – The Gamble
Volume 5 – The Result

OTHER THRILLERS
The Lady Pirates

www.robertcort.net

Chapter 1

Richard Caxton, Ian's father, had just entered the lounge and was checking the time on his wristwatch. It was just after six o'clock. "Damn," he said to himself, "I'm missing the evening news." Watching *The Six O'clock News* on television was a habit with Richard. He liked to catch up on what was happening in the world.

He pressed the remote and sat down on the sofa. A few seconds later, the first picture he saw was of a multi-vehicle pile-up on a motorway. He turned up the volume.

The commentator was describing the huge crash that had occurred at about 4.30 that afternoon. "It occurred in dense fog," he was reporting, "between junctions 23 and 22 on the southbound carriageway of the M1. It's an extremely serious accident and first estimates say there are numerous casualties. Many people have either died or been injured. This section of the motorway cuts through the dense Charnwood Forest, so it happened at a particularly difficult section for the rescue services to reach. The police have just closed the northbound carriageway at junction 22, so they, the fire brigade and ambulances, from both Derby and Leicester, can attend. Two rescue helicopters have just landed…"

"Oh, my goodness. Elizabeth!" shouted Richard.

Ian's mother immediately came into the lounge. "What's

that?" she asked, looking at the television whilst rubbing her hands on a tea towel. She'd been preparing dinner.

"A big pile-up on the M1. Somewhere in Derbyshire. Lots of fog in the area."

"Oh dear. Anybody hurt?"

"Man reckons lots of people have died or been injured. People drive far too close and fast nowadays, especially in fog!"

Elizabeth sat down next to her husband. She had a worried look on her face. "I do hope nobody we know is involved!"

THREE HOURS EARLIER

It was just after 2.40pm when Ian Caxton parked his car in the large multi-storey car park in Derby's city centre. Using the car's satnav, he estimated it was about a ten-minute walk to the Derby Museum & Art Gallery.

He and his wife, Emma, arrived in reception at 2.56pm.

As they were expected, they were promptly escorted through the museum and into The Joseph Wright Study Room. There, Lucy Johnson, the curator, and an elderly gentleman were looking at one of the display screens. Lucy was smartly dressed in a grey suit and cream blouse. When she looked up and spotted Ian and Emma walking towards her, she smiled and spoke to the gentleman. Both greeted the new arrivals, and after Ian and Emma were introduced to Mr. Bristow, they all made their way into Lucy's office.

Emma guessed Mr. Bristow was in his late 70s. Slim, well-dressed in a smart tweed overcoat, he had an air of confidence that reminded her of Ian's father.

"Welcome back to Derby and our museum," said Lucy, with a smile. "I hope you had a lovely time in the Peak District."

Emma gave a brief summary of their visits and finished

by saying they were also going home with a bag full of Bakewell puddings for the freezer. Everybody laughed.

Ian's Joseph Wright painting was displayed on the same easel where he'd placed it three days ago. He'd only intended for the museum to give their opinion of the picture's authenticity. However, Lucy had shown it to Mr. Bristow, an avid collector of Wright's work. He'd immediately decided he wanted to add it to his collection and had offered £125,000. Ian had agreed to the price and was both surprised and thrilled.

They all walked over to inspect it.

"It's an excellent painting," said Mr. Bristow, who then pointed to the restored area. "I gather there's been a small amount of restoration work, but it's obviously been done by a professional. Someone who cares and knows what they're doing. Doesn't distract from the painting's quality, or its value, in my opinion."

Ian couldn't identify Mr. Bristow's accent, but there was just a hint of one. "The restorer is Peter Jarrett. He used to work for Sotheby's when I worked there. He now works on his own and has a long waiting list of clients."

"Well, young man, here's your banker's draft for 125,000 pounds. Don't spend it all at once!"

Everyone smiled.

"Thank you, sir," said Ian, glancing at the draft. "I hope the painting gives you many years of pleasure."

Mr. Bristow laughed. "Lucy here, and this museum, they're the ones that'll get the pleasure... when I've popped my clogs. They'll inherit all of my Joseph Wright collection."

"Not for many years yet, we hope, Ernest," said Lucy, with feeling.

"Are you people going back to London tonight?" asked Mr. Bristow. He had a more serious expression on his face.

"Yes, we've got plans for the weekend. Mind, we want

to come back here again in the summer. It's a lovely part of the world."

"Travelling by car?" Mr. Bristow's question had a slightly more unsettling tone.

"Yes," said Ian, hesitantly. "We've parked in the multi-storey. Travelling back via the M1."

"Just be careful. The weatherman has predicted more fog between here and Leicestershire tonight. Could be a pea-souper."

"Thanks for the warning. I think we'd better make a move."

They all shook hands and said their goodbyes. Ian and Emma left the museum and headed back towards the car park.

The predicted thick fog was already rolling in.

Chapter 2

"This fog is getting much thicker," announced Emma as they walked along the pavement. She was worried about them having to endure the long drive home in such horrible weather. "It's also damp and bitterly cold."

Ian pushed up the collar of his overcoat.

After a few minutes, Ian noticed they were walking past the front of the hotel they'd stayed at four nights ago. He stopped and pensively looked at the entrance. "Maybe we should see if they've got a room for tonight. Another 24 hours wouldn't interfere too much with our plans."

"It'll be a lot safer than driving home in this fog," replied Emma, gently pulling at Ian's arm and leading him up the three concrete steps.

Ian pushed open the dark blue wooden door. The reception area was noticeably warmer and had the same welcoming atmosphere as before.

"Good evening, sir," greeted the friendly young receptionist, as Ian and Emma walked over towards the reception desk. "Can I help you?"

"Hello… Julie," responded Ian, reading her name badge as he rubbed his cold hands together. "We stayed here four nights ago and were wondering if you had a vacancy for this evening?"

The receptionist pressed some keys on her computer. "I'm sorry, I'm afraid we're fully booked… except for one single."

"Oh," said Ian, looking at Emma. She had a dismayed expression on her face, having just spotted a lovely log fire burning in the lounge.

Ian pondered on the situation before asking the receptionist, "Are there any other local hotels you could recommend?"

"There's 'The George'. It's about a five-minute walk. They usually have some vacancies. However, the main problem this evening is there's a big conference starting tomorrow at the Council House. My guess is most local hotels are going to be fully booked."

"Okay, thanks," replied Ian. He stepped away from the reception desk and moved over to a toasty warm radiator Emma was warming herself by. "There's only one single room. Where are you going to sleep?" he said, grinning.

"Very funny. I was thinking you'll have to sleep in the car!"

Ian took a deep sigh. "So, what are we going to do now?"

"I don't know," responded Emma, staring through the open lounge door. Her attention was still being drawn to the inviting log fire. "I really don't want to travel home in this weather. It's far too dangerous."

Whilst they pondered on the problem, another woman was speaking with the receptionist. Ian could hear Julie explaining their plight.

After a moment, the woman strode over to join them. "Hello, I'm Debbie Taylor, the manager. I gather you're looking for a room for the night."

"Yes," responded Ian. He hoped this was going to be good news.

"I've just taken a cancellation, a double room. The guests cannot get here due to the fog. Julie can book you in now."

Ian and Emma had relieved expressions on their faces as they followed Debbie back to the reception desk.

Julie had heard the discussions and was already tapping keys on her computer.

"Thanks very much," said Ian to Debbie. "You've saved us from a precarious drive back to London in this fog."

Debbie smiled. "You're welcome. Enjoy your stay," she said before walking back towards the manager's office.

Ian explained to Julie that they'd stayed in room 204 four nights ago. Julie checked her computer and transferred the same details to tonight's booking: room 208.

Once booked in, Ian informed Emma he was going back to the multi-storey to collect his car. He'd park their car in the hotel's car park and bring their bags up.

About an hour later, after they'd unpacked their bags, they were sitting facing the warming fire in the cosy lounge, drinking a hot pot of tea.

Whilst Emma stared at the flickering yellow flames, Ian was eavesdropping on a conversation between a group of four people sitting directly behind him. His curiosity had been aroused when one of the women mentioned a major vehicle crash on the motorway.

"There were police cars and ambulances all over the place," said the woman. She had a raised and commanding voice. "It was total chaos. Jeremy and I, well, we really didn't think we would get here. Isn't that right?"

Ian guessed the woman was asking Jeremy to confirm her statement, but the next voice he heard was the same woman. "We were diverted. God knows where! Good job we had the satnav, otherwise we might still be lost somewhere in the back of beyond."

Ian heard a man's voice ask a question, but couldn't make out the exact words. He leaned forwards and whispered to Emma. "Did you hear that?"

"Mmm," Emma whispered back. "I think everyone in the lounge heard her!"

Ian smiled, then became more serious. "A major crash on the motorway. We could have been involved in that."

Emma took a deep breath. "A great decision of mine, then, to stay here tonight!"

Later that same evening, Ian and Emma were back in their room watching *The 10 O'Clock News* on the television.

The programme was dominated by the crash on the M1 motorway. The commentator was describing the multi-vehicle pile-up. "It occurred this afternoon, at about 4.30, between junctions 23 and 22 on the southbound carriageway of the M1. Dense fog had been a major factor and has continued to hamper emergency services all evening. It's an extremely serious accident and at least 15 people have died; many more are seriously injured. This section of the motorway cuts through the dense Charnwood Forest area, so it occurred at a particularly difficult section for the rescue services to reach. Both carriageways are closed and the Leicestershire and Derby fire brigades and ambulances have been working tirelessly all evening. Rescue helicopters have also been involved, when the weather allowed. The motorway is expected to remain closed until further notice. I've got Derbyshire's Chief Constable, John Atkins, standing next to me. I'll ask him about the current situation…"

"Oh, wow!" cried out Emma, staring at the screen. She was startled to see the carnage.

Ian turned down the television's volume and spoke to Emma with an alarmed edge to his voice. "4.30! That's about the time we should have been passing that spot."

"Oh, Ian! It's all so horrible."

"I know. We've been unbelievably lucky."

Chapter 3

Derbyshire, and the East Midlands, was not an area Ian knew. He rarely needed to travel to this part of the country. So, the next morning, after checking out of the hotel, he and Emma were sitting in his car, having just reset the satnav. Ian had inserted their home postcode and was now waiting for the device to programme an alternative route avoiding the closed section of the motorway. A few seconds later, the new route was displayed. It was just after 10.30am.

Although the previous day's dense fog had abated, there was still a murky gloom as Ian steered their car out of the hotel's car park.

About 15 minutes into the journey, they joined the southbound A50 trunk road. The traffic was busy and moving at an unusually slow pace. News of yesterday's crash and today's gloomy weather were probably making drivers more cautious.

Ian continued to slavishly follow the satnav directions, changing roads when instructed. Neither he nor Emma had a clue where they were; they just hoped the satnav knew what it was doing. Eventually, Emma spotted a sign for the M1 motorway, junction 21. They both gave a relieved cheer and Ian happily drove the car towards the southbound entrance.

The weather conditions were still dismal and overcast, but nothing like the 'pea-souper' of yesterday. Drizzly rain and spray, being thrown up by the vehicles driving ahead, was now blurring Ian's view. He switched on the windscreen wipers.

They were both still a little unnerved after yesterday's ordeal, and Ian decided to keep the car's speed below the motorway's limit. He wanted to get home quickly… but safely.

They arrived home just after 5.30pm. Emma had fallen asleep for the last hour, so when Ian turned his car into their driveway, she awoke with a start.

"Oh, wonderful," she announced, as soon as she recognised where they were. She stretched her arms and stared out through the side window. The lawn was a little longer, but otherwise everything in the garden appeared to be the same. Mind, they'd only been away for a handful of days, but to Emma, it had seemed like an age.

Ian parked in front of the large double garage and switched off the engine. "I could do with a large glass of wine," he said, rubbing his tired eyes.

Emma unclipped her seat belt and opened the passenger door. "Okay, I'll leave you to bring in the bags. I'll deal with the wine."

Five minutes later, the car was locked and Ian had deposited the holdalls in the hallway. He wandered into the kitchen and immediately spotted two large glasses of white wine on the breakfast bar. Emma was staring at the answerphone.

"Have we got any messages?" asked Ian, picking up both glasses and joining Emma.

Emma accepted the glass he was offering. "Yes. My mum's left a message, but there's also a strange one from Vic. I'll play it again. See if you can understand it."

Ian took a sip of his wine whilst Emma pushed the 'play' button. Immediately, Viktor's unmistakable voice said, "Hi, Ian... and Emma. It's Vic. Look, I have a bit of a problem. Well, actually, it's Penny's problem really. Not a problem as such, but more of an issue, I think. I don't want to say any more... not over the phone, but can you give me a buzz, please? Hope all's okay with you both. Cheers for now. Vic."

Ian stared at Emma. "Mmm," he said, with a quizzical look on his face. "Play it again."

Emma pressed the 'play' button again and both listened to the message once more.

"I'll give him a ring in the morning. I wonder why he didn't ring my mobile," said Ian, taking another sip of his wine.

"Maybe he did and we were out of range." Then, after sipping her own wine, she said, "The message was left three days ago. We were probably in... Matlock then."

Ian nodded and thought. "Yes, that's true. Anyway... I'm starving. What do you fancy for dinner?"

The next morning, Ian was sitting at his desk. He had just dialled Viktor's mobile number.

"Hi, Ian, thanks for coming back," responded Viktor. "Have you been away? I tried your mobile."

Ian explained where he and Emma had been and, also, about the sale of his Joseph Wright painting. He then asked Viktor what the problem he'd mentioned in his message was.

"I don't want to discuss it on the phone. Can we meet up? I can come down to Esher... or, how about you and Emma come to us for dinner? You'd both be welcome to stay overnight."

"Emma's not been to your apartment, so that would be great. She'll really be impressed. When were you thinking of?"

"Er. Well, I'll need to speak to Pen first. Can I drop you an email?"

"Of course. I'll need to talk to Emma, too. So, your problem's not urgent?"

"Well… yes… and er, no. Sorry, Ian, you'll understand better when we meet face-to-face."

"Okay. I'll wait for your email." Ian switched off the call. He was none the wiser, but it certainly sounded like there was a problem… and Penny too. How was she involved? Was it something to do with her and Sotheby's?

Chapter 4

Ian received Viktor's email, and after a bit of to-ing and fro-ing, a date and a time for the dinner date was agreed.

Emma had been surprised, and a little excited, when Ian told her of Viktor and Penny's invitation. She knew Ian had visited their apartment before and, also, remembered he'd told her they lived in a penthouse apartment in the London Docklands area. He'd also told her of the amazing views from the lounge and dining-room windows. In addition, there was access to a roof-top garden which gave more far-reaching, 360-degree views.

Even so, Emma was still bemused by Viktor's earlier answerphone message. She wondered what it really meant. Was Penny in trouble, or was there a problem with her and Viktor's marriage? She couldn't see why, because they'd always seemed very close. It didn't sound like there was a business issue either. If there was, why had she been invited? No, it was all a little odd and certainly mysterious. Even Ian said he hadn't a clue.

Was it all just a storm in a teacup... or was it something much more serious?

It was a wet and sunless day when Ian and Emma caught the 2.32pm train from Esher to London Waterloo. Neither fancied another trip in the car, especially driving in such grisly weather... and into London. They were sitting in the First-Class carriage, and Ian was staring at the passing grey countryside. He was thinking about the apartment in Monaco, and how much warmer and brighter it would be over there. He hated the British weather, especially the seemingly endless, depressing and dismal winters. We really need to get back into our old routine of frequent visits... and indeed, more holidays in general, he thought.

"I've just been looking at the weather forecast for London tomorrow," Emma said, interrupting his train of thought and placing her mobile on the table. "It's suggesting today will be the last day of this dreary weather. Tomorrow is likely to be colder, but sunnier, with a clear blue sky."

"Okay. That's a bit better," replied Ian, now looking across at her. "At least you'll be able to see the great views from Vic's apartment."

Now that Emma had obtained Ian's full attention, she leaned forward and asked, "Do you still not know what Vic's message was about?"

Ian shook his head and grimaced. "No. It must be something unusual, Vic's not usually that evasive. We'll just have to wait. My main concern is him saying it was more of a problem for Penny. Makes me think it may have something to do with Sotheby's."

Ah, thought Emma. She knew Ian was still emotionally connected to his former PA. They'd worked together for several years and Penny had even asked him to be her 'father of the bride' on her wedding day. Penny's own father had passed away a few years earlier. He'd also pushed Sotheby's board to promote her to replace him when he'd handed in his letter of resignation. Although Penny was not as experienced as others, the board did concur with Ian's recommendation and she was duly promoted.

However, Emma still occasionally wondered if their relationship was more than that, but she didn't have any evidence for this thought... it was just a niggly feeling... a woman's intuition? However, maybe Ian only saw Penny as the daughter he'd always longed for. She knew he loved and cherished their son, Robert, but...

"I've just been talking to you," said Ian, waving a hand in front of Emma's face.

"Sorry, Ian. I was miles away. What did you say?"

"I was saying we ought to go back to Monaco... or, maybe on holiday, somewhere warmer."

Emma was now registering Ian's words. "Yes, yes, it would be nice to have a few days in the sunshine. Where are you suggesting?"

"There's always the apartment, but otherwise, I've not got anywhere specific in mind. Just to get away from this depressing weather."

"Okay. Let's talk about it when we return home."

The train started to slow down and Ian looked out through the window. "I reckon we're about five minutes away. Better tidy up."

Fifteen minutes later, they were sitting in a taxi, heading towards Docklands. Ian had given the driver Viktor's address but knew, from his last visit, that they'd have to walk the last few yards as there was a 'pedestrian only' walkway at the side of the apartment building.

Ian also telephoned Viktor and told him where they were. He responded by saying he'd meet them in reception and arrange their security passes.

Chapter 5

As Ian and Emma approached the main entrance to the apartment block, the two large glass doors automatically opened. Emma led the way through but immediately stopped when she saw the huge atrium area opening out in front of her. The vast space was enclosed by a modern steel frame construction, at least two stories in height. Two sides were solid, cream-painted walls, adorned with four large modern art pictures. The remaining two sides were dominated by large, floor-to-ceiling windows, allowing lots of natural light to flood in. Even with today's gloomy conditions, only one of the three large chandeliers was required to be illuminated.

Both stood on the light grey marble flooring, whilst Emma pointed to the property's mixed collection of unusual and intriguing features.

"Admiring our wonderful building, are you?" announced Viktor, as he strode towards them.

"Hi, Vic," responded Ian, shaking Viktor's hand. He'd seen it all before, but was still impressed. "Emma wants to move in!"

Ignoring Ian's comment, Emma stepped forward and Viktor gave her a brief hug. "Wow, Vic, this is wonderful."

"We still think it's great. Wait till you see the views from the apartment windows. Mind, today, it's not so good. Hopefully tomorrow will be better. Anyway, here are your security passes, so if you follow me, I'll fly you to the moon!"

As they walked towards the security desk, Emma looked at Ian with a quizzical look. Ian was carrying their overnight holdall bags and leaned over to whisper, "He said that to me the last time I was here."

Emma was none the wiser.

Once through security, Viktor led them to a bank of elevators. They only had to wait a few seconds before one of the doors opened and they all stepped in.

Viktor pressed the illuminated button next to the number 29, which Emma noticed was on the top floor. The doors closed, and the elevator quickly, but very smoothly, accelerated upwards. Emma could feel the speed of the ascent through her legs. After three floors, the subtle blue lighting suddenly changed and daylight appeared. Emma turned around and realised it was a glass-sided elevator, which now gave murky views of the neighbouring Dockland skyscraper buildings. As the elevator rose higher, the River Thames became visible. Unfortunately, the thick low clouds were restricting the distant views.

The elevator slowed down and then stopped. The doors opened, and Viktor led the way along a brightly decorated corridor until they came to a door displaying the number 29d.

"This is our home," said Viktor. He unlocked and pushed open the door.

Emma and Ian were led across the hallway and into the lounge area.

"This is fabulous, Vic," said Emma, walking towards the pair of large windows to take in the view.

"You can usually see for miles... well, on a clear day," announced Viktor, walking across to join Emma. "Hopefully, you'll get the benefit tomorrow."

Ian hadn't spoken until now. He wanted Emma to get the same fabulous first impression he'd experienced. "Where's Penny?"

"Ah, yes. That's part of what we wanted to talk to you about. She'll be back shortly. She's over at Jonathan Northgate's apartment."

Emma stared at Viktor and then at Ian. She knew all about Ian's bitter rivalry with Jonathan Northgate. At least the bits he'd told her about.

"Northgate!" exclaimed Ian, putting down the two overnight bags. His face showed immediate alarm. "What's she doing there!?"

Ever since these arch-rivals had confronted each other earlier in Ian's career, in New York, Jonathan Northgate had been Ian's nemesis… and he was still determined to get his revenge. Ian had warned Penny the guy was useless, all hot air… but, nevertheless, dangerous and ruthless. When Ian had turned down the CEO role at Sotheby's and resigned from the company, to his shock and horror, Sotheby's had then turned to Northgate as their second choice.

"Let's wait until she returns," responded Viktor. "She'll be able to explain the problem far better than me. In the meantime, I'll brew us a pot of coffee."

As Viktor walked back towards the hallway, Ian and Emma decided to follow.

When Emma saw the large kitchen area, she immediately noticed the modern, almost showroom, pristine surroundings. "This kitchen is wonderful," she said, surveying the cupboards, cooker, hob and worktops. It reminded her of the apartment in Monaco. "It still looks brand new."

Viktor filled the electric kettle and switched it on. A tray containing a cafetière of ground coffee beans, four mugs and a plate of biscuits, was already sitting on the breakfast bar.

"That's Penny. She insists on everything being clean and tidied away," said Viktor as he walked over to the large American-style fridge-freezer and removed a jug of milk.

Ian smiled. He remembered back to Penny's desk at work. It was always tidy and well organised.

It was at that moment they heard the main door close. Penny walked into the kitchen and gave hugs and kisses to their guests. "Just give me a minute. I want to hang up my coat."

Meanwhile, Viktor poured hot water into the cafetière and picked up the tray. "We'll go into the lounge. It'll be more comfortable to sit and talk in there."

Ian and Emma followed Viktor. Penny soon joined them, and they all sat down.

"Well," said Ian, anxious to know what this mysterious problem was… and why was Penny visiting Northgate's apartment!? "You'd better explain why we're here."

Chapter 6

After Viktor had poured the coffee and everyone had helped themselves to milk, Penny started to explain her situation.

"It all started just over a year ago. Jonathan mentioned that he was living in an apartment in Docklands. I said that was a coincidence as I live here too. We then discovered our apartment buildings are only about 100 metres apart. He told me he was renting and living alone. His American wife and children still live in the family home in Upstate New York. He returns to New York during his holiday leave."

Ian looked intently at Penny as he sipped his coffee. Emma was also staring and wondered what was about to unfold.

After taking a sip of her coffee, Penny continued. "Then, about nine months ago, Jonathan asked me if I would do him a favour. Needless to say, I was a little wary and suspicious. We were getting on well at work, but that's as far as I wanted our relationship to go." Penny looked across at Viktor, who gave her a broad smile.

Emma raised her eyebrows, but said nothing.

"However, it turned out to be quite innocent. He told me that his neighbour had a key to his apartment, and whilst Jonathan visited his family in America, the neighbour visited every other day to feed his collection of tropical fish.

However, this obliging neighbour had just told Jonathan that his employer wanted him to relocate to Paris, so he wouldn't be able to deal with his fish in the future. What Jonathan was asking me, i.e., his favour, was would I pop in and feed the fish whilst he was away? He said it would only be a temporary measure... until he'd found someone else to help on a more permanent basis. Anyway, I agreed... and also thought I might have a sneaky peek at his apartment at the same time. So, on the first visit, I had a nose around and, to my huge surprise, I saw a painting on his lounge wall that I'd seen before... at Sotheby's! I even remembered it had been the responsibility of one of my team, Emily, to prepare it for auction. I checked our files and discovered the picture, which was titled 'Brown Surprise' by Sir Alfred Munnings, had sold for 3.3 million pounds. However, it hadn't been purchased by Jonathan, but by a private buyer in Dubai. So, the question I now asked myself was, is this picture a copy or the original? I read all Emily's notes on the picture. One comment said that on the back of the frame, an old faded auction number 36 was just visible. Sotheby's file also contained photos of both the rear and front of this painting."

"Interesting," murmured Ian to himself.

"The next day, I went back to the apartment. Jonathan was due back in two days' time, so I had to move quickly. This was my last chance. I looked a lot closer at the picture this time, particularly at the rear. The old faded auction number 36 was in exactly the same position as Emily's photograph. Okay, I thought, so maybe this is the original, so what? Maybe Jonathan has a good reason for the painting to be there. Not that I would be brave enough to ask him, having been sneaking around in his lounge!"

"It certainly sounds very 'fishy'," said Ian, with a smirk on his face.

"Ha, ha," responded Emma.

Viktor and Penny both briefly smiled.

"No, in all seriousness," continued Ian, "there could be criminal activity going on." He hoped so and started to wonder how he could find out. He'd give anything to get his revenge on Northgate. A long-awaited reprisal would be so deserving!

Viktor now spoke. "I was wondering if I ought to speak, unofficially, to a policeman I know at the Met, Detective Sergeant Andrew Baker. He works in the Art and Antiques Unit. Anyway, we can talk about that later. Penny's story isn't finished yet." He looked across at Penny, who was drinking the last of her coffee.

"So, I was in a quandary," continued Penny. "After chatting it through with Vic, we decided to leave it for the time being. After all, what could we do? I did, however, say to Jonathan that I didn't mind continuing to look after his fish, if he wanted me to. That way, I could still have legal access to his apartment. He said he hadn't had time to find anyone else, so he jumped at my offer. Then, three weeks ago, he told me he was going back to America for ten days. He gave me his spare key and left last Friday. I called in to the apartment two days later. Another surprise! The painting, which had previously been hanging in the lounge, had gone. It had been replaced by a surreal picture by a modern artist I'd never heard of, Oliver Poulter. This time I took a photo with my mobile and, next morning, checked to see if Sotheby's had been involved... and, yes, we had! I read all our records and the picture's details. Having been painted in 2002, it was auctioned by Ally McLoud's department two months ago. Once again, it was not purchased by Jonathan but by a private buyer, this time in Abu Dhabi. My guess is Jonathan's picture is the original again, but being a modern painting, we can't really check without a full investigation."

"No," said Ian, pondering on the situation.

Penny, Viktor and Emma all stared at Ian, waiting for him to say more.

After a few seconds, he responded, "Penny, can you give me copies of everything you've got on the painting's paperwork? Also, we need to get a duplicate of the apartment's key." There was another short pause before Ian continued, "I don't think we need to involve the police at the moment, Vic. However, your police detective friend may come in useful later. Finally, I need to speak to a colleague none of you will have heard of… and I think it's best if we keep it that way."

Both Penny and Viktor were relieved that Ian had decided to take charge. Emma, however, was far more concerned about what Ian was planning to do… and who, indeed, he would be speaking to. She hoped it wasn't going to be another Andrei-like situation!

Whilst Penny collected the empty coffee mugs, Viktor carried the tray into the kitchen. Emma sat quietly and continued to stare at Ian.

Ian, meanwhile, was pondering on all that he'd heard over the last hour. Yes, he knew this was THE opportunity, maybe the last chance he'd ever have, to finally nail that jumped-up, useless bag of wind. What he would give to see Northgate in the dock, before being sentenced to, what, five, seven or even ten years in prison? If he were the judge, he'd send him down for the rest of his life… and throw away the key!

Chapter 7

Next morning, the weather had improved. The murky, damp atmosphere and heavy clouds of yesterday had disappeared and were replaced by a clear blue sky and a chilly breeze.

When Ian walked into the kitchen, Penny was already there, unloading the dishwasher.

"Morning, Penny," announced Ian, sauntering across to stand nearby. "That was a wonderful meal last evening."

Penny placed some of the plates on the island and looked at Ian. "Thanks. Did you sleep well?"

"Yes, the bed's really comfortable. Didn't wake up once. Can I give you a hand?"

"No, I've nearly finished. However… Okay. You could put the crockery over there on the worktop, please," said Penny, pointing to the area opposite the double oven. "I can then put them straight into the cupboards."

Whilst Ian picked up the pile of plates, he continued talking. "So, how's everything at Sotheby's for you now?"

"The work side's going really well. My team has certainly supported me, which is great. I know you said I was capable of doing the job, but, for me, it was a huge step. For the first six months I didn't think I was going to stick it out. Vic, however, persuaded me to give it more time, and it's worked out fine."

"I'm pleased. I knew you could do the job, but I must admit, I also felt I was leaving you in the lurch, especially when I heard that Northgate had been appointed. I still can't believe the company did that. The guy's a buffoon!"

Penny smiled. "I get on well with him… and he's made a number of successful changes. Maybe he's improved since you worked together in New York."

"Mmm," responded Ian. He wasn't convinced. "Not unless he's had a brain transplant!"

Penny laughed out loud.

"Hello. What's so funny in here then?" Viktor arrived in the kitchen.

"Your high-flying wife has just been telling me about life at Sotheby's."

"And Ian's accused Jonathan of having had a brain transplant!" added Penny, still smirking.

Viktor laughed and then responded, "Maybe he's received one of the Great Train Robbers' brains."

All three now laughed. Then Penny asked Ian where Emma was.

"Last time I saw her, she was still hiding under the duvet. I'll go and see if she's emerged yet." At this Ian walked back towards the guest bedroom.

"Let's have breakfast in the dining room," suggested Viktor. "The island might feel a little cramped for four."

"I agree. We can set it up now. I know Emma was looking forward to seeing the view."

"It might be warm enough to take them up onto the roof garden later. For a short while, at least."

"It looks warmer than it will feel, but yes, we can go up there for a few minutes."

By the time Emma finally appeared, the dining room had been fully prepared for breakfast. Nobody wanted anything cooked, so there was a selection of cereals, yoghurts, fruit and slices of bread waiting to be toasted.

Ian suggested it was like staying at the Savoy.

As soon as Emma saw the sun shining through the window, she dashed over to take in the view. "Wow, Penny... Vic, this is wonderful. You can see for miles. I recognise the Shard... and Tower Bridge."

"From the lounge window," interrupted Viktor, "You can see where the Thames estuary flows into the sea."

"I must see that!"

Ian interrupted, "Can I suggest we eat this wonderful breakfast our hosts have generously prepared for us first?"

"Sorry," said Emma, who immediately sat down. "It really is a bird's-eye view."

"We'll take you up to the roof garden as well. You get a 360-degree perspective from there," said Viktor, pouring himself a glass of orange juice.

"Yes please!" exclaimed Emma. She anticipated it would be an unbelievable vista.

"Unfortunately, there's always a breeze," interrupted Penny, "so it'll probably be too cold to stay there for too long."

"I still want to see it though. I've got a thick coat."

After breakfast they all visited the roof garden. Penny was right, there was a noticeable chilly breeze, but Emma was determined to stay as long as she could. The temperature was certainly cold, but the air was clear and they could see for miles. It felt, thought Emma, like they were standing in the basket of a hot-air balloon, hovering in the sky.

Unfortunately, after about ten minutes, even Emma had to give in and return to the warmth of the apartment.

Viktor made hot coffees, whilst Ian and Emma packed their bags. It was almost time for them to leave. They'd arranged for a taxi to collect them in 45 minutes. There was just time to finalise their discussions on the Northgate paintings situation. Ian promised he'd try to investigate what had happened to the two paintings immediately after they'd been sold at auction. He also told the others that he had a connection in Dubai who would probably help. Finally, he was going to talk with a colleague and arrange for some level of surveillance. However, he wouldn't expand on what this was likely to entail.

Penny had given Northgate's apartment key to Viktor. It was his task to get a copy cut.

When Ian and Emma exited the apartment building, Ian knew his plan of action. He was keen and determined to make sure that Northgate would finally pay for the treatment he'd received whilst they'd been working together in New York.

For Ian, it wasn't enough to see Jonathan Northgate's career come crashing down, he also wanted to witness Northgate's egocentric life being totally ruined!

Chapter 8

In Antigua, May and Oscar were sitting in the kitchen eating breakfast. They'd just returned from their regular early morning swim in the Caribbean Sea. It was just over a year since they were married and six months since all the changes to the villa had been completed. To May, the villa was now more comfortable and, domestically, much more practical. There was a lot more space for all their (her) clothes and a large office from which to run their businesses. Guests were now treated to a welcoming ensuite bedroom and the new double garage provided shelter and security for both their vehicles.

"I'm going to see old Charlie Hall this afternoon," announced Oscar, placing a spoon on his plate after swallowing the last two pieces of his melon. "He phoned me yesterday. Told me a neighbour wants to sell a picture. Apparently, the neighbour needs some money to top up his pension."

"That's good," responded May, pushing her long black hair back over her shoulders, "because I'm seeing Wesley, at 2.30, so we can travel together. You can drop me off at his gallery... and afterwards we could meet for a drink at 'Ambrose's Bar'."

"Great idea. Have you had any more interest in the Richie Hope landscapes?"

"Wei Qi, my contact in Shanghai, emailed to say he has four galleries interested."

Oscar nodded. He wished he'd achieved this amount of interest when he'd first arrived in Antigua. Mind, he knew May's experience and connections had always been better than his. "I'm sure Wesley's over the moon with all the sales you're generating."

May smiled. "Yes, he is, but it was you who initiated the interest. Without your inspired endorsement I wouldn't have considered these types of paintings for the Chinese market. Anyway, do you know anything about Charlie's neighbour's picture?"

"No, not really. Other than Charlie thinks it will be an interesting challenge."

"A challenge!" announced May, smiling. "It sounds intriguing. Maybe I ought to come with you."

"As you know, Charlie's only involved in a small amount of local art trading, so anything not Antiguan, or worth over a thousand dollars, is much too large for him to handle. His favourite remark is 'dats all too much of a challenge for me, man'."

May laughed at Oscar's cheeky Antiguan accent. "Okay. You can tell me more when we meet in the bar."

Later that afternoon, after dropping May off at the 'Shell Gallery', Oscar arrived outside Charlie's property. It was a small detached wooden house with a corrugated metal roof and peeling window frames. Similarly constructed properties were located on either side. Set seven streets back from the local beach, this was not a wealthy part of town. The road originally had a hard surface, but over the years, it had slowly been worn away, resulting in a number of water-filled potholes. Nevertheless, it was a quiet area and Charlie had enjoyed living there for 30 years. The last 12 on his own after his wife, Winny, had passed away.

This district was not one of Oscar's favourite areas, but he knew it was reasonably safe during the day. He parked his Jeep directly outside Charlie's house on a dry mud plot close to the house's covered front porch. When Winny was alive, this patch would have been a small garden, containing a riot of coloured flowers. However, Charlie didn't have the same interest, so the garden was ignored and now just consisted of baked soil and the occasional lingering weed.

Oscar set the car's alarm and locked all the doors before making the four steps to the front door. After two raps on the faded green-painted door, he stood back and waited.

It was a few moments before Charlie appeared from the side of his house. "Hi, man," shouted Charlie, shuffling over towards Oscar. He was probably in his early 80s, still bright in mind though his old legs were not as sprightly as they used to be. His dark brown face was wrinkled, and his grey hair was now only growing in tight tufts just above his ears. "Come round d' back, I've got us some lemonade."

The two men shook hands and then Oscar slowly followed Charlie back along the path at the side of the house. The rear of the property was once a small garden, but now consisted mainly of a concrete-slab patio. Charlie pointed to a pair of old wicker chairs and both men sat down. Between the chairs, a small wooden table was placed, containing a jug of iced lemonade and two glasses. Charlie poured the lemonade and offered one of the filled glasses to Oscar.

After taking a sip, Charlie began to speak. "Thought I'd better tell you about me neighbour, before we went to see 'im. Lives dare." Charlie pointed to the wooden property directly behind Oscar. "We've been neighbours for 'bout ten years, not close friends, but we speak occasionally."

Oscar sipped his own drink while Charlie continued with his introduction.

"Mathis Laurent, dat's 'is name. 'E's from France. Moved

'ere from Guadeloupe. Don't know why 'e came 'ere. Always lived on 'is own. Last week I was sitting 'ere, minding me o' business, when 'e called to me from over d' fence. 'E's never done dat before. Made me jump! I wondered what 'e wanted so went over to talk to 'im."

Oscar smiled and wondered when Charlie would get to the point. He was famous for his ramblings. It was during one of Charlie's long-winded speeches to Wesley that Wesley had first introduced Charlie to Oscar. It was just a short time after Oscar had arrived on the island. Wesley thought it would be useful for Oscar to meet another art dealer, but it also proved a good excuse for Wesley to escape Charlie's latest rant.

Oscar's mind had temporarily drifted away, but when he heard Charlie mention the name Monet, his attention was recaptured. "Did you say Monet?"

Charlie looked at Oscar with a queried look. "Yes… you not been lis'nin', man?"

"Sorry, Charlie," said Oscar, a little embarrassed.

"What I was saying is, when I went over to d' fence, Mathis told me about a picture 'e wanted to sell. 'E knew I did a bit of buying and selling, so wanted me 'dvice. 'E then said that when 'e lived in a place called Vétheuil, dat's in France… before moving to Guadeloupe, 'e'd been given a paintin' by a woman friend. 'E said Vétheuil was made famous by Monet's paintings… long before Monet moved to Giverny."

Oscar was surprised that Charlie knew anything about Giverny.

"Mathis said 'e'd originally thought the picture wasn't very good… all splodges and splashes. 'Owever, 'e kept it as it reminded 'im of 'is friend… and now 'e wants to sell it."

Oscar leaned back in his chair and pondered on the situation. It sounded like a waste of time. "Do you know who the artist is?"

"Nope. 'E just told me dis woman friend 'ad painted it. You can ask 'im all these questions when we go round dare. I told 'im I couldn't 'elp 'cos I only dealt with local artists. I den thought of you."

"Okay. Thanks." Oscar stood up and drank the last of his lemonade. "Should we go round now?"

Charlie looked up at Oscar and smiled. "Slow down, man… me old legs aren't as nimble as yours."

Fifteen minutes later, Oscar, Mathis and Charlie were standing in front of a colourful oil-painted abstract picture hanging on Mathis's lounge wall.

Still looking at the picture, Oscar was the first to speak. "You say you obtained this picture directly from the artist. When was this?" He turned to face Mathis. He guessed Mathis was probably in his late 60s. He was tall and slim with short-cropped grey hair. He was casually dressed in a white collared shirt and light brown chinos. His house appeared to be clean and very orderly.

Mathis rubbed his chin with his right hand and thought back in time. "Probably about 1990. I worked part time in Joan's garden for about six years and, when I told her I was moving to Guadeloupe, she gave me this picture. She told me that I'd worked hard, especially looking after her sunflowers, and wanted me to have this picture as a reminder." Mathis pointed at the painting. "These are supposed to be sunflowers. Nothing like the ones I grew though. She painted a lot of pictures like this which she also called 'Sunflowers'. She was an American, so I assumed that was the reason."

Oscar was impressed by Mathis's clearly spoken English, despite a French accent that was still recognisable. He was, however, a little doubtful as to where all this was going. The only sunflower paintings he knew anything about were painted by Van Gogh. These were nothing like Van Gogh's. "What was Joan's surname?" he asked.

"Mitchell, Joan Mitchell. Ever heard of her?"

Oscar slowly shook his head from side to side. He would be the first to admit that abstract paintings were not his preferred interest.

Charlie, meanwhile, just shrugged his shoulders. He too was none the wiser.

"Come over here," ordered Mathis, and he walked over towards a nearby table. Oscar and Charlie duly followed.

The table was covered with reports and articles removed from magazines and newspapers. Mathis pointed to the collection and Oscar picked up two, as did Charlie. They both began to read:

Joan Mitchell's current record was set in 2018 by the abstract painting titled 'Blueberry' (1969), which sold for $16.6 million at Christie's in New York.

In a resounding testament to the enduring legacy of American Abstract Expressionist Joan Mitchell (1925–1992), history once again unfolded at Sotheby's New York Contemporary Evening Auction. Mitchell's oil on canvas painting, 'Sunflowers' (1990–91), achieved a groundbreaking sale of $27.9 million on the evening of November 15, 2023.

Joan Mitchell's unique abstract artistic language is due to her life-long appreciation for the beauty of the natural world. 'Sunflowers' not only captivates with its vibrant strokes but also stands as a testament to Mitchell's enduring influence. This remarkable piece, part of the Collection of John Cheim, had been acquired as a gift by the present owner from the artist in 1992, adding an extra layer of significance to its journey through the art world.

Securing a distinguished position as the fourth most expensive female artwork ever sold at auction, Joan Mitchell (1925–1992), stands triumphant with her emotionally charged masterpiece, 'Untitled' (circa 1959). In November 2023, this extraordinary work, marked by gripping shades of crimson, purple, khaki green and deep blue, garnered an astounding $29.1 million, establishing a remarkable personal record for the esteemed artist.

After they'd put the papers back on the table, Oscar and Charlie looked at each other. They were astonished. Both had their eyes and mouths wide open.

"Wow," said Oscar, as he turned to face Mathis. Mathis had a huge grin on his face.

"'Kinell!" responded Charlie. He was truly amazed.

When Oscar and Charlie had recovered from their surprise, it was Oscar who spoke. "This is out of my league… probably Wesley's too. These sales all took place in New York, and seeing that Ms. Mitchell is an American, that's where you're going to get the best price… if the painting's authentic."

Mathis's face suddenly changed from a grin to a scowl. "It definitely is authentic!"

"Look, I'm not saying it isn't, but you'll need proof and evidence that she gave it to you. Have you got any paperwork showing a transfer, for example?"

Mathis thought for a moment and slowly shook his head. "All I can remember is her presenting it to me. There were three other people in the room at the time."

"Do you remember the names of these people?"

Mathis pondered on the question. "No. They were just Joan's arty colleagues. They weren't local."

"Were they fellow artists? All women?"

"Not sure about whether they were proper artists. I wasn't into art. Two were women and one a man."

"How do you know this painting is called 'Sunflowers'?"

"That was what she told me it was called, but as I say, a lot of her pictures at that time had the same name… or were untitled."

"For this sort of highly regarded artist there must be a catalogue raisonné. That's a book which lists all Joan Mitchell's authorised paintings. Has anybody enquired about your picture?"

"No. Hardly anyone knows of its existence."

"Mmm, okay. The only thing I can suggest is I speak to a colleague who used to work at Sotheby's in New York and see what he suggests. In the meantime, I want you to go through all your old files and papers. Any scrap of information could be extremely useful. Also keep that picture extra secure… it looks as though it could be worth 20 million dollars… at least!"

Chapter 9

It was just after 5.30pm when May walked into 'Ambrose's Bar' looking for Oscar. Oscar had arrived 15 minutes earlier and was sitting at the bar chatting with Amos, the bartender and owner. Oscar had been introduced to Amos by Wesley, during his early days on the island. It was also the bar which he and Gladstone had often frequented.

"Hi," said Oscar, when he spotted May walking over to join him. "Let me get you a drink."

"Thank you. A cold lager would be lovely."

Amos duly poured the drink and handed it to May. They then wandered over to Oscar's favourite table, outside on the balcony. It was the table where he and Gladstone had spent many hours sipping their beers, discussing art deals and enjoying 'man to man' conversations.

The late afternoon sunshine had disappeared and dusk was setting in. It was still lovely and warm, like most evenings, and a cooling sea breeze was drifting across the balcony.

After sitting down, both stared at the beach view. The peaceful sea's dark golden hue would shortly change to an inky-black colour. The soft reflection of the moon would then highlight the tranquillity of the calm sea.

"I spent many hours with Gladstone admiring this

view," said Oscar, thinking back on the many conversations he'd had with Gladstone. He knew it was mainly due to Gladstone's friendship that he'd progressively felt more 'at home' in Antigua than during his later years in Hong Kong.

"It's beautiful, Oscar. The sea looks so calm and relaxing… and look, those two people walking along the beach, they look like silhouettes. It's a wonderful scene, so romantic and quiet." May looked across at Oscar and gave him a loving smile.

Oscar smiled back. No more Gladstone, he thought, but this was a new chapter in his life. His business partner was also his wife. How good was that! "Do you know, May, I really enjoyed my business dealings and social time with Gladstone. He introduced me to this island, its culture and the local art market. Wesley and Garfield also helped… and now… well, I'm totally settled in Antigua." He smiled. "I'm even getting used to mañana and the general slower pace of life. I couldn't go back to Hong Kong. Antigua is definitely my home, and I hope, in time, you'll feel the same."

"It's certainly a different culture," responded May, placing her glass back on the table. "There are a few things I still miss from my Hong Kong and China days, but there are so many positives living here. I can still do most of my business with colleagues and clients via the internet. Other than the few deals I do with Wesley, I've left the rest of the Caribbean market to you."

"Do you have any regrets?"

May leaned back and pondered Oscar's question. "When you invited me to visit for a holiday, that's all I thought it was going to be. An appealing holiday with a lovely friend, a break from the routine… from the treadmill. But you opened my eyes to a different type of life. A life with, maybe, a loving husband, a lifestyle that was not dominated by working long hours and solely targeted at wealth creation. I saw living here, with you, as an exciting new challenge, an adventure… and that's really what's happened. No, Oscar, my life now is so wonderfully different. I can't see me leaving this lovely island either… or having a future without you."

Oscar leaned over the table and gave May a kiss. Yes, thought Oscar, these last two years have certainly been a new chapter in my life.

After a few moments, May broke the silence. "How did your visit to see old Charlie Hall's neighbour go?"

"Oh, yes. That was a surprise… a really fascinating meeting. I need to give Ian a ring." Oscar then went on to explain about Mathis and his potentially mind-blowing painting.

"Wow," said May, once Oscar had finished. "I think I came across the name Joan Mitchell in Hong Kong. However, I don't recall ever selling one of her paintings. Are you going to help Mathis?"

"I most certainly am. I've agreed 15% commission on the eventual sale price after costs."

"15% of 30 million dollars would be a nice piece of work."

"Yes, indeed, but the market for abstract paintings is not an area I know. It's really specialist and you need to know what you're doing. Also, auctioning in New York, I've never done that before. I'm hoping Ian will be able to give me some advice because he worked there before he arrived in Hong Kong. Mind, lots of things must have changed since those days."

May pondered for a moment and then replied, "I know a colleague in Shanghai who mainly deals with abstract art. I can ask him, but I don't recall him saying he'd bought or sold at an auction in New York."

Oscar picked up his glass and drank the last of the lager. "I need another drink. You're a much slower drinker than Gladstone!"

Next day, Oscar telephoned Ian. It was early morning in the UK, but Ian was already in his home office. After a few banter exchanges, Oscar came to the point of his call. He summarised his meeting with Mathis and asked Ian for his thoughts.

"That's a biggie, Oscar. A bit out of your league," responded Ian.

Oscar couldn't see Ian's teasing smile.

"That's what I said to Mathis, but for three to four million commission, Ian Caxton, I'm definitely prepared to give it my best shot."

"The New York market has changed considerably since I worked there, but I still have a contact I can ask."

"That would be great. I really don't know where to start. I've told Mathis he's got to find provable evidence relating to the picture's provenance. Tomorrow I'm going to check out whether I can find a catalogue raisonné, but, even if I do, I'm doubtful I'll find his painting there. Mathis told me nobody has ever approached him about the picture."

"Not the end of the world, but it'll save you a lot of leg-work if it is recorded."

"Great. Thanks, Ian."

"Ah, must go, Oscar. That's my mobile ringing. I'm expecting an important call. I'll let you know what my colleague says."

Chapter 10

When Ian answered his mobile phone, he was pleased to hear it was George Bailey, the private detective he'd employed.

"Hello, George. What good news have you got for me?"

"Everything's set up, Ian. All the surveillance and security equipment is in place. I'll give you a buzz in about ten days."

"Excellent!" exclaimed Ian. "Don't tell me any of the details over the phone."

"As I say, I'll contact you again. We can then meet to review what I've found out."

"See you in about ten days' time. Thanks for the call."

Ian switched off the connection. He had a broad smile on his face. "Now, Mr. Northgate," he said to himself, "let's see what you're really up to!"

Ian's next call was to Penny's mobile. After three rings, Penny answered. "Hi, Ian, everything okay?"

"Couldn't be better. Just be careful when you feed the fish; your every move is going to be observed."

"Okay," responded Penny, but then after a pause on the line, "thanks for the call."

"Bye, Penny. Chat again soon."

The following day, Ian telephoned a former colleague at Sotheby's in New York.

When Bruce Campbell answered his phone, he was surprised to hear Ian Caxton's English dulcet tones. "Well, Ian Caxton, you're a blast from the past. How's you doing in Hong Kong?"

Ian immediately recognised Bruce's booming southern American accent. Born in the state of Georgia, Bruce had grown up in Atlanta before moving to university in Texas. Straight after graduating, he'd joined a top art gallery in New York before then moving to Sotheby's at the same time as Ian had arrived in New York. Ian explained he'd moved on from Hong Kong and gave Bruce a summary of his career to date.

"Wow, boy, you've been around," responded Bruce. "Me? I'm still with the old firm. Hoping Sotheby's will think I'm ready for early retirement soon. Anyway, one can wish. So, buddy, what can I do for you?"

"Heard of Joan Mitchell?" asked Ian. He knew Bruce probably had, but wanted to sow a seed of intrigue.

Bruce laughed at his end of the line. "Sure have, buddy. She's the real deal in the States at the moment. People are spending fortunes on her splat, dab and slashes. You got one of her pictures? Could be worth 20 mill."

"Not me, Bruce, but a colleague thinks he may have. It was a gift by the artist to the owner in about 1990."

"That's all the provenance?"

"So far, but my colleague is digging."

"This painting, is it in the UK?"

"No, Antigua."

"Antigua! What the hell's a JM painting doing there?

"The owner is French and moved to Antigua years ago, after he left France where he was Joan Mitchell's gardener."

"Gardener! C'mon. Is today April Fools' Day!?"

"Okay. I know it all sounds… er, incredulous, but my colleague wouldn't be wasting my time if he didn't think it was potentially authentic… I promise. Any chance you can help us?"

"That's easy, 'old boy'." Bruce often used these sorts of English phrases to tease Ian. "Get your guy to get in touch with the Joan Mitchell Foundation. They're based here in the 'Big Apple'. Google it on the internet. They invite owners to complete and return a catalogue raisonné submission form. The form can be downloaded. Mind, warn your colleague there's no guarantee that the submission will result in its inclusion in the catalogue raisonné. As usual, they have sole discretion over whether or not to include a painting. Even if they agree to include it, they won't fully authenticate any picture without all the usual history."

"Mmm, I agree. It's still all about provenance."

"Nothing changes in the US art world, buddy, even for abstracts. Just gets more technical and complicated. Tell your colleague that once he gets it authenticated, I'll sell it quicker than I can eat my mum's apple pie!"

Ian smiled. Nothing seems to have changed with Bruce, a real great guy. "I certainly will. Great chatting, Bruce. I'll call on you next time I'm in New York."

"You do that, buddy. Don't leave it too long, cos I might have moved on."

"Cheers," responded Ian and closed the call.

After placing his mobile on his desk, Ian opened up his computer and typed in 'Joan Mitchell Foundation'. From the website, he clicked on 'Catalogue Raisonné' and explored over 500 Joan Mitchell pictures. Her earlier work in the 1940s, he noted, mainly consisted of simple landscape paintings, but from the 1950s onwards, her painting style slowly evolved towards expressionism and then into abstract art.

Under the website's heading, 'Biography', he read that Joan was born in Chicago in 1925 and graduated from the School of the Art Institute of Chicago. Upon graduating in 1947, she was awarded a travel fellowship which enabled her to visit France for one year. There she met, and was influenced by, a number of local abstract expressionists. These artists had become the representatives of the second generation of the movement, painting in a free, vigorous, rough-textured style.

After returning to the United States in 1949, Joan settled in New York and became an active participant in the 'New York School' of painters. By the early 1950s, she'd established a reputation as one of the leading young abstract expressionist painters. From then on, she divided her time between New York and France. Finally, in 1959, she settled permanently in France, initially living and working in Paris but in 1968, she moved to Vétheuil, a small town northwest of Paris, where she worked continuously until just before her death in 1992.

After exploring more of the website and gleaning more information, Ian leaned back in his chair and pondered on the situation. He could see some of the positives in Joan Mitchell's earlier work and, to some extent, her middle period, where her pictures had progressed towards French expressionism. However, the abstract work in her later years he wasn't so keen on. Yet, these were the paintings that were now selling for many millions of pounds. Did this make sense, or was it just like all the other 'fads'? Some artists suddenly come into vogue and their pictures can sell for millions of pounds, but suddenly, sentiment changes and a different artist becomes the 'must have'. Such is the fickle and volatile world of art.

Chapter 11

The following day, Ian telephoned Oscar and relayed all the information he'd obtained from Bruce Campbell and the Joan Mitchell Foundation website. He suggested Oscar should look at the website himself, in particular, the section on the catalogue raisonné.

This, Oscar agreed to do and thanked Ian for his information. He promised he'd let him know how everything was progressing.

When Oscar switched off the call, he looked over to May and summarised the telephone discussion. They were both sitting in their recently created home office where their desks faced each other.

"That's good of Ian. What are you going to do now?" asked May. She was keen to know what Oscar was planning.

"This Joan Mitchell Foundation website seems the best place to start. Apparently, the catalogue raisonné can be found there, and I can download a copy of the submission form. I'll then be able to see what information is required, speak to Mathis and show him what we need to do."

"Has he got any further with searching through his old papers?"

"No. However, I think the three people who were in Joan's property when she presented the picture to Mathis

44

could prove invaluable as a starting point towards establishing provenance."

"1990, you said. They may all be dead by now."

"Oh, thank you, May. Any other similar 'positive' suggestions?" asked Oscar, with a scornful look on his face.

May smiled. "Seriously, it's been over 30 years since Joan Mitchell died."

"I know, but I'm hoping some of that group were much younger than Joan. They might still be alive today."

"Good point. They may indeed."

"Anyway, my next step is to look into every detail on the Joan Mitchell Foundation website."

For the next two hours, Oscar read every word printed on the Foundation's website. This included the catalogue raisonné, where he examined every painting dated after 1989. Unsurprisingly, Mathis's picture wasn't there. There were other examples of abstract paintings titled 'Sunflowers', but none of these matched Mathis's painting. Oscar realised there weren't going to be any short-cuts... just a lot of hard work. Still, for the amount of commission he'd been promised, he knew it wasn't going to be that easy.

"Any luck?" asked May, who had now returned to their office with two mugs of coffee. She placed one on Oscar's desk.

"No. Thanks for the coffee. There are other paintings titled 'Sunflowers', but they don't match Mathis's 'Sunflowers'."

"I've had a glance at the Foundation's website myself," said May, returning to sit behind her own desk. "They seem very protective and want to control everything about the history of Joan Mitchell. Maybe you should try emailing them and explain your situation."

"Good point. However, the problem is I don't want to open my hand too fully at this time. I certainly don't need other people suddenly descending on Mathis."

"Okay. So… what about just asking the Foundation if they have any further information about Joan's life, colleagues and friends in the early 1990s. Tell them you're a History of Art student and are writing a thesis on their heroine."

"Yeah… that could get the ball rolling. Great idea. Thanks. I'll do that now."

Oscar proceeded to draft his email. After several changes, he asked May to read it.

"Yes, that looks okay," responded May. "After all, you've got nothing to lose."

Oscar leaned forward and placed his finger on the keyboard. Without further delay, he pressed the 'send' button.

It was four days later when Oscar received a reply from the Foundation. The message was polite, but brief, and only gave Oscar the barest of information. They also referred him to other published books and articles. Signing off, they wished Oscar the best of luck with his thesis and would be delighted to see a copy once it was finished.

Oops, thought Oscar. At least I didn't tell them the timescale of the thesis. He then pondered the rest of the information they'd given and made a note of the book titles and articles mentioned. We're another step forward, he thought to himself, but a long way away from the finishing line.

He then investigated the internet for the books the Foundation had mentioned. He discovered two of them on an American second-hand bookshop website and ordered them immediately. Delivery was predicted to be within the week.

Two days later, Oscar had a slice of luck. Mathis telephoned and told Oscar he'd found two old black-and-white printed photographs. One of the photographs, Mathis explained, was of him being presented with the painting by Joan. The second was of him holding the painting with Joan, and her two female colleagues, smiling and standing beside him.

Oscar had immediately dashed off to Mathis's house. There, using his mobile phone, he'd taken three pictures of each photograph and immediately uploaded them to his Google account. Now he was getting somewhere! But, the big question remained: who were these two colleagues... and were they still alive?

Chapter 12

Ian arrived at Waterloo railway station and headed straight for the 'Underground' sign. He'd made arrangements to meet with George Bailey, the private detective, to discuss the surveillance of Jonathan Northgate's apartment. During yesterday's telephone conversation, George informed Ian that he had some details to discuss. Ian agreed to a meeting and George had suggested the 'Sherlock Holmes' pub in London at midday.

After purchasing a return ticket on the Underground, Ian caught the next train and alighted at Charing Cross station. Once back in the daylight, he strolled along the Strand and turned into Northumberland Street. Within just a few minutes he'd arrived outside the famous 'Sherlock Holmes' pub. The black-painted facade and double bay windows with small engraved panes gave a feeling of stepping back in time to the Victorian era. All it needed now, thought Ian, was carriages drawn by horses clip-clopping along the cobble street and an eerie mood created by a thick London fog.

Ian pushed on the heavy wooden door and entered the bar. Although now smartly furnished and decorated, the room still had an old Victorian atmosphere. The walls were adorned with Holmes memorabilia and a separate room housed a small museum.

It was just after 12 noon, but already there were a number of customers either sitting at tables or standing at the bar. He'd already spotted George sitting at a table close to one of the engraved windows. He was drinking the last of a cup of coffee. Ian walked over to join him. "Hi, George. An unusual meeting venue."

George was about 50 years of age, of medium build and still had a full head of dark brown hair. Smartly dressed in a double-breasted blue suit, he looked more like a businessman than the stereotypical detective. He smiled and shook Ian's hand. "I'm a great fan of Conan Doyle's books and love the atmosphere of this place. What can I get for you to drink?"

"A cappuccino would be great."

George went over to the bar and ordered two cappuccinos. Meanwhile, Ian admired the comfortable studded leather bench seats and surveyed the room. He could see a variety of framed exhibits on the walls. Not a great reader of Sherlock Holmes stories himself, nevertheless, he could feel the history, character and atmosphere of the place, despite knowing all the books were fiction.

"Here you go, Ian." George placed a large mug of frothing coffee directly in front of him. "Have you ever been in here before?"

Ian sipped his coffee and said, "A long time ago. I think it's been refurbished since then."

"I'm a great fan of Conan Doyle. I first read his books as a teenager. Holmes, Watson and Moriarty. Wonderful stuff. Anyway, we're not here to discuss them, it's Mr. Northgate you're interested in."

"Yes, it is," responded Ian, anxiously waiting on George's report.

"Okay. We've placed three hidden cameras in his apartment. Two in the hallway and one in the lounge. We've also bugged his mobile. He doesn't have a landline."

Ian wondered how George had managed to conceal a miniature device inside Northgate's smartphone. On reflection, he didn't want to know. "So, what have you found out so far?"

"Nothing from his phone calls, but one interesting occurrence. Last Thursday, he brought home an abstract painting, removed the existing picture in the lounge and replaced it with the new painting. Next morning the old picture was parcelled up and carried out of his flat."

"Interesting," said Ian, sitting back in his seat. "It figures. However, I need to know what happens to the painting next. Also, can your lounge camera zoom in on the new picture?"

George removed his mobile from his inside pocket. "Already done," he announced and pressed some buttons. He showed Ian the screen. "Here's the painting. I've zoomed in on the signature as well. I'll email you copies."

Ian leaned over and looked closely at the screen. "Yes, email both pictures, please."

George pressed a few more buttons. "They should have arrived in your inbox."

Ian checked his own mobile. Both photos had arrived. "Excellent!" He looked at the zoomed-in picture of the signature. "Mmm, Alex Colon. Not an artist I've come across before."

Whilst Ian looked at his phone, George sipped his coffee and asked, "Useful?"

"A good start," responded Ian, logging off his emails. "I'll need to investigate this picture's history. See where it's been in the last 12 months."

"You want me to carry on with the surveillance?"

"Oh yes. I'm particularly interested to know where Northgate takes the paintings."

"That's not a problem. The chip we've put into his phone

also tracks the phone's roaming." George pressed some more buttons on his phone. "Right. I've just sent you a map. It shows the phone's location at any time, on any given day, since the chip was installed."

"That's amazing. So, if I follow Northgate's phone's journey for last Friday, I might get an idea where he took the painting."

George nodded. "Assuming he took his device with him."

"Nobody goes anywhere without their phone nowadays," said Ian, smiling.

"I have two phones… and get both regularly checked out for bugs."

"Are you serious?" asked Ian. He wondered if he should get his own phone checked.

"I had my phone bugged once. It was three years ago. A wealthy woman employed me to follow her husband. She was convinced he was having an affair. After a week, the husband knew I was following him. He'd already employed a female detective, called Ellie, to spy on his wife! I found out later that Ellie had bugged my phone and was tapping into all my telephone conversations with the wife. Incidentally, neither husband nor wife was actually having an affair, but Ellie told me later to get my phone checked!"

Ian smiled. "You can't trust anyone. Not even a private detective!"

"I can trust Ellie now… she's my partner!"

"If you can't beat them, join them, eh?"

George smiled. "I assume these paintings are being stolen and sold on?"

After sipping the last of his coffee, Ian replied. "That's what I hope he's doing, but we need proof!"

On the train journey home, Ian sent Penny a text. 'Hi. Met with "our friend" today. He gave me some interesting information. Will let you know the details. Can you see if Sotheby's were recently involved in a sale of an abstract painting by Alex Colon?'

After pressing the send button, Ian sat back in his seat and looked out the window. The sun was low in the sky creating long dark shadows shrouding the passing countryside. Ian pondered on his meeting with George. He knew in his bones that Northgate was up to no good, an illegal activity, but he needed more evidence. Were the paintings Northgate was collecting the originals? Where were they going... and to whom?

Chapter 13

Two days later, Ian sat in the main bar of 'The Grapes' public house in Maddox Street, just a few minutes' walk from Sotheby's London gallery in New Bond Street. He'd agreed to meet with Penny to discuss the latest developments in the Northgate paintings situation.

Ian had only been back to this pub once since he'd left Sotheby's. Now, as he sipped his beer and looked around the room, his thoughts drifted back to his first meeting with Andrei all those years ago… at this very table. His life had completely changed since that memorable encounter… just as Andrei had predicted it would. He still missed his friend and business colleague but accepted that time moves on. 'Out of sight, but not out of his memories', was how he would always remember his friend.

"Hello, Ian." Penny was standing next to him.

Ian immediately stood up and gave Penny a hug and a kiss on the cheek. "Sorry, I was miles away. I didn't see you come in."

They both looked at each other for a moment and smiled, then Ian said, "What can I get you to drink?"

Penny sat down and started to undo her coat. It was cold outside, but cosy and warm in the pub. "A glass of sparkling water would be lovely, please."

Two minutes later, Ian placed the glass of water in front of Penny. Resuming his own seat, he picked up his beer and proffered a toast. "Cheers."

Penny clinked her glass with Ian's. "Good health."

After sipping his beer and placing it back on the table, Ian said, "You're looking good and I like the shorter hairstyle. Vic's obviously been looking after you."

Penny smiled and replied, "Thank you. However, I think it's more about me looking after him."

They both laughed and then Penny spoke, "That Alex Colon painting, Sotheby's sold it at auction three weeks ago. It was bought by a client for 1.2 million pounds. The client lives in Qatar."

Ian nodded but wondered what was going on. "Mmm, so, what's Northgate's game? Is it a coincidence that the three buyers we know about are all based in the Middle East? Is Northgate deliberately targeting these buyers? If so, why?"

"It's all very worrying, Ian," said Penny, staring at the rim of her glass. "Something's just not right. Is Jonathan stealing these pictures? If so, why? It doesn't make sense. He's got his CEO's salary, and I've heard his wife comes from a wealthy family in America. Why would he need the money?"

"Could be for a number of reasons. Drugs, blackmail… who knows? Anyway, this afternoon I'm going to visit the premises where Northgate keeps taking his paintings. That might give us a clue."

Penny stared at Ian with a curious look. "You know where he's taking them?"

"My colleague has fitted a device inside Northgate's phone. It records everywhere the phone goes. The other Friday, we know Northgate left his apartment with one of the paintings, but he didn't go to Sotheby's. He went to a location near Euston station. I'm going there this afternoon."

Penny raised her eyebrows. "This could be dangerous, Ian. Are you sure you want to take the risk?"

"All I plan to do this afternoon is establish where Northgate went. Nothing more than that." Ian picked up his beer and sipped some of the contents. He looked at Penny and decided she didn't need to know any more for the moment.

"Just be careful, Ian. We don't know what type of people Jonathan is dealing with."

A little after 3pm, Ian arrived at the junction of Euston Road and Charlton Street, between Euston and St. Pancras stations and close to the large red brick facade of the British Library. From Euston Road, Ian strode along Charlton Street glancing at his mobile. He was following the map George had given him. The left-hand side of the street had an eclectic collection of mainly three and four-storey brick buildings, with shops on the ground floor. On the far side of the road the properties were of similar size, although somewhat obscured by a long row of mature deciduous trees.

When he was nearly halfway along the street, Ian began to slow down and stopped at what he thought was the point that Northgate had entered a building. He stood back and stared at the white-painted frontage. It appeared to be a block of offices with a firm of estate agents as neighbours on one side. Ian wandered towards the entrance door and spotted a shining stainless-steel name plaque stating, 'Cotton Enterprises'.

Ian wanted to look in through a window but was foiled by the frosted glass. He then decided to see if the door was unlocked, and if it was, see what was inside. He pushed on the grey painted door, and to his surprise, it opened easily and quietly. Stepping inside, he was in a dark corridor. He couldn't hear any sounds of activity and wondered if the building might be unoccupied. But if so, why was the front door unlocked? He sneaked along the corridor and came to a door on his right that was slightly ajar. He looked in, but the room was empty. The next door had a sign saying 'Reception', so he pushed on this door. It slowly opened with a creaking sound. Ian stepped through into a small room with a counter directly in front of him. Behind the counter were two empty desks, and leaning against two of the walls were about 20 framed pictures.

"Can I help you?" said a strong female voice standing directly behind him in the doorway.

The voice made Ian jump, and he turned around quickly to see a large woman probably in her late 50s. She had short grey curly hair, folded arms and a scowl on her face. Ian began to explain, "I have an appointment with Tony Baxter."

"No Tony Baxter works here. Who's he work for?"

"Cotton Associates, solicitors. Is this the right place?"

"No. No solicitors here. Where did you get this address?"

"From Tony Baxter. He said their address was 68, Charlton Street. I saw the Cotton name on your plaque outside and thought these were the premises."

"Well, they're not. 68 is further down the street."

"Okay. Sorry." Ian began to move towards the door, but the woman filled most of the doorway, arms still folded, scrutinising his face.

"Sorry, could you let me come past?" Ian was trying to make his best condescending appeal.

The woman continued to glare at him for a few more moments before standing back leaving just enough room for Ian to squeeze past.

"What's going on?" A man had appeared in the corridor.

Ian glanced at him before heading towards the door he'd earlier entered.

"No problem, Eric," said the large woman. "This guy's got the wrong Cotton address."

Ian quickly exited the premises and headed up the street. After a few moments, he stopped and looked back. Nobody was watching him. Mmm, he thought, why are Cotton Enterprises storing all those paintings?

Ian crossed the street and walked back towards Euston Road. He used the row of London plane trees to hide him from the Cotton Enterprises property's windows. He stopped behind the trunk of one of the largest trees and took out his mobile. He took two photographs of the building and planned to email copies to George Bailey. He wanted George to find out what exactly was going on at Cotton Enterprises.

Chapter 14

Oscar had received the two second-hand Joan Mitchell books he'd ordered from America. For most of the day, he'd been slowly ploughing through the first. There was lots of information about Joan's life as an artist and her changing style of painting over the years. Unfortunately, very little was included about her social life and he'd failed to identify any of the people that appeared in Mathis's photographs. He'd certainly acquired a deeper knowledge and greater understanding of the artist but was still desperate to discover anything about her friends and colleagues in France.

After reading all of the first book, he decided to have a break and wandered into the kitchen to make himself a mug of coffee.

May was preparing their evening meal and when she saw Oscar's dejected face, she walked over to give him a sympathetic kiss on his cheek. "No good?" she asked.

"No," responded Oscar. "I thought I'd have a break and a coffee. Can I make one for you as well?"

May went back to her food preparation and said, "That would be nice. Thank you."

Oscar boiled the kettle and prepared the cafetière. A few minutes later, he poured the coffee into two mugs, placing one close to where May was working. He sat down at the table and observed May at work.

May looked across at Oscar and asked, "Have you read both books?"

Oscar, still staring at May, had his elbows on the table and his chin resting in hands. "No, just the first one. I'll start the other after my coffee."

"Maybe you'll have better luck with that one."

"We'll see," responded Oscar doubtfully.

"You know this is always the hardest part, trying to uncover every part of the provenance. You'll get there. You usually do."

Oscar smiled. "Yes, you're right." At that, Oscar stood up in a more confident mood, picked up his coffee mug and strode back towards his office.

Back at his desk, he opened the second book. Slowly flicking through the pages, he found a number of photographs of Joan's paintings. Some were in black and white, but most were in full colour. Turning back to the beginning, he looked at the list of chapter titles. Suddenly he stopped when he came to chapter 21. It was titled, 'Life in France'. He quickly flicked through the book again until he came to the right page. After a sip of his coffee, he began to read.

About 20 minutes later, May joined him in the office. Seeing Oscar engrossed in the new book, she asked, "Better luck?"

Oscar laid the book down and looked up at his wife. "Possibly. I've found two chapters about Joan's life in France. They mention some people she was friendly with and some of her art colleagues, but there are no photographs other than the house where she lived."

"Maybe Mathis will recognise some of the names."

"Maybe," responded Oscar. "I certainly don't recognise any of the names of the artists mentioned, but I'll google them and see what I can find."

May sat down at her desk and, after pushing her long black hair back behind her shoulders, she opened up her laptop. "Give me some of the names and I'll look them up."

Oscar looked at his notes and told May three names.

The room was now quiet except for the tapping of May's computer keys. After a few minutes, she stopped and stared at the screen. "There's an old black-and-white photo of Elizabeth Dubois. She's painting a picture."

Oscar got up, collected his mobile phone and came to look at May's screen. Leaning over May's shoulder, he peered at the photograph. "It's a possibility. Let me compare it to Mathis's photos." Oscar switched on his mobile, opened the photos app and scrolled through his collection of pictures. "He we are. Mathis thinks these pictures were taken in about 1990. When was your picture dated?"

"It doesn't say. Mind, I think this woman looks similar to her," said May, pointing to the woman now displayed on Oscar's phone.

Oscar smiled. "You could be right. What else does your article say about Elizabeth Dubois?"

"It says she was born in England in 1957 and married Louis Dubois in 1980. Divorced in 1989. No children. Lived in Vétheuil until 1998 when she moved back to England. Now lives in Surrey. The rest is all about her paintings, although none of her work has sold for more than 5,000 pounds."

"Surrey, you say? I think that's where Ian lives! It also sounds as though she's still alive."

"There we are, some good news at last," announced May, smiling and leaning back in her chair.

Oscar smiled back and, after leaning down, gave his wife a kiss on her forehead. "Well done, you. I need to speak to my old pal, Ian Caxton."

Chapter 15

Oscar checked his watch and calculated what time it would be in the UK. He reckoned it was about 8pm, so decided he'd make his call to Ian.

"Ian Caxton," said Ian, answering the phone.

"Hi, buddy, your favourite chum from the Caribbean."

"Oscar! Great to hear from you. How's May?"

"May's great, thanks… and Emma, and England's next cricketing captain?"

Ian smiled. "Yes, we're all good too. So, what can I do for you?"

Oscar explained it was about the Joan Mitchell painting they'd recently discussed. He went on to explain the recent development and about Elizabeth Dubois living in Surrey.

"Okay," replied Ian. "So, you want to contact this woman?"

"Yes, that's the idea. I'm hoping she can confirm Mathis's story and maybe add some more information."

"Surrey's a big county. You've not got a specific address?"

"No. I thought you might know someone who could help me."

"Err, okay, Oscar, I have an idea. Email me all your information and I'll see what I can do."

"Thanks, Ian. You're a star. When are you coming to see

us again? Come over for Christmas and bring young Robert. I'll show him the Sir Vivian Richards cricket stadium."

Ian laughed. "I'll speak to Emma and let you know. Sounds like a great idea."

"Excellent. Speak to you later. Cheers."

"Bye, Oscar." Ian switched off the connection.

"I'll speak to Emma? What's that all about?" asked Emma, sitting next to Ian on their sofa.

"Oscar's invited us all over to Antigua for Christmas."

"Sounds lovely. However, there are our parents to consider."

"I know. Maybe we could visit in January, before Robert goes back to school."

"It's a possibility. I'll check out the dates."

"Meanwhile I've got to speak with George Bailey and see if he can help out with Oscar's problem."

The following morning, Ian telephoned George. He suggested a meeting, as he wanted to discuss not only Oscar's problem but also the office premises he'd visited in Charlton Street.

Two days later, the two men met up in the 'Sherlock Holmes' public house again. Ian firstly mentioned his findings at Cotton Enterprises' offices and asked George if he could find out what was going on there. Secondly, he outlined Oscar's problem.

"Okay," responded George. "The Cotton Enterprises thing is straightforward. I'll get on to that this afternoon. The Elizabeth Dubois location shouldn't prove a problem either. I'll ask my partner, Ellie, to look into that. Woman to woman... might be easier that way."

"Thanks, George." Ian handed over a large white envelope. "Here are some papers and photos Oscar sent. I'll also email you copies. Can I suggest Ellie sends her findings directly to Oscar? His contact details are in the envelope too. I'll tell Oscar about Ellie's involvement."

"Fine. Now there's also been further developments with Mr. Northgate and his paintings."

"Has there? What's he been up to this time?" Ian leaned back in his seat and drank the last of his now cold cappuccino.

"Yesterday, he brought another painting back to his apartment, but the existing Alex Colon painting is still hanging on his wall. Couldn't identify the new picture; it's still wrapped in brown paper."

"Mmm." Ian scratched his head. "Anything from his phone calls?"

"Nothing linking him to these pictures. Maybe he uses a separate phone for those calls?"

"Possible, I guess. We really need to understand what's going on... and why."

Chapter 16

Ellie Morgan, now in her early forties and a former police detective, became a business partner with George Bailey just over three years ago. They came into contact when she and George found themselves on opposite sides of a husband and wife affair investigation. Both established that neither husband nor wife were actually having an affair, but the two detectives didn't speak to each other until Ellie told George she had bugged his phone! George was impressed with Ellie's business methods and unassuming style and suggested they should work conjointly. George proposed a six-month trial, but after only three months, both agreed they were gelling well. Each brought different skills and experiences, and their interaction was producing great results.

When George told Ellie about Oscar's problem, she agreed to carry out the investigation. She was currently finding out where Elizabeth Dubois lived. Her route, via council tax records and other more secret resources, soon established that the woman was living on her own in Gomshall, a quaint and pretty village, located in the Surrey Hills, roughly halfway between Guildford and Dorking. She was living in an old cottage at 22 Green Lane. Ellie then identified the ex-directory landline telephone number, and 15 minutes later, she'd made an appointment to visit

Madame Dubois… tomorrow morning.

The following day, Ellie caught the 9.35 train from Waterloo station. Just over an hour later, she arrived at Gomshall station. Following her notes and using Google maps on her mobile, she was soon knocking on Elizabeth Dubois' front door.

The door was opened by a tall portly woman with an attractive smile. She looked down at Ellie, who was at least ten centimetres shorter. Staring at the caller, she waited for Ellie to introduce herself.

"Hello, Madame Dubois? I'm Ellie Morgan. We spoke on the telephone yesterday," announced Ellie, hoping she had the right person. This woman was much larger than she'd remembered in the photographs.

"Hello, Ellie. Do come in," responded Elizabeth Dubois. She had a middle English pronunciation. No sign of any French accent. "Please, nobody has referred to me as 'madame' in over 30 years. Just call me Elizabeth."

They shook hands, and Ellie followed Elizabeth along the corridor and into the back living room. The room, which was obviously once smaller, had been extended to include a larger kitchen. It was now an attractive open-plan arrangement. Practical, but still very cosy.

Elizabeth turned around and spoke. "I must admit, when you called yesterday, I was surprised, but also a little intrigued. I haven't spoken to anyone about my time in France since I arrived back in England. Anyway, I've prepared some coffee. Do sit down. I'll bring it over, then you can ask me all your questions."

Ellie unbuttoned her jacket and sat down on a chair next to a pair of small wooden tables. She placed her briefcase on the floor at her side.

"Here we are," said Elizabeth, carrying a tray containing a cafetière, a small jug of milk, two mugs and some biscuits.

She placed the tray on one of the small tables. "Do help yourself."

Ellie smiled and poured herself a black coffee.

Elizabeth poured her own but added half the contents of the milk jug. "Right then, where do you want to start?"

Ellie opened her briefcase, lifted out two A4 size photographs and passed them over to Elizabeth. Elizabeth picked up her reading glasses and placed them on her nose. She then inspected each photograph in detail. After a few seconds, she smiled and said, "Mmm, I was a lot thinner in those days. Takes me back, they do. Life was very different then." She handed the pictures back to Ellie.

"Do you remember this photograph of the man being presented with the painting?" asked Ellie, placing one of the pictures back on the table in front of Elizabeth.

Elizabeth stared down at the photo for a second time. "Oh, yes. He was Joan's part-time gardener. Good-looking man. Don't remember his name, but he was leaving, going away to somewhere… in the Caribbean, I think. Joan was heartbroken, I remember that. She said he was a conscientious gardener and a lovely man. Looked after all her sunflowers. That's why she gave him one of her sunflower paintings. Told him it would remind him of her garden and his life in France. I hope he's still got the picture, because it'd now be worth a fortune."

"Do you know who the other woman is in the picture?"

"Oh, yes, that's Camille Barbier. She died… must be about ten years ago now."

"Didn't a man take the photos?"

"Yes, Claude Boucher. He was the eldest of all Joan's pupils. If I remember correctly, he died about the same time Joan did.

"Were you all Joan's pupils?"

"Not seriously. We were mainly friends of Joan. She gave

us some tips. I think I was the only one to take painting seriously. Not that I've been very successful, but I still enjoy dabbling. Converted the front bedroom upstairs into a studio. Lovely light comes in there."

"Have you still got any of Joan's paintings?"

"I wish! No, I did once own two, but sold them before I came back to England. They must be worth millions now."

"If I told you the gardener's name is Mathis Laurent, would that ring any bells?"

Elizabeth stared out of the window and repeated the name. "Mathis… Mathis. No, I cannot connect that name with the gardener. But as I said earlier, I really cannot remember his name at all. I used to see him working in the garden, but we never spoke."

"Do you know of anyone else who was witness to Joan presenting the painting to the gardener?"

Elizabeth slowly shook her head. "I don't think so. I can't remember anyone else being in the house when these photos were taken."

"Do you know if Joan gave Mathis any paperwork confirming her gift?"

"I wouldn't have thought so. It was just a gift. There was no buying and selling involved. No receipts, or anything like that."

"If I summarise everything you've told me today and put it in a statement, would you be prepared to sign it?"

"If it helps that gardener… Mathis, with proving his ownership, of course I will. Good luck to him. After all, Joan was heartbroken when he left."

Chapter 17

Ian had already informed Oscar of Ellie Morgan's involvement in tracing and interviewing Elizabeth Dubois, so it came as no surprise when Oscar received an email directly from Ellie.

Ellie's email summarised her investigations, her visit to the Surrey home and discussions with Elizabeth. She'd also attached two separate documents. One was a signed statement by Elizabeth confirming she was present when Joan gave Mathis his painting. The second was Ellie's invoice.

Oscar read the email and the signed statement with a broad smile on his face. He knew this was a crucial step towards proving the painting's provenance.

"You look excited," observed May. She was sitting at her desk and watching Oscar scrutinising his computer's screen.

"Brilliant news," responded Oscar. "Ian organised a private detective to trace Elizabeth Dubois. I've just received her report."

"And it's all good news?"

"Yes, largely. Elizabeth is the only witness still alive, but she's given a statement which confirms everything Mathis told me."

"What are you going to do now?"

"I'm not sure. I need to tell Mathis, and we also need to finish completing the catalogue raisonné submission form to the Joan Mitchell Foundation."

"Do you think you've got enough information now?"

"To be honest, I don't know. I'm not sure what more information the Foundation will want or if they'll need any technical evidence. Modern paintings are a new area for me."

"Yes. It appears to be a lot trickier with modern paintings. I read on their website that the submissions go directly to the Joan Mitchell Catalogue Raisonné project research staff. They don't appear to offer any extra guidance."

"I know... and they have sole discretion as to whether or not they'll include a painting in the catalogue raisonné. Without that, we're dead."

"Didn't Ian give you a contact in New York? Can he help?"

"Probably, but more people getting involved might just prompt them to turn up at Mathis's address. That would push me out. I need to make sure I stay in control."

The following day, Oscar visited Mathis. He was guided into the lounge where Joan Mitchell's painting was still hanging on the wall. After they sat down, Oscar explained Ellie's report and the significance of Elizabeth Dubois' statement.

Mathis smiled. "You have been a busy boy. Where do we go from here?"

"We certainly need to update our submission to the Joan Mitchell Foundation. Have you managed to find any more information we can include?"

"Maybe I've got some good news," said Mathis, with a teasing smile on his face.

"You have! Great," responded an excited Oscar. "What have you got?"

"I suddenly remembered, the other day, that, more or less, the last words Joan said to me, before I left for Guadeloupe, were to write to her and tell her I'd arrived safely. Initially, I forgot about her request, but after about a month in

Guadeloupe, I suddenly remembered and sent her a letter. I thought that would be the end of it, but she did reply."

"Wow! Have you still got the letter?"

Mathis gave Oscar another broad grin. "Yes I have. In fact she wrote to me twice."

At this, Mathis stood up, walked over to the table and picked up a blue cardboard folder. "I completely forgot that I'd kept these. I found the folder in an old suitcase in the attic." Mathis handed the folder over to Oscar.

Oscar gently eased out the old and delicate letters. He nervously unfolded the first one and read the contents. It was hand written in French. (translated):

My dear Mathis,

It was so wonderful to read your letter. I'm so pleased you arrived safely and you are enjoying life in Guadeloupe. I have a new gardener, but he's nowhere near as conscientious as you were. I do miss you and your smiling face.

I hope you look at my painting every day and it reminds you of the lovely times we shared in my garden.

Please write to me again when you have more news.

Fondest,

Joan.

Oscar put the letter gently down on the folder, opened up the second one and started to read:

My dear Mathis,

Oh what a lovely surprise when I received your letter yesterday. It cheered me up no end. My health is failing and it's probable that I'll be moving to Paris soon. If I do, I'll let you know my new address.

Fondest,

Joan.

Oscar placed the second letter down on the folder and wiped a tear appearing in his eye. "These are lovely, Mathis. I think this woman really liked you."

Mathis smiled and then his bottom lip trembled. "I was very fond of her and still feel sad that I left. She died two years after I arrived in Guadeloupe. That was the last letter I received from her. I was told she'd died in Paris, but I didn't find out for many months after."

"I'm so sorry," replied Oscar. He picked up the letters again and asked Mathis if it was alright to photograph them.

"Yes, of course. You go ahead. Maybe they'll help with your submission."

Oscar gently unfolded each letter again and laid them flat on the folder. He removed his mobile and took several pictures of both letters.

When Oscar returned to his villa, he went straight to his office to finalise his and Mathis's submission to the Joan Mitchell Foundation. As well as including several different photographs of the painting and a copy of Elizabeth Dubois' statement, he also attached copies of both the letters Joan Mitchell had sent to Mathis. Whilst the second letter didn't add anything towards the provenance, Oscar decided it did reinforce the special relationship that existed between Joan and Mathis.

Finally, when he'd finished, he asked May to check it. This she did, and after reading the letters, she too had a tear in her eye.

"Oh, Oscar, that's so sad. I'm sure the Foundation will jump at including Mathis's painting. I do hope so. You've done a wonderful job. Is Mathis pleased?"

"He appreciates we're giving it our best shot. Mind, even if the Foundation agrees to the submission, I'm not totally convinced Mathis will sell his painting now. Those letters have brought back happy memories, and he seems more passionate and sentimental now towards it. I guess we'll just have to wait and see."

Chapter 18

Ian sat in his office looking at his computer. He was studying Sotheby's latest catalogue advertising the next auction to be held in three weeks' time. However, his concentration kept drifting as he was still waiting for the latest report from George Bailey.

After about 15 minutes, he decided there wasn't really anything of interest in the catalogue. Also, on page 2, he'd spotted an uninspiring photograph of a grinning Jonathan Northgate, which he immediately took exception to. Typical, he thought, get Penny and her team to do all the work and then try to take all the credit. Still, what's new with this egotistical clown?!

"Ian?" Emma called from the kitchen.

Ian closed down Sotheby's website, stood up and wandered through the hallway to the kitchen. "You called," he announced, sounding a little jovial.

Emma was staring at the calendar and, without looking up, said, "It's about Oscar's invitation. I've been looking at our calendar and was wondering what you thought. We're already committed for your parents to visit for three days over Christmas, and then we go to my parents for the new year. Robert doesn't go back to school until January 19th, so we could have a couple of weeks in Antigua."

"That sounds good. Should I speak to Oscar and see if he and May are free then?"

"Yes," said Emma, a little hesitant. She was still focussed on the calendar. "Better suggest we leave them on the 16th. It's usually an overnight flight, and I need to make sure Robert is properly packed before he goes back to school."

"That's cutting the time we're going to have with Oscar and May because the earliest flight out to Antigua we could do is the 2nd."

"It would still be a nice break, and you know Oscar likes to see Robert."

"Okay. I'll email him."

As Emma replaced the calendar back on the hook on the wall, she asked, "Have you heard any more from George?"

"No. I was going to give him till tomorrow and then chase him up."

"Do you really think Jonathan Northgate is involved in some sort of crime?"

"To be honest, I don't really know. It all sounds very odd. Why does he keep arriving back at the apartment with different paintings? I emailed a colleague in Dubai, some weeks ago, and gave him the details of the Munnings horse picture, the one Penny told us about. Also, I gave him the name and address of the buyer, so I'm hoping he'll be able to find out if the buyer actually received his painting."

"This colleague, is he in the art business?"

"Yes, it's Joey Sanderson. I first came across Joey in Hong Kong. He's owned a gallery in Dubai for... must be about 15 years. He might already know the buyer."

"Do you think, other than Penny, anybody else at Sotheby's is aware of the situation?"

"I wouldn't have thought Penny would have mentioned it to anyone, but, of course, security may have already been watching. I'm still concerned about Penny though. I told her right from the start not to trust Northgate."

"But Penny told you she was getting on well with him?"

"Yes, but I still keep warning her. The guy's dangerous and cannot be trusted. I want to see that conceited creature finally given his just deserts!"

The following morning, Ian was in his office and had just opened up his computer. In his email inbox, he spotted a reply from Joey Sanderson:

Hi Ian,

Long time no see. Thanks for your email and all your news. Interesting change of career. I thought you would have been the boss of Sotheby's by now. I guess there's another story there.

Things here in Dubai are really good. The place is expanding rapidly and so is my business. I'll soon be able to retire!

That Munnings painting you mentioned. Interesting situation. I know Karim very well, we've done some business together over the years. However, he spends a lot of his time abroad, that's why I've taken some time to reply.

It was a tricky conversation I had with him, as he received the painting within ten days of the auction. He seems completely happy with it and, I must admit, the painting looks the real deal. If it's a copy, it's brilliant, and at face value, it's fooled me. I guess the only way to find out properly is for the picture to be forensically inspected. I've not mentioned this to Karim, but I'm sure my conversation with him has got him thinking.

I'll let you know if he decides to have the picture examined.

All the best,

Joey.

So, thought Ian. The plot thickens! It still could be a good copy, but we're not going to be sure unless it's forensically inspected. But, even then, the result might not be totally clear. There's a number of brilliant forgeries out in the market fooling the art world. Could this be another example?

Chapter 19

Ian met with George Bailey two days later. They'd agreed on the phone to meet at 'The Bear' public house, close to Wimbledon railway station. George had suggested this venue as he had an appointment with another client in the town earlier the same morning.

Ian knew it was only a short train journey for him, and after George had described the venue as being a traditional English pub and a former coaching inn that once provided refuge for the infamous highwayman, Dick Turpin, he was intrigued. George always seemed able to find a meeting place that had both character and history.

It was just after one o'clock and both were sitting on a wooden bench seat next to an old wooden table on which sat two pints of beer. On their left-hand side was a large window, which gave them a view of the main road. The tables in the bar area were well spread out, so it was easy to have a conversation without being overheard.

After taking a large drink of his beer, George began to speak. "I checked out Cotton Enterprises. That office you went to in Charlton Street is just a front. Their main set-up is in Poland. There, they employ some of the best painting copiers in the world."

Ian was just about to have a drink of his beer when his

hand suddenly stopped in mid-air. He stared at George with his eyes wide open. "Poland! That's a new one on me."

"Originally, the organisation was based in Russia, but following the outbreak of the Ukrainian war, they transferred all their operations to Poland. My contact says they're sending out about four paintings a month."

Ian took a deep breath and slowly shook his head. "Where do they get all the original paintings from?"

"Mostly from America and the EU, but some do originate from the UK."

"Northgate!"

"I've still not made a direct connection, but it's a strong possibility. Cotton Enterprises appear to be responsible for photographing every minute detail of the original painting acquired in the UK. That way, the copy can be shipped to the auction buyer in just a few days. Most of the originals eventually find their way to Eastern Europe where they're sold on the dark web. Sometimes, paintings are stolen from museums or private collections, to order. This is usually when the museum doesn't have the picture on display and kept in store, or when the private collector isn't at home. The paintings are professionally switched and no one appears to be the wiser."

"This is unbelievable." Ian was suddenly wondering if this was something Andrei could have been involved in during his earlier days.

"They also like paintings that are sold at auction to buyers who are money rich but not technically clever enough to realise what they're buying. Hence your Middle Eastern buyers."

"After all, they're trusting the auction house to send them the original painting."

George nodded. "Quite."

Ian explained his email from Joey Sanderson in Dubai.

"Perfect example," responded George. "I guess until these paintings are properly investigated, nothing's going to change."

"But we've still not got a definite link with Northgate. It seems pretty certain he's involved, but we need proper proof."

"That's my next task, Ian. Leave it with me."

On the train journey back to Esher, Ian pondered on what George had told him. This was all getting very serious; it was more than just Northgate now. There was this world-wide criminal operation, probably running into millions, if not billions, of pounds. He certainly didn't want to get tangled up with this sort of organisation. Leave that to the proper authorities... but, of course, this was still a great opportunity to get his revenge on Northgate. Even, maybe, his final chance!

Ian stared out of the window at the passing country-side. Suddenly, he remembered that George had mentioned paintings being sent from America. Could Northgate have been doing the same thing when they were both working in New York?

Chapter 20

Oscar was still waiting for a reply from the Joan Mitchell Foundation, following his submission of Mathis's painting. It was now ten days since he'd sent the email, and although he'd received an automated acknowledgement, he was still anxiously waiting on their final decision.

When he'd recently spoken with Mathis, the former gardener was a little more relaxed. Yes, he wanted the Foundation to formally agree that his painting was definitely by the hand of Joan Mitchell, but as he told Oscar, the more he looked at the painting, the more he felt closer to his former employer and friend. He still felt guilty and sad that he wasn't aware of how ill Joan had been during the last 12 months of her life and, to some extent, he was blaming himself for leaving Vétheuil when he did.

Oscar tried to persuade him that, in all probability, he wouldn't have been able to save Joan or even prolong her life. After all, she'd died of lung cancer. However, Mathis countered this argument by saying that Joan was only 67 when she died, and two years earlier, she seemed fine. So he was now convinced that leaving when he did had a detrimental effect on her health.

Oscar didn't have any more ideas or evidence to comfort his colleague and just hoped that, in time, Mathis would realise

that, despite her dying early, Joan had enjoyed a great life…
and for almost five decades had been a very successful artist.

Two days later, Oscar finally received a letter, via email,
from the Foundation. It read:

Dear Mr. Ding,

*Thank you for your painting submission and photographs on
the behalf of the owner, Mathis Laurent. It's not a painting we've
come across before, although we know Joan Mitchell painted a
number of pictures she titled 'Sunflowers'.*

*The statement from Elizabeth Dubois and the two letters
addressed to Mr. Laurent are intriguing and do suggest that this
painting could indeed be part of the work completed by Joan
Mitchell. The photographs also confirm that the picture is very
much in the style of Joan's paintings whilst she lived in Vétheuil.*

*Nevertheless, for us to consider the matter more fully, we would
like to inspect the painting for ourselves. Is it possible that it could
be delivered to our offices in New York? The address is at the top
of this letter and should be sent for the personal attention of Harry
Clarke, Deputy Head, Research Team, Joan Mitchell Catalogue
Raisonné project.*

*Please note. Our decision as to whether to include your paint-
ing in the catalogue raisonné shall be solely an expression of our
opinion, and shall remain within our sole discretion. The decision
to include a painting does not constitute a warranty or guarantee
as to the painting's authenticity or provenance, and may not be
relied upon as such by the owner or any future purchaser of the
painting. Nor shall a decision not to include a painting be a dec-
laration that it is inauthentic. We reserve the right to change our
decision as we see fit.*

Yours sincerely,

Harry Clarke,

Deputy Head, Research Team.

Oscar read the letter for a second time and then looked across at May, who was working at her own desk. "I've just received a reply from the Joan Mitchell Foundation."

"Oh great! Is it good news?" asked May, standing up and walking around her desk to look at Oscar's computer screen.

"See for yourself," said Oscar moving his mouse to bring the letter back to the start.

May slowly read the letter and then looked at Oscar. "It's not exactly saying yes, but certainly not a no. What are you going to do now?"

"I need to speak with Mathis… and get his thoughts. I'm not sure he'll want to send the picture to America. I may have to take it myself."

May walked back to her seat and sat down. "This is all costing you time and money, and if Mathis has decided not to sell, then what?"

"I don't know. I never discussed my costs at the outset; we just agreed on a commission level when it was sold. But if he's decided not to sell, why would I incur the extra costs of taking the picture to New York?"

"Didn't you say at the beginning that Mathis was looking to sell because he wanted to increase his pension income?"

"Yes, so I don't think he can afford to pay me just for my expenses. He's either got to commit to the sale or we'll have to call it quits."

"There's still no guarantee that the Foundation will accept the painting after they've seen it in the flesh, so to speak."

"I know, but I still think we should have enough information to get the painting authenticated, but will the Foundation finally agree to it being added to their catalogue raisonné?"

"Then, of course, there'll be the forensic examinations," responded May. She didn't want to put Oscar off, but thought she needed to remind him of all the costs.

Oscar nodded. "I need to speak with Mathis and spell out all the facts."

Chapter 21

Oscar telephoned Mathis and made an appointment to visit him. He'd told Mathis that the Foundation had responded and he needed to discuss the next steps.

It was a hot day, even by Antigua standards, when Oscar drove over to meet with Mathis. He had the canvas roof of his Jeep folded down and the warm air was blowing all around inside the car. He was still pondering on his discussion with May and the approach he was going to take with Mathis. However, when he pulled up at the front of Mathis's property, he had a good idea of what he was going to say.

Mathis greeted Oscar with his usual smile and escorted him into the lounge, the coolest room in the house. A large jug of lemonade with added ice cubes was waiting for them on the table.

Whilst Oscar sat down on a sofa, Mathis poured two large glasses and handed one to him. Oscar thanked him and took a sip before placing it on a small table next to his seat. He then started to speak. "I sent you a copy of the Foundation's reply. In essence, they've not said yes but, crucially, not said no. They would like to see the painting for themselves. That means the picture going to New York. What are your thoughts?"

Mathis was sipping his drink and then placed it down on the table next to him. "I'm not sure now, Oscar," said Mathis, glancing across at the painting hanging on the wall. "It's all getting much more complicated than I thought it would… and, of course, there's no guarantee that once the Foundation sees my painting they're going to agree to it being published in their catalogue raisonné."

"I agree. So the question is, where do we go from here? I thought you wanted to sell this painting to increase your pension and improve your standard of living."

Mathis blew out a deep sigh. "It's not that simple now. That statement from Elizabeth Dubois and me finding those old letters have really made me think. It's not just a black-and-white situation."

Oscar was trying to calm his inner frustrations. "Okay. I realise you now seem to have a more sentimental attachment, but we need to make a decision. Either we carry on and get the picture to the Foundation in New York or we call it quits… now. I've incurred a number of expenses and don't see the point of incurring more if you're not committed to the sale."

Mathis was quiet and stared at Oscar for a few moments. Suddenly, his face became more sympathetic. "I can understand your position, Oscar. You'll only get paid when that picture is sold. But for me, it's more than just the money… although the money is a serious factor; it would set me up for the rest of my life. However, I hadn't realised how much I meant to Joan. She never said anything like what she said in her letters when I worked in her garden."

"That's never going to change. You'll still have your memories, and I could try and persuade the Foundation to just keep copies of Joan's letters on file, and you leave the originals to them in your will."

Mathis smiled. "That would be nice."

"However, you've still got to make the big decision."

Mathis sipped some of his lemonade and stared across at his painting. He stood up and walked across to the far wall, standing about a metre away from the picture. He placed his right hand on the frame and stared at the strange coloured splashes of the abstract work. "You know, I never really understood why Joan's work commands such high prices. These are supposed to be sunflowers, but they look nothing like the ones I grew. It's not the quality of the painting I see, Oscar. It's Joan standing next to her easel and painting it. She put her heart and soul into her work."

Oscar stood up and walked over to join his colleague. He placed his hand on Mathis's shoulder and stared at the picture. "The art world is strange. What is a quality piece of artwork? Some would say Canaletto, others Rembrandt. Then there's Turner or Picasso, Pollock or even Joan here. What do they all have in common? They're all revered artists for very different reasons. People pay millions for their work. Often it's not for the quality of the work, but the rarity and as an investment. That's where Joan's work is standing today. Tomorrow, it may all change, but for the moment, her work's wanted as an investment... and remember, right now, people are prepared to pay millions of dollars."

The room was now quiet except for a ticking clock. Mathis, still staring at his picture, said, "I've never been to New York, or even America. They say it's a big city with huge skyscraper buildings. Have you been there?"

"Not to New York, no."

"Maybe we should go and see it for ourselves... and take this picture to the Joan Mitchell Foundation."

Chapter 22

Ian decided to look once again at the forthcoming auction catalogue on Sotheby's website. He had an idea. Slowly turning the pages, he eventually came across what he was looking for, Lot 24. It was an abstract painting by Oliver Squires, titled, 'The Green Dress'. The picture showed a red-haired woman sitting on a wooden chair, staring out of a window. She was wearing a part-ripped green dress, which exposed her bare back. The chair appeared to be floating in the air, and the surrounding walls and floor were painted with different-coloured rectangles and triangles. It had a reserve price of £1.2 million. Ian then googled Oliver Squires and established that he was a young artist who was slowly building up a solid following. His last two paintings had sold for £525,000 and £777,000, and the art world was saying he could be the new Willem de Klooning. Ian wasn't sure about this last comment, but who knew? He certainly wasn't an expert when it came to abstract artists.

He needed to speak to Joey Sanderson.

Ian checked the time and calculated it was about 4.30pm in Dubai. He then removed his contact book from his top right-hand drawer and flipped through the pages until he came to the letter 'S'. He found Joey's entry and dialled his telephone number.

A pleasant-sounding female answered the call. Ian introduced himself and asked if he could speak to Mr. Sanderson. A few moments later, he was listening to a voice he hadn't heard for at least ten years.

"Ian Caxton," announced Joey, with an elated tone to his voice. "We haven't spoken for ages, and this is the second communication in a month! To what do I owe this honour?"

After brief general exchanges, Ian finally got to the point of his call. "Joey, I'm looking for a favour. You know from my email that I'm concerned about paintings being bought at auction in the UK but the buyer potentially being defrauded and only receiving an excellent copy. It's a bit like what we had in Hong Kong with the Chén group."

"Yes, I remember that group. I was thinking about them after receiving your email about Karim's painting. By the way, Karim's going to get his Munnings picture forensically analysed."

"Good. Can you let me know the result, please?"

"Of course. If it's a fake, Karim's going to sue Sotheby's. Probably a good job you're not in charge."

"I know, but I'm concerned that someone high up in the organisation is involved."

"Sounds like you're taking this situation very personally?"

"Yes, I am. It goes all the way back to New York, before I arrived in Hong Kong."

"Okay, so what exactly is the favour?"

Ian explained that he wanted to arrange for £1.5 million to be transferred to Joey's personal account and the money to be used to buy the Oliver Squires painting: Lot 24, at the forthcoming Sotheby's auction on the 29th. He wanted to follow what then happened to the painting. "I don't want your company name associated with the bidding. It's got to be an individual, someone like Karim, fronting the purchase on my behalf."

"I wouldn't want Karim involved, but my PA, Bakir, would probably do it for you. Incidentally, why me and Dubai?"

"These people are very keen on obtaining original paintings, bought at auction. Particularly from wealthy and trusting innocents in the Middle East."

"I see where you're coming from. Oliver Squires, you say? I've heard that name. Isn't he supposed to be the next up-and-coming abstract artist?"

"You're more up to date with abstract paintings than I am, Joey. If I get a good deal at the auction, I'll let you have first refusal at the auction price."

"What, for a fake!? Thank you for nothing."

Both men laughed, and Ian said, "Thanks. I'll wire you the money and email you all the details."

Chapter 23

"Oscar. It's great to hear from you," said Ian, after he'd answered the phone and realised it was his friend from Antigua. "How's things?"

"Things are really good… Well, they are now. Mathis has finally agreed for us to take his picture to New York. We've got an appointment with Harry Clarke, he's the deputy head of the Joan Mitchell Research Team."

"That's great. So your submission worked?"

Oscar explained his recent communications with the Foundation.

"At least they've not said no. Sounds promising."

"I hope so. I've got a lot of money riding on this one, Ian. Mind, Mathis has become much more sentimental since he read your detective's statement from Elizabeth Dubois and him finding those letters. I'm still not 100% sure he's going to sell. Which is why I've telephoned you, Ian. I'm interested in contacting your colleague in New York."

"Bruce Campbell? Yes, he's still working for Sotheby's."

"Good, because I thought it would be a great idea for Mathis and me to meet with him. You said he was really positive when you spoke to him."

"He says Joan Mitchell paintings are in demand… and fetching seriously high prices at auction in New York."

"That's great, because I'm hoping he'll be able to convince Mathis to sell... if the Foundation authorises it of course. Mind, the provenance certainly stacks up, so I'm really confident."

"I'll email you details of Bruce's telephone number and email address. I'll also email Bruce and tell him to expect a call from you."

"Thanks, Ian. By the way, are you coming out to see us at Christmas?"

"It might be early in the new year, if that's okay? We're already committed with parents over the Christmas period. Emma's juggling dates."

"That should be fine. Let me know when you've finally sorted out your diary. Thanks again, Ian. Bye for now."

"Bye, Oscar. Let me know how you get on in New York."

"I will. Cheers." Oscar switched off the call and leaned back in his chair. Now, he thought, time to contact Mr. Bruce Campbell.

The next morning, Oscar opened his email inbox and spotted Ian's email with Bruce Campbell's contact details. He then wrote the following email:

Dear Mr. Campbell,

I'm hoping Ian Caxton has informed you of my forthcoming meeting with the Joan Mitchell Foundation. He previously suggested you might be interested in my client's painting, if it was authorised and you still recommend selling at auction in New York.

Our meeting with the Foundation is in seven days' time, on the 16th. I was therefore wondering if we could take this opportunity to meet with you? You obviously understand better the workings of the American art market and Sotheby's auction requirements.

After the Foundation meeting, my client and I propose to spend

three days looking around your wonderful city, so if you're avail-
able can you please let me know which day would work best for
you?
    I look forward to your reply,
    Yours sincerely,
    Oscar Ding.

Only two hours later, Oscar heard a ping from his computer, indicating an incoming email. He opened it up, and, to his surprise, it was a reply from Bruce Campbell. In summary, Bruce said he was looking forward to meeting Oscar and his client. He suggested they call at Sotheby's late morning, on the 17th. He would then take them for lunch and answer any questions about the American art market.

Oscar was elated and quickly replied, confirming he and Mathis would visit Sotheby's late morning on the 17th.

Just after 8pm, on the 15th, Oscar and Mathis's plane landed at John F. Kennedy International Airport. It had been a long day, as they'd had to change flights at Miami. They were both tired and weary and just wanted to climb into bed. However, it was another hour before their yellow cab dropped them off at their hotel in downtown Manhattan. Both collected their room keys and agreed to meet in reception at 9 o'clock, for breakfast. Tomorrow was the 16th and they were expected at the Joan Mitchell Foundation at 11 o'clock.

At 8.55am the following morning, Oscar sat in reception reading a free newspaper he'd found laying on his seat.

"Ready for breakfast?" announced Mathis, standing in front of Oscar.

Oscar looked up and smiled. "Yes. I'm hungry. It's ages since we last ate."

The two men walked down the corridor and entered the

dining area. Although it was fairly busy, they were quickly shown to an empty table. It was a buffet arrangement, so both men could select exactly what they wanted. Oscar decided to go for the 'American' and tea, whilst Mathis selected various pastries, toast and black coffee.

"Big day," said Oscar, breaking the silence and placing some of his scrambled eggs into his mouth.

Mathis returned a nervous smile. "Yes," he said hesitantly. "Do you think there'll be any problems?"

"There shouldn't be. The provenance all stacks up, but the Foundation will need to be absolutely certain. Their reputation's on the line."

Mathis slowly nodded and placed a portion of pastry into his mouth.

At 10.52am, the yellow cab pulled up outside 137 W. 25th Street. Oscar paid the fare, and both men got out. Mathis was careful not to catch his picture on the door frame, even though it was double protected in bubble wrap and a canvas bag.

Oscar looked up and down the street. All the buildings seemed relatively uniform. Mostly six stories high and built of concrete and glass. Above the first floor, most appeared to be occupied as offices. Each building's ground floor, however, had large display windows, behind which were office receptions, shops and a few restaurants.

The two men pushed on the large glass entrance door and walked into a bright and modern reception area. Oscar announced they had an appointment with Harry Clarke, and they were invited to sit on a large blue leather couch.

Five minutes later, a tall dark-haired man in a light grey suit strolled over to join them. Oscar thought he might be about his own age. He nudged Mathis. They both stood up.

"Hi! I'm Harry Clarke. Welcome to the Joan Mitchell Foundation." Harry held out his hand.

Both shook Harry's hand and Oscar introduced himself and Mathis.

"Come a long way… from the Caribbean, I hear. I assume you've got the painting in that bag?"

Mathis now spoke for the first time. "Yes… and it's been a nervy 24 hours carrying it all the way from Antigua."

"Okay. Well, let's get it up to my office and take a look," said Harry, still smiling. He led the way through the reception area. "I'm on the fifth floor, so we'll use the elevator."

Five minutes later, Harry pushed on an oak door that led the group into a large, plush office. Harry walked across the thick green carpet to a sizeable oak table. He suggested Mathis should unpack his picture and place it there. This Mathis did.

Once the painting was unpacked, Harry walked over to inspect it. He removed a small torch from his pocket and leaned down, slowly shining the beam all over the picture. After a few moments he asked, "Mind if I pick it up?"

"No. Carry on," responded Mathis. It was a bit late now, he thought, to be hyper protective.

Harry lifted the painting and angled it towards the window light. After a few moments, he turned it over and inspected the back.

During the rest of the inspection, Harry didn't make any more comments. Oscar and Mathis, meanwhile, just stared and held their breaths.

Finally, Harry placed the picture back on the table and broke the silence. "Certainly looks like Joan's work… but, unfortunately, so do a lot of good fakes."

Oscar didn't like this last comment. "It's not a fake. It has excellent provenance."

Harry smiled at Oscar and then said, "Let's sit down."

All three sat down next to the table.

"Yes, the provenance you sent us is… okay," continued

Harry, looking again at the painting, "but our forensic team will need to fully analyse this picture before we can make any definitive decision."

"How long will that take?" asked Oscar. He hoped it could be completed before they left New York.

"When are you guys planning to fly home?"

"In three days' time. Our flight leaves JFK at 1pm."

Harry nodded his head. "Come back in two days; we'll have an answer by then."

Chapter 24

Just over 24 hours later, Oscar and Mathis arrived outside the imposing 30-plus-storey building. The address was 1334 York Avenue.

They both stared up at the modern glass-fronted building, which had a large and impressive sign above the two revolving entrance glass doors. It simply stated, 'Sotheby's'.

Both were impressed, and Oscar felt excited. This, he thought, was what the art world was all about. Some of the greatest pictures ever painted had been auctioned here… and some had been sold for in excess of a hundred million dollars!

Mathis looked at Oscar and said, "This is wonderful. I'm feeling really nervous."

Oscar smiled and patted his colleague on the shoulder. "Come on. Let's go and see what Bruce has got to say."

The two men pushed on one of the revolving doors and entered a spacious and modern reception area. Mathis stopped and stared all around him.

Oscar carried on to the reception desk where he announced he had an appointment with Bruce Campbell. The woman smiled and made a telephone call. She then told Oscar, "Mr. Campbell will join you in a few moments."

"Thank you," responded Oscar, and looked around to see where Mathis was.

Mathis walked over to join his colleague. "I've never been in a place like this before."

"It's the atmosphere and history. Must be amazing to work here," responded Oscar. He enviously thought about Ian working here.

"Mr. Ding and Mr. Laurent?" announced a strong voice from behind them.

Both Oscar and Mathis turned together and looked at a large man with a well-tanned face. He was dressed in a navy suit and multicoloured tie. Despite the air conditioning, he was perspiring slightly.

Oscar held out his hand. "I'm Oscar, and this is Mathis."

Bruce gripped Oscar's hand firmly and then did the same with Mathis. "I'm Bruce. Great to meet you guys," he said, when he'd finally released Mathis's hand. "All the way from Antigua, I gather. Not been there. Only place in the Caribbean I've been to is the Bahamas. You been there?"

Oscar knew the Bahamas was not, technically, in the Caribbean, but this was not the time to quibble and discuss its exact location. "No," said Oscar and he looked at Mathis.

Mathis responded. "I went there once, but it was a long time ago. This is my first visit to New York."

"Really! Okay. There's lots to see. I'll tell you all about that later. First, I've organised a table at our Italian restaurant on the first floor. It's great for a light lunch and brews awesome coffee. Come on."

Bruce turned around and strode out ahead. Oscar and Mathis had to walk quickly to keep up. A few minutes later they were sitting at their table. The Sant Ambroeus, Sotheby's restaurant, was in a bright and modern room, although Bruce informed them that the mahogany panelling decor was influenced by the Italian coffee bars of the 1950s.

After ordering their drinks, they each started to look at

their menu. Eventually, Oscar decided on the 'Chicchirichi', a chicken panini, whilst Mathis selected the 'Insalata Centocolori', a mozzarella, avocado and tomato salad. Bruce chose his regular 'Tonno Classico', a tuna and tomato Paninetti with fries.

"Okay, guys. Let's talk about your painting." Bruce was eager to hear what Oscar and Mathis had to say. "I assume you've left it with the Foundation?"

For the next ten minutes, Oscar and Mathis explained the history of the painting and the more recent developments with the provenance.

"You guys have certainly been busy. So, you're now just waiting on the Foundation's answer," said Bruce, leaning back in his seat. "Certainly, if you get the okay from Harry and his team, I can definitely get you a few possible buyers. I've already put out a few feelers. You're looking at about 15 to 20 mill… minimum."

Oscar looked at Mathis and then to Bruce. "Are you suggesting a private buyer rather than auction?"

"Not necessarily. I've just tossed a stone in the water at this stage. That's the immediate feedback I got. Obviously, it still depends on what the Foundation has to say."

Mathis stared at Bruce, but remained silent. Oscar wanted Bruce to push and encourage the possible sale. "Do you think we'd get a better price at auction?"

"Yep, I'd say so, but then you've got to factor in the added auction costs." Bruce explained how Sotheby's auction system worked and compared these extras and timescales with a direct sale.

Oscar looked at Mathis. "What are you thinking?"

After a moment, Mathis looked directly at his colleague and gave him a wry smile. "This sounds very good, but it's all academic. We can't decide on anything until we get the Foundation's result. Then I'll be able to make my final decision."

Chapter 25

Ian's next meeting with George Bailey was disappointing. The detective's report only informed Ian that Jonathan Northgate's activities had gone very quiet. No more paintings had arrived in the apartment and none had been delivered to Cotton Enterprises.

Despite this potential setback, Ian still made the transfer of £1.5 million to Joey Sanderson's personal account. He still felt confident that the Oliver Squires abstract painting, Lot 24, would be too much of a temptation for Northgate. He also decided to telephone Viktor and ask him if he was available to go along to the auction.

"Of course I'll go," responded Viktor. He was intrigued and assumed this had something to do with the Northgate investigation.

"I'm only interested to know what Lot 24 is sold for," said Ian. He didn't want to go into too many details over the phone.

"Okay. I'll let you know as soon as the picture's been sold."

"Thanks, Vic. I owe you one."

Both said their goodbyes, and Viktor switched off the call. Mmm, he thought, let's have a look at that auction catalogue. He switched on his computer and brought up

Sotheby's website on his browser. After linking to the auction on the 29th, he paged through to Lot 24, where he read all the promotional information. When he'd finished, he considered the main details: Abstract painting by Oliver Squires, titled 'The Green Dress'. Reserve price £1.2 million. Viktor folded his arms and began to smile. What are you doing, Mr. Caxton? You don't even like abstract paintings, he thought.

After Ian ended the call with Viktor, he looked across to Emma, who was typing on her computer's keyboard. "Fancy a few days in Dubai?"

Emma immediately looked up in surprise. "Dubai! Is this something to do with Joey Sanderson?"

"Yes. I've persuaded him to purchase a painting on my behalf. It's coming up for auction at Sotheby's in three days' time. I'm banking on Northgate stealing it and a copy being delivered to Dubai. If that happens, I want to see which picture arrives at his gallery."

"Are you sure Northgate will be interested?"

"No, but I'd bet a few pounds he won't be able to resist it."

"So, you think a copy will arrive in Dubai and Jonathan Northgate keeps the original?"

"Not for himself, but he'll pass it on to Cotton Enterprises. The organisation will produce the copy and keep the original."

"Why is Jonathan involved? Have you found out his reasons yet?"

"No. George is still investigating." Ian scratched his head and hoped George would come up with more information… very soon.

Emma stood up and walked over to the side of Ian's desk. "Is Penny aware of what you're doing?"

"No. As far as possible, I'm keeping my activities away from her and Vic. Mind, I do have a small job for her to do before the auction."

Later that evening, Ian telephoned Penny. He suggested they meet for lunch the following day at a quiet French restaurant close to Berkeley Square, a ten-minute walk from Sotheby's.

Ian arrived at the restaurant at 12.35 and was shown to his reserved table. He ordered a gin and tonic and said he was waiting for his guest.

Penny arrived at 12.50 and was shown to Ian's table by the maître d'. Ian stood up, and they gave each other a hug and kisses on the cheek.

Penny removed her coat and, after placing it on the back of her chair, sat down.

"You're looking well," said Ian, still smiling at his former PA. "What can I get you to drink?"

"Thanks. I better stick to mineral water. I've got a team meeting later this afternoon. Don't want to be breathing alcohol fumes all over my colleagues."

The maître d' was still standing next to Penny's chair and said he would send his colleague over with the lady's drink and the menus.

"So, Mr. Caxton, why do I deserve this treat?" asked Penny, with a glint in her eye.

Ian smiled and looked around the room. "Two reasons. One, I always enjoy your company and treating you to a meal…"

Penny leaned back in her chair and smiled.

"…and secondly, I've got a little job for you."

Before Penny could query Ian's last comment, they were interrupted by a waiter delivering Penny's drink and two menus. Once the waiter had walked away, Penny asked, "Something to do with Jonathan?"

This time it was Ian who smiled. "How did you guess?"

Penny picked up her glass and took a sip. "How's your investigation progressing?"

"I think we agreed that the less you knew of what I was doing, the better it would be for you. I still largely want to keep it that way. However, I need to ask a favour." Ian then explained about the Oliver Squires painting, 'The Green Dress', and it being for sale in the next Sotheby's auction.

"My team was involved in putting together the catalogue. I know which picture you're talking about, but, Ian, it's an abstract. You're not usually interested in modern art?"

"Let's just say, I know who wants to buy it and why. It's then, supposedly, going to be shipped to Dubai. But I think your Mr. Northgate will intervene and it'll be a copy that arrives in Dubai."

Penny raised her eyebrows in surprise and glanced around her. She then leaned forward and whispered, "What do you want me to do?"

Ian put a hand in his side jacket pocket and removed what looked like a silver pen. "I got this from my detective colleague. It's a special felt tip that writes using invisible ink. The wording can only be read using a special ultraviolet torch. What I want you to do is write the word 'original', on the back of the canvas. About five centimetres high should suffice."

Penny reached across the table and took the pen from Ian's hand. She looked at it suspiciously and then unscrewed the cap. The tip looked like a normal felt-tip pen. She placed the tip on her menu and made a scribble. When nothing appeared she looked at Ian smiling.

Ian put his hand into his other side pocket and removed what looked like a small torch. Checking nobody was watching, he pointed it at Penny's menu. A strong purple light immediately shone and illuminated the scribble Penny had drawn.

They both had wry smiles on their faces.

Penny placed the pen into her handbag, and after Ian had put the torch back into his pocket, he picked up his menu. "I think we'd better order some food."

Chapter 26

Later that same afternoon, after her team meeting, Penny was walking along a corridor heading towards the specially secured room where Sotheby's stored items due shortly to be auctioned. Hidden up the sleeve of her jumper was Ian's pen.

She was apprehensive and wondered what she'd say if someone challenged her. Since she'd been promoted, it was rare for her to visit this room; it was usually one of her team who had the responsibility for checking on any queries.

Arriving outside the room's secure door, she was just about to press the code on the security pad when she was suddenly startled. Stepping back quickly, her heart racing, she noticed the door slowly opening. To her astonishment, it was Jonathan Northgate exiting the room. He didn't immediately notice Penny; he was too engrossed examining photographs on his mobile. When he finally looked up, Penny spoke first. "You made me jump!" She smiled and placed her left hand over her heart.

"Sorry. Just checking on three paintings," he replied, trying to keep his voice as normal as possible.

"Is there a problem?" asked Penny, attempting to hide why she was there.

"No. It all seems fine. I looked at the catalogue earlier

and thought I'd have a closer look at some of the paintings. Are you going in there?" asked Jonathan, still holding the door ajar.

"Yes. I wanted to check on Lot 12's frame… to see if it had been properly tidied up. Angela noticed it had been damaged in transit." Penny hoped she sounded convincing.

"Everything looks okay and ready for the auction. Good idea to check for yourself though."

Jonathan stood aside to let Penny enter. "When you've finished, can you come up to my office? There are a couple of issues I'd like to discuss."

"Yes. I'll only be here for a few minutes. I'll then come straight up."

At this, Jonathan walked away and Penny quickly stepped into the secure room. Once she'd heard the door latch click, she gave a deep sigh. That was a close one, she thought and turned around making sure nobody else was in the room. When satisfied, she locked the door and reset the lighting for an extra ten minutes. The room was a large windowless space. Facing her were several tall sliding metal racks and two substantial empty tables standing at the far end of the room. The tables were normally used to store items of pottery, ceramics and any other free-standing items. Today the room was only being used to store pictures for Thursday's auction.

Penny walked towards the row of racks. On the end of each rack, a notice had been attached. Each notice listed all the paintings being stored and their allocated Lot numbers. Advancing along each row, she soon found the notice that included Lot 24, 'The Green Dress'. Pulling on the frame's metal handle, the rack slowly eased backwards, gliding on rubber wheels. She searched through the eight paintings displayed. Halfway along was a sign saying, Lot 24 "The Green Dress". She looked closely at the abstract picture and noticed Oliver Squires' signature in the bottom right-hand corner. Lifting the painting off its retaining hooks, she carried it over to the nearest of the two tables and placed it face downwards. After blowing away a few specks of dust, she carefully removed the silver pen from her sleeve and wrote the word 'original' in the top left-hand corner. Leaning down to examine her work, she was reassured when she observed no evidence of her writing. Pushing the pen back up her sleeve, she picked up the painting and returned it to its original position on the rack hooks. Now satisfied the picture was properly level, she pushed the rack back to its precise storing position and hurried towards the door. Breathing heavily, she released the internal lock and cautiously peered into the corridor. Satisfied the coast was clear, she switched off the room's lights and gently closed the door. Still breathing heavily, she waited anxiously until she heard the familiar click from the security lock.

Seconds later, she was striding triumphantly towards the elevator and onwards to the meeting with her boss.

Chapter 27

Oscar and Mathis had just arrived outside 137 W. 25th Street. They were expected for their follow-up meeting with Harry Clarke. Both men were nervous and apprehensive as they stood in front of the large glass entrance door.

"This is it," said Oscar, taking a deep breath.

Mathis looked at his colleague with a tense smile. "I know it's Joan's painting. It's been in my possession every day since she gave it to me."

Oscar pulled open the glass entrance door. "Let's hope the Foundation finally agrees with you."

Both entered the now familiar bright and modern reception area. Oscar walked over to the reception desk, announced their names and said they had an appointment with Harry Clarke. The receptionist smiled and picked up her phone. She also pointed to a cream leather couch and suggested they should sit down.

Both men duly followed her instruction.

When Oscar sat down, he gazed around the room and thought about all the powerful organisations like this Foundation. They were the ultimate deciders on the fates of hundreds of paintings, potentially worth tens of millions of dollars. Were the pictures originals or copies? Did they make mistakes? This was the crunch decision moment for

Mathis's picture. He glanced at his colleague and wondered what he was thinking? Mathis appeared to be calm, just staring down at his hands, but was he worried?

"Mr. Ding?" A young woman in a navy blue suit appeared at the side of the couch.

Oscar was suddenly aware of his name being announced. He looked up to see an attractive woman. He stood up and answered, "Yes."

Mathis remained sitting but looked up to study the new arrival.

"Hello, I'm Donna, Mr. Clarke's PA. Will you both follow me?"

Mathis stood up and gave Oscar a nervous smile. Here we go, he thought and both of them followed Donna towards the elevator. The doors were already open, and after they'd entered, Donna pressed the button for the sixth floor.

Oscar looked across at Donna and said, "When we were last here, we went to Mr. Clarke's office on the fifth floor."

"We're going to the board room, not Mr. Clarke's office."

"Oh, okay," responded Oscar, looking at Mathis, but his colleague just gave a shrug of his shoulders.

When the doors opened, they all walked along a brightly lit corridor. On both walls, a number of paintings were proudly being displayed. Oscar thought two of the pictures looked very similar to Mathis's picture. He wondered if all of them were Joan Mitchell originals.

At the end of the corridor, Donna stopped in front of a large oak door. On the right-hand side, a copper plaque stated 'Board Room'. Donna gave the door a firm knock and pushed it open. After stepping into the room, she waved for Oscar and Mathis to follow.

The room was huge and grand. Three walls were decorated with more Joan Mitchell pictures, whilst directly facing them was a bank of large windows. Sitting at the far end of a large oak table was Harry Clarke with two female colleagues. Behind one of the women was an easel displaying Mathis's painting.

All three stood up. Harry Clarke walked across to greet the new arrivals. "Welcome back, gentlemen. Let me introduce you to my colleagues, Belinda and Sally. Both work in the research department and have personally been investigating your painting."

Both women stepped forward and shook hands with Oscar and Mathis.

Oscar was surprised. The two women appeared to be much younger and more smartly dressed than he'd expected. He'd anticipated older men in white lab coats, not stylish white cotton blouses and navy blue skirts.

"Please, gents, sit down. We've got a lot to discuss," said Harry, pointing at two vacant chairs.

Both men sat down and waited for Harry to continue.

"These ladies have spent a lot of time reviewing your picture." Harry pointed to the painting behind Belinda. "They'll explain their findings."

Sally was the first to rise and stood next to the painting. Her New York accent sounded clear and confident. "Firstly, I have to say that until two days ago, we didn't know of this painting's existence. Initial thoughts were it must be a fake…"

"It certainly is not a fake!" announced Mathis, with an annoyed tone to his voice.

"Please bear with me," pleaded Sally, with a reassuring smile. "As I said, that was our first thought. You'd be surprised how many fakes we come across. Joan's work has been copied and faked a huge number of times. However, once I examined the picture in more detail, I realised it could possibly be a new find. The painting style, brushstrokes and composition seemed very typical of Joan's work.

I also analysed specks of paint and compared them with our records of pictures painted by Joan at about the same time you said Joan presented it to you. The pigment chemical structures are almost exactly the same. I then looked at the canvas and, again, this tied up with the type of canvas and thread weave Joan was using at that time. It could even have come from the same roll."

Oscar quietly smiled to himself. However, he wondered if there was a 'but' still to come.

Harry intervened and thanked Sally. "We also carried out a number of tests using the latest technology. Belinda will explain her findings."

Belinda walked over, stood next to the painting and began speaking, "We have to be absolutely certain when we make our decisions. As you're aware, Joan's paintings have sold for many millions of dollars. Any mistake on our behalf could lead to multi-million dollar legal actions being made against us. That's why we use the most up-to-date technological machinery. As Sally said earlier, fakes and copies are numerous, but even the best fake doesn't get past our technology."

Oscar glanced at Mathis. His colleague's face seemed much calmer.

"I won't bore you with all the details," continued Belinda, "but we do use optical microscopy, x-ray fluorescence, infra-red spectroscopy and chromatography-mass spectrometry."

Mathis raised his eyebrows and shifted in his seat. He was wondering what this attractive young woman was talking about!

"The x-ray was very interesting; it showed that the artist changed her mind several times before deciding on this final picture we see today."

"Is that a problem?" asked Oscar. He hoped not, but...

"Not in this case. The artist just made a few changes to

the initial lay-out. It's rare for a genuine painting not to have some final amendments. Fakes and copies very often don't show any such amendments."

Mathis sat back and folded his arms. He wanted to hear the final result.

Belinda continued, "In summary, your painting showed no adverse features."

"Thank you, Belinda." Harry stood up and replaced Belinda, standing next to the easel. "So, gentlemen, all is good… so far."

Oscar's tiny smile retreated. Here we go, he thought.

"When we see a strong painting such as yours," said Harry, now pacing behind his two colleagues. "We have four key factors to consider, style, materials used, provenance and exhibition history. You've heard my two colleagues talk positively about the style and materials used. However, now we have two difficult areas to consider. Provenance and exhibition history. There is no exhibition history, nor any auction catalogue records, no sales listing and no files appearing on the internet. Until a few days ago, the art world didn't even know of this painting's existence. You say, Mr. Laurent, it was painted decades ago and remained solely in your possession all that time. Certainly, the photographs you provided us with do suggest a similar-looking picture was given to you by Joan herself, but there is no documentary proof that states it is this same picture."

Harry arrived back by the painting. He picked it up and turned it around so the rear canvas faced his audience. "No information on the canvas or frame. No clues to the painting's history. That's unusual."

Oscar stood up. He was angry, and whilst Harry was replacing the picture on the easel, Oscar walked over to the other side of the painting. "Look, Harry, we've told you this picture has been in Mathis's possession all the time since

Joan gave it to him. Her letters even refer to it. Yes, there are no exhibitions or auction entries; this was a gift from friend to friend. It's rare, I agree, but it's also the truth!"

"Okay, Oscar, please return to your seat. I've not finished yet."

Oscar duly sat down and waited for Harry to resume.

"You might say I'm being picky," continued Harry, wiping his brow. "You've explained the reason for the painting's lack of provenance and why there wasn't any exposure to the art world, but we're talking about the art market here. Joan's paintings are sold for tens of millions of dollars. I'm just pointing out what we and the art market need to consider."

Oscar reluctantly nodded to Harry and waited for him to continue.

Mathis stared at Harry. He wasn't happy with what he was hearing.

"In conclusion, gentlemen, we're prepared to put all the facts we've uncovered in a report for you. We cannot categorically state, 100%, that this picture was painted by Joan. However, we can include a comment that says we do not believe it is either a fake or a copy. We will waive our final decision on whether it will be added to our catalogue raisonné. If we do eventually include it, it will be described as 'attributed to Joan Mitchell'."

Chapter 28

Oscar and Mathis stood silently outside the entrance to the Joan Mitchell Foundation building. They were hoping to hail a passing cab. Mathis was holding his painting, repacked and secure in its travelling case. He was angry. He felt the Foundation didn't believe his story. Yes, there was little actual proof of its history, but he knew he wasn't lying.

Oscar was still annoyed. He thought the organisation was just running scared of committing and stating it was painted by Joan. He knew they had a lot to lose and little to gain financially, but surely, that was their job? They'd even stated the painting wasn't a fake or a copy! What else could he and Mathis do? Would this decision devalue the painting? Had they both been wasting our time?

"They didn't believe me," said Mathis, breaking the silence. He was staring down at his feet.

Oscar took a deep breath, pushed his hands deep into his jacket pocket and looked at his colleague. He needed to raise Mathis's hopes. "I think they did believe you. Just didn't want to fully commit. We need to speak to Bruce and tell him the news. See what he's got to say. After all, it's not all bad news. He may have an idea."

Oscar spotted a cab cruising in their direction. He

stepped into the road and raised his hand. The cab pulled up and the two men climbed in.

Twenty minutes later, they were standing outside Sotheby's.

"Let's see what Bruce has got to say," said Oscar, pulling open the glass door. They both entered the reception area where Oscar gave his name and asked the receptionist if he could speak to Bruce Campbell.

The receptionist telephoned an extension. A few seconds later, she told Oscar that Mr. Campbell would shortly join them.

Oscar said, "Thank you", and returned to stand next to Mathis. "Bruce is coming."

Mathis nodded, but said nothing.

A few minutes later, Oscar spotted Bruce walking towards them. He nudged Mathis.

"Hey, guys, great to see you again." Bruce gripped Oscar's hand firmly and then did the same to Mathis. "I presume that's the special painting in there," said Bruce, pointing to the travelling case. "Have you got some good news?"

"That's what we want to talk to you about. It's not all great news," responded Oscar.

"Okay," replied Bruce, a little despondent. He could see both men were looking a bit down. "Let's go up to my office. I want to have a look at that painting… then you can tell me what the problems are."

Bruce turned around and strode out ahead, and again, Oscar and Mathis had to walk quickly to keep up. A few minutes later, they entered Bruce's office. By American standards, it was not huge, but it was nicely furnished in mostly teak. Behind the desk, was a large bookshelf containing both Art and Travel books. Against a large window, was a round table and four chairs.

"Let's sit at the table. Mathis, I'd like to see your painting. I want to see it without any preconceived ideas."

Mathis unbuckled the case and removed his picture, placing it on the table.

Bruce picked it up and looked at it closely. He then replaced it on the table and stared at it from a small distance. "First reaction... looks good. Certainly has Joany's style and... yep, the brushstrokes and composition seem fine. I can't fault it at the moment. What did the Foundation say?"

Oscar summarised what Harry and his two colleagues had said. Bruce listened quietly and only commented by nodding or changing his lips' pose.

When Oscar had finished, Bruce looked at Mathis. "Bit of a kick in the goolies."

Mathis smirked and said, "They didn't believe me. Thought I was lying."

Bruce looked again at the picture. "I don't think so. It's just that the provenance is a bit weak. There's no real history for them to see. No documentation or real evidence. When are you going to get their report?"

"They've promised to email both of us a copy in the next few days," said Oscar. "A written version will be posted and sent to Mathis's home address. We go back to Antigua tomorrow."

Bruce leaned back in his chair. "Look, guys... I don't think all is lost. The Foundation seems to be about 95% there. Nothing less than 100% is good for them. Let me have a copy of the report, and I'll see what I can do. Do you want to leave your painting with me? It'll be fine in our security. I'll obviously give you a receipt."

Oscar thought this was a great idea, but waited for Mathis to respond.

Mathis looked at Oscar. "What do you think?"

"Makes sense to me," responded Oscar. "It'll be secure in Sotheby's care. Bruce can show it to any potential buyer and you won't have to carry it all the way back to Antigua."

"It won't be on my wall at home. I'll miss it... but, yes, what you both say makes sense." Mathis stood up, looked at the picture one more time and walked away from the table. "It's like saying goodbye to a friend, to Joan."

Bruce and Oscar stood up and joined their colleague. Bruce said, "If we sell it, I'll make sure you get an exact copy."

When Mathis looked at Bruce, he gave him a sad smile. "Thanks. But it won't have been painted by Joan."

Two days later, Mathis finally arrived back home. There had been problems at Miami airport, and he was exhausted. He placed his luggage in the hallway and walked into the lounge. He immediately stared at the empty space on the wall. He began thinking about Joan and wondered what she'd have said. Would she have agreed with what he'd done? He hoped so, especially after she'd become aware of his financial situation.

He was almost broke and desperately needed the money.

Chapter 29

Viktor arrived at London's Sotheby's auction room just as the gavel came down on Lot 15. He found an empty seat in row seven. Looking around, he guessed the room was probably about 90% full. On his right-hand side, he noticed the bank of telephones were all in use. He wondered which one Ian's buyer would be connected to. Opening the catalogue, he searched for Lot 16 and listened whilst the auctioneer tried to manoeuvre potential buyers to higher bids.

It was 35 minutes later that Viktor turned his catalogue page to Lot 24. The auctioneer started to speak. "Now, ladies and gentlemen, we come to Lot 24, an abstract painting entitled, 'The Green Dress'. The artist is Oliver Squires, a young and up-and-coming, new artist. Can I have a bid of 500,000 pounds?"

Viktor looked at the people in his immediate vicinity. Nobody appeared to be in a rush to make a bid. All was quiet, too, with the people manning the telephones.

The auctioneer looked around the room, searching for a raised hand. "Oliver Squires' last painting sold for a much higher amount than this. Do I hear 450,000 pounds?"

Viktor heard a woman behind him say, "450,000 pounds."

"We now have a bid of 450,000 pounds. Do I hear 475?" asked the auctioneer, happy the bidding had finally started.

Viktor noticed a young man, holding one of the telephones, raising his hand.

"Thank you. We now have 475 on the telephone. Do I hear 500,000 pounds?"

This time a man in a dark grey suit, two places along the row where Viktor was sitting, raised his hand and announced, "600,000 pounds."

There was a murmur from the audience.

"Thank you, sir. Now we're moving on nicely. Do I hear 700,000 pounds?"

Slowly, the bidding crept up between the three bidders. When the bid on the telephone reached one million, the man near to Viktor shook his head.

"The bid of one million pounds is now against you, madam. Do I hear 1.1 million?"

"One million, and 50 thousand pounds." Viktor heard the woman shout.

"We now have a bid of one million and 50 thousand pounds." The auctioneer, and most of the crowd, now looked across at the young man talking on the telephone. He was still in discussion with the caller.

"The bid is against your client, Jeremy," the auctioneer announced. He knew the names of the six people manning the phones.

"One million, one hundred thousand pounds," Jeremy suddenly announced. He had a satisfying smile on his face.

More murmurs in the crowd.

"The bid is now at one million and one hundred thousand pounds. Madam?"

Viktor couldn't see the woman, but he guessed she was shaking her head. The auctioneer gave her a few more seconds to reconsider. "Do we have any further bids?" He looked around the room and across at the telephone users. Finally, he announced, "Do we have any bids over one million and one hundred thousand pounds?" Once again, he scoured the room. People were looking around to see if there would be another bid, but nothing was forthcoming.

"In that case I'm selling Lot 24, 'The Green Dress' by Oliver Squires, for one million and one hundred thousand pounds." The gavel came down with a resounding strike.

Viktor rose from his seat and made his exit. He had a telephone call to make.

When he arrived outside in New Bond Street, Viktor removed his mobile phone from his jacket pocket and telephoned Ian. After brief pleasantries, Viktor said, "One point one million, on the phone. I hope it was your man."

Ian had been sitting in his office when he took Viktor's call. Now he telephoned Joey Sanderson, in Dubai. After the receptionist answered the call, Ian was immediately connected to Joey. "Hi, Ian. I've got some good news. Bakir bought your picture. The cost, plus Sotheby's cut, will be transferred once we get the formal invoice."

"Thanks, Joey... and pass on my thanks to Bakir. Can you email me a copy of the invoice, please? I want to read the exact wording and see if the conditions have changed. Also, can you let me know when Bakir receives the painting."

"Yes, of course. You still think the painting we'll receive is going to be a copy?"

"I'm banking on it. Emma and I will be travelling out to Dubai to see for ourselves. By the way, did Karim get his Munnings picture forensically analysed?"

"He's not said any more to me, but I know he's been abroad for a couple of weeks."

"Any chance I can meet with him when I visit Dubai?"

"Let me know your plans, and I'll see if he's available."

"Thanks, Joey. Speak to you again shortly."

"Good luck, Ian."

After the call, Ian immediately telephoned George Bailey and asked him to keep an extra special eye out for any new arrivals at their 'associate's' home address.

Chapter 30

Both Mathis and Oscar duly received their emailed copies of the report from the Joan Mitchell Foundation. There were no surprises; the report confirmed what Harry and his associates had stated at their meeting.

Oscar telephoned Mathis from his home office. They discussed the report's contents and particularly the conclusions, but were neither elated nor disappointed. The report spelled out, in black and white, what they were expecting. Oscar said he would email copies of the report to Bruce Campbell and Ian. He wondered whether Ian might have any thoughts or suggestions.

Mathis told Oscar he was still unhappy with the Foundation, particularly implying his story was a lie. Oscar reminded him what Bruce had said. He didn't think the Foundation was calling him a liar; it was just their way of saying the provenance and exhibition history was too weak.

Oscar suggested Mathis should look again through all his old papers. Maybe he could still unearth something useful. Mathis said he was doubtful but agreed to look. After all, there was nothing to lose.

Oscar spent the rest of the morning emailing copies of the report. With Ian's email, he also included more information about the two meetings with Bruce. For Bruce, the report was attached to a covering message which simply said the report was enclosed. He felt a little more optimistic with Bruce's involvement and waited anxiously to see what transpired.

"Are you ready for lunch?" May entered the office.

"Yes, I've just finished sending my emails to Bruce and Ian. There's not much more I can do for the time being."

"Let's talk in the kitchen. Your salad's getting warm."

Oscar smiled and followed May into the kitchen where they sat down at the breakfast bar. Two plates of tuna salad were waiting to be eaten.

"Do you think Bruce will be able to help?" asked May. "He knows the American market and has probably come across something similar before."

Oscar placed his fork on the side of his plate and looked at May. "That's what I'm hoping. He didn't seem too distraught with the Foundation's conclusion. I'm eager to hear from him. It's Mathis I'm more worried about. He's still unhappy, thinks the Foundation is calling him a liar. I don't see it like that, but, of course, Mathis has more emotional ties with his painting than others might."

"Yes, I can see that. It's a difficult position for him. What's he doing now?"

"I've asked him to look again at all his old papers. Twofold really. Firstly, it will keep his mind occupied and feeling less defeated… and secondly, he may stumble across something he missed before."

"What about that detective in England? She unearthed some useful information. Maybe she could speak again to that former friend of Joan's. From when they lived in France."

Suddenly, Oscar had a big smile on his face. "That's a great idea! Thanks. I'll email her this afternoon."

When Ian received Oscar's email, he immediately read the Foundation's report and Oscar's summary of the conversations with Bruce. He was disappointed for his friend and pondered on the situation. The trouble was, he was too remote and behind the times with the American art market; that was Bruce's field of expertise. Nevertheless, he would try to imagine what he would do in the same situation. In the meantime, however, he had his own challenges with the Northgate saga. That very morning, George had telephoned to say he had some news. A meeting was agreed for four days' time. George said he had an appointment at nine o'clock in Kingston upon Thames, so they'd agreed to meet at lunchtime at 'The Queen's Arms'. George said the pub was about a five-minute walk from Kingston railway station.

Ian closed down his computer and looked across at Emma. She was sitting at her desk. "I've just received an email from Oscar."

"Oh, good. How is he… and May?"

"It wasn't that sort of email. He's got a problem with that painting I mentioned to you. Apparently the Joan Mitchell Foundation won't authenticate it. They agree it looks like a piece of work by Joan and say it's neither a fake nor a copy, but because Oscar's client, Mathis, was gifted the picture and has owned it since that time, the provenance and history is weak. There's no proper documentation and Mathis has never tried to sell or exhibit it, or even get a valuation."

"Didn't you tell me a detective had helped find out some information for him?"

"Yes, George's partner, Ellie. She interviewed a friend of Joan Mitchell's, from when they both lived in France. Maybe Oscar should talk to her again. I'm not sure what else to suggest, except to put his faith in Bruce. I'm pretty sure Bruce will come up with a good answer, maybe even an acceptable solution."

Chapter 31

On the day of his meeting with George Bailey, Ian caught the train and alighted at Kingston station. Following George's instructions and Google maps, he walked the five-minute journey and arrived outside 'The Queen's Arms' public house at 12.45. The pub looked inviting with large bay windows containing numerous small panes. However, when Ian approached the door, he spotted posters advertising regular live music and televised sport. Ian wondered why his colleague had suggested such a pub. After all, he was looking for a quiet conversation.

Once inside, however, Ian noticed the posters referred only to evening and weekend entertainment. At the moment, the room was quiet with just a few locals standing and chatting next to the bar. Others were sitting at two separate tables. Most of the walls were decorated by more posters and pictures promoting an Irish theme.

Ian spotted George and wandered over to join him. "Well, this is another surprise. Who's the famous character this time?"

"Hello, Ian." George stood up and shook Ian's hand. "A number of famous bands and singers have performed here, but that's not why I suggested it. It's usually quiet at lunchtime and their real ales are good. Let me get you a drink."

They both walked over to the bar and Ian surveyed the various names on the beer pumps. "What do you recommend? I caught the train, so I'm okay for a couple of pints."

"Depends on your taste, Ian. What do you like? Heavy, light, mild… and, of course, being an Irish themed pub, there's Guinness too."

"Better stick to light. I don't want to arrive home drunk."

George laughed and ordered two glasses of 'Harvest Gold'.

As they walked back to the table, Ian sipped his beer. "This is really good."

"They're all good here, Ian."

Both men sat down, and after George finished the final drops of his previous glass, he started to speak. "Right, down to business. As you know, we've been following your Mr. Northgate via a device inserted into his mobile. Also, we've recorded his comings and goings at his apartment. Until two days ago, nothing out of the ordinary had happened over the last couple of weeks. However, on Monday, he returned with a new painting and hung it on his lounge wall. I've got a photo for you to see. It's in my briefcase. Next morning, the painting was taken down, wrapped up and taken to our friends in Charlton Street, Cotton Enterprises."

George picked up and opened his briefcase. Ian eagerly waited for George to show him the photograph.

"Here it is. Ring any bells?"

George handed Ian an A4 size photograph. It was a picture of an abstract painting. Ian laughed and then excitedly announced, "Gotcha!" He was looking at 'The Green Dress', painted by Oliver Squires!

"Is that what you were hoping for?"

"It certainly is, George. Pity I couldn't see the rear of the canvas before he carried it off to Cotton Enterprises."

"I've got a copy here in my case." George leaned over and removed another photograph.

"Unfortunately, it won't show me what I'm looking for," said Ian, looking at the picture. "I was able to arrange for a colleague to use the invisible ink pen you gave me to write a message on the back."

George smiled and said, "Original."

"What!? How do you know that?"

"Let's just say we have our ways, Ian. Here, take a look." George produced another photograph. This time the background was dark, but the rear of the canvas was lit by an ultraviolet torch beam and the word 'original' could clearly be seen.

Ian smiled and slowly shook his head. "You got into his apartment overnight?"

"Not me, Ian. I was in bed at home. Ask my wife."

Now Ian laughed. "Okay, point taken. I need to follow the painting's journey."

"No problem there. A tiny electronic transmitter has been carefully hidden inside the frame." At this, George removed his mobile phone and opened a special app. He showed Ian a Google map with a red flashing dot halfway along Charlton Street in London. The premises of Cotton Enterprises.

"This is unbelievable, George. So you can follow this painting wherever it goes?"

"Anywhere in the world."

Ian picked up his beer, sat back in his seat and drank about a quarter of the contents. After replacing the glass on the table, he looked across at George, now sipping his own beer. "This is unbelievable, George. We're getting into the world of James Bond!"

"Technology's moved on massively since Mr. Bond's day. You'd be surprised what micro-technology is now available."

Ian thought for a moment and wondered where all this information was taking him. His only ambition was to pin down the activities of Northgate. To get his revenge, his reprisal, not to get involved in a Mafia-style world of art thefts and fraud. "Look, George, I need to think about all this. It's taking us much deeper into a world I never intended to be part of. It's only Northgate I'm after."

George collected his photographs and placed them back into his briefcase. "I'll keep these for safekeeping. You know where they'll be. We'll continue to keep tabs on Mr. Northgate until you tell us otherwise."

Ian nodded. He had a lot to think about. "Thanks, George."

Chapter 32

Bruce Campbell had received Oscar's email. Attached to it were copies of all the documents Oscar had submitted to the Joan Mitchell Catalogue Raisonné project and the Foundation's reply. After glancing at the submission papers, he was concentrating on the Foundation's report, which he read with a mixture of interest, curiosity and... a little disappointment. Once finished, he realised this wasn't going to be the easy sale he'd first envisaged. Nevertheless, as his father always told him, 'There's more than one way to skin a cat'! Nope, we now have a bigger challenge, but, hey, that's the fun of the job! There's a lot of commission riding on this one and I've no intention of giving up at the first hurdle. Okay. Let's get moving. I need to make some phone calls... and quick!

In Antigua, Oscar was pondering on what he was going to do next. He'd sent his email to Ellie, in England, and hoped she might come up with a new idea. He was also waiting on Bruce and Ian to respond to his emails. It was all frustrating and costing time and money. He wasn't even sure if Mathis's painting would attract a buyer now, never mind the 25–30 million dollars he'd hoped it would sell for in the beginning.

A little dispirited with the situation, he wandered into his kitchen intending to make himself a mug of coffee. He was on his own in the villa, as May had a meeting with Wesley at the Shell Gallery. He filled the kettle and was about to boil it when he decided he needed to be more positive and proactive. Abandoning the coffee, he grabbed his car keys and headed out to visit Mathis.

Thirty minutes later, he was ringing Mathis's doorbell.

"Hey, Oscar, come in. I've just brewed some coffee," announced Mathis, after he'd opened his front door.

They walked through the hallway and into the lounge. Oscar immediately spotted the empty rectangular blank space on the wall. "You've not replaced the painting I see," said Oscar, staring at the bare wall.

"No. If I can't sell it, I'll be putting it back over there."

"Bruce will certainly be able to sell it. The problem is, for how much?"

Mathis shrugged and headed out of the room. "I'll get the coffee."

Oscar noticed a pile of papers and folders on the table. He wandered over to have a look. He was hoping Mathis might have found something to help their cause.

"Not found anything, yet," said Mathis, re-entering the room with a tray and two mugs of coffee. He placed the tray on a small area of the table not already covered in papers. "Anyway, why have you called?"

Oscar picked up one of the mugs and took a sip. "To tell you I've emailed Ellie, Bruce and Ian… plus, I thought I might be useful in helping you go through all these old papers."

"Bit of a thankless exercise really, but it's given me a chance to throw out some rubbish. Anyway, two pairs of eyes are better than one."

Over the next hour, the two men looked through the

pile of papers. Those written in French, Oscar put to one side. His knowledge of the language was not even rudimentary!

"I don't think I'm being much help," announced Oscar, despairingly. "Most of this correspondence is in French."

"I did live there for most of my early life."

"We didn't study French in Hong Kong. The only foreign language I know is English."

Mathis smiled. "Mmm, same with me!"

"At least we have something in common," said Oscar, who decided to look for numbers on invoices, hoping a valuation of sorts might show up. "Are these all the old papers you've got?"

"Not all, but it is the majority." Suddenly, something caught Mathis's attention.

"Have you found something?" asked Oscar, hopefully.

"Nothing to do with the painting, but it's a copy of an invoice I gave to Joan for my gardening. I've written 'paid' and the date on the bottom."

Oscar looked over Mathis's shoulder, but gave up, when he could see it wouldn't help them in their search.

Another 30 minutes and they'd finished. Nothing helpful had been found.

"What about the other papers?" asked Oscar. He was bored with the exercise now but wanted to make sure everything had been looked at.

"At least these have all been sorted, so I'll take them away and return with the others." Mathis collected the three neat piles and left the room.

Oscar sipped the rest of his coffee, but grimaced when he realised it was now stone cold.

"These are the last lot," announced Mathis, walking back into the room. He placed two cardboard folders on the table.

Another hour and the task was complete. Nothing remotely linked to Joan Mitchell's painting had been found.

"Ah well," said Oscar, with a resigned sigh, "at least we've now exhausted that possibility. I guess we'll just have to wait for Ellie, Bruce or Ian to come up with something more helpful."

Chapter 33

When Ian arrived home after his meeting with George, he had no intention of telling Emma everything George had told him. He knew Emma was concerned with his determination to seek his reprisal with Northgate, so to tell her about the Mafia-style organisation Northgate was involved with wouldn't be a clever move. It would only bring back memories of his dealings with Andrei, and he certainly didn't want to do that. Instead, he just mentioned that George was monitoring the situation and had informed him that Northgate had 'The Green Dress' painting in his possession.

"Why don't you just report all this to the police?" was Emma's immediate reaction. "You've got proof that he's stolen it."

"Not quite. We still need to know which painting arrives in Dubai. My strong guess is it will be a copy, but until we're sure, I certainly can't afford to get the police involved."

"I wish you weren't involved with this, Ian. Why can't you just let bygones be bygones?"

"This isn't a schoolboy argument, Emma. In New York, Northgate tried to get me the sack... and nearly succeeded! If that had happened, you and I wouldn't have met. No, Northgate is going to get his just deserts... and I'm going to make sure it's really going to happen!"

Emma decided she had said her piece and left the office. However, just as she entered the hall, she called back, "I hope you know what you're doing, Ian... for the family's sake!"

Ian stared out of the window and said to himself, "So do I, Emma. So do I."

A couple of minutes later, Ian switched on his computer. He wanted to see if he'd received an email from Joey, in Dubai. He hadn't. However, he did spot the earlier email from Oscar, asking for his help with Mathis's painting. He started to type his reply.

Hi Oscar,

Sorry to hear the result from the Foundation. In many ways it's good news, but not quite good enough. The only suggestions I can think of are:

1. *Somehow Mathis needs to come up with extra information that strengthens the picture's provenance. I know that's obvious, but without it, you won't be able to get the Foundation to change their mind.*

2. *What about Ellie? Why don't you email her and suggest she does a bit more digging for you?*

3. *Bruce is probably your best bet. Get close to him. Find out what he's thinking. He'll want to sell the painting as much as you do. He's also got the right connections, knows the market and might even be able to get the Foundation to change their mind. He's good, Oscar. Trust him.*

Sorry I couldn't be of more help.
Keep me informed.
Best,
Ian.

Ian pressed the 'send' button and leaned back in his chair. He started to reminisce about Bruce Campbell and the great times they'd shared in New York. He'd learned a lot from Bruce, especially when he was still 'a little wet behind the ears'. Also, Bruce's involvement had partly helped him out of the mess with Northgate. Yes, he had a lot to thank Bruce for… and a lot of wrath to hit Northgate with.

"Ian," Emma called from the kitchen. "Dinner's going to be about ten minutes."

"Thanks. I'll be in shortly."

In Antigua, back at his villa, Oscar heard his mobile make a 'ping' noise, informing him an email had arrived. After opening it, he read Ian's message. Although a little disappointed, he took notice of Ian's recommendation to get closer to Bruce… and to trust him! Hmm, thought Oscar, maybe Bruce will make it all happen!

Whilst reading two other new emails, his mobile started to ring. Changing to the telephone app, he noticed a number he didn't recognise. "Hello," he said cautiously.

"Hey, Oscar. Is that you?"

Oscar immediately recognised Bruce's strong, southern American accent. "Hi, Bruce. Sorry I didn't recognise your number."

"That's okay. Look, I've just read the papers you emailed me. I might be onto something, but first, I've got a question. Did you know Mathis changed the picture's frame sometime after the photo of Joan presenting him with the picture was taken?"

"What!" exclaimed Oscar.

"I guess that's a no. Yep, the painting we've got has a different frame. Can you find out why? It might be useful. Also, I've got a couple of potential buyers interested. One is a massive JM collector, so we might be in there. Look, got to go. Let me know about the frame and why. Cheers."

Before Oscar could say his thanks and goodbye, Bruce had gone. Well, thought Oscar, placing his phone down. Why didn't Mathis mention it... and when was it done?

He telephoned Mathis.

"Hello, Oscar," said Mathis, when he recognised Oscar's number.

"Mathis, I've just had Bruce on the phone. He wants to know about the change of picture frame... and so do I!"

"What change of frame?"

"Mathis!"

"Hang on whilst I think. Oh, yes. Yes, I remember now. It was when my belongings arrived in Guadeloupe from France; one of my bags was damaged. The contents were fine but the picture frame was split in a couple of places. Fortunately, the painting was okay, so I didn't do anything immediately. It was when I got the first letter from Joan that I decided to get the frame repaired and put the picture on my wall. I got a quote, but as I didn't really like that frame, I decided to buy a different one instead. Anyway, what's that got to do with the painting?"

"Maybe nothing, but can you remember where you bought the frame?"

Mathis laughed. "That's easy, the gallery was called 'Boucher Gallery'. Boucher was my mother's maiden name. That's why I used them."

"Can you remember when this was?"

"Yes. As I said earlier, it was just after I received Joan's first letter. That'd be about 1990. Could have been early 1991. Do you think this frame is relevant?"

"I'm not sure. Bruce thinks so. He wouldn't have asked me otherwise."

After ending the call, Oscar decided to do some

investigations for himself. Maybe, just maybe, he thought, Bruce could be onto something. He opened up his computer and googled 'Boucher Gallery, Guadeloupe'.

Immediately he was taken to a live entry and clicked on the gallery's website link. He was pleased to see the gallery was still in existence. All looking good, he thought. Scrolling down the page, he noted down the address and telephone number.

13 Centre Commercial L'Etoile – Marina, Pointe-à-Pitre 97110, Guadeloupe. Téléphone numéro +590590908146.

He checked the opening times, but today they were closed. A job for tomorrow, he thought, and closed down his computer.

Chapter 34

Warsaw's Central Business District (CBD) is currently represented by the streets of Jana Pawła II Avenue, Solidarności Avenue, Hoża, Krakowskie Przedmieście and Nowy Świat. It is located just south of the Gdański Railway Station and close to the Vistula River to the east. The area has been transformed in recent years following the building of a number of modern offices. In addition to these modern buildings and futuristic skyscrapers, this area is home to second-generation offices developed before 2000 and also historical buildings that form an integral part of the capital city's centre. One such building is now occupied by a new and advanced technological company, recently located there from Russia. Translated from Russian, the company's name is AZN Enterprises. AZN's name doesn't appear on any nameplate or registered documents. The business is hidden in the basement of a long-established Polish computer company. AZN, originally, had been partly financed by the Russian KGB. It was deliberately set up to undermine and sabotage the Western art industry. For several years it was based about 15 miles from the centre of Moscow. However, due to the ever-increasing KGB influence and following Russia's invasion of Ukraine, it made secret plans to relocate its organisation to Poland. With the KGB's shift in priorities, this gave AZN the opportunity to move almost overnight. Three lorries were loaded with all AZN's technical equipment and, via three different border crossings, it moved overnight into the new Warsaw premises. Within the week, the firm was back up and running. The 12 members of staff were moved swiftly as well, and were now living in lavish new apartments located within a five-mile radius of the new AZN premises. Since the move to Warsaw, the business has continued to grow, slowly increasing its activity of faking and copying original paintings.

However, and unknown to them, a small group of highly paid surveillance mercenaries had been employed by the Polish government to spy on AZN's activities, waiting for the right moment for their police force to strike. That moment was imminent.

Szymon was dressed in black clothes and wore rubber gloves. On his back was a black rucksack. A black woollen balaclava was temporarily stored in one of the rucksack's side pockets. It was just after 2am, and he was walking in the shadows of the tall buildings along Solidarności Avenue, carefully and constantly, observing all around him. The street was quiet; the moon and stars were hidden by a thick blanket of cloud. All the street lights had been turned off five minutes ago.

As he approached a drab grey concrete building, he placed the balaclava over his head. Seconds later he was standing in front of a dark blue unmarked door, except for a large protruding brass handle. He removed a set of keys from his right-hand trouser pocket. Knowing which two keys to insert, he easily undid the two deadlocks. Noiselessly, he pushed back the door and entered a dark hallway. The burglar alarm pad was immediately in front of him and a red light was flashing. He had 20 seconds to deactivate it. The code was changed every day, but he knew today's code and quickly entered eight numbers. The flashing red light stopped, but there was still a secondary system which led down to the basement.

He switched on a small powerful torch and walked along the corridor. The special soles on his shoes made no noise and left no identifiable impression. A few steps later he arrived in front of a dark green door where he faced two more locks and an alarm pad. He knew the pad had to be deactivated before the keys were inserted. He entered a different set of eight numbers and the pad light flashed green. He took out another set of keys and unlocked the door. Slowly he pushed the door open and peered in. It was pitch black except for six tiny red lights flashing from one of the two visible banks of computers. He slowly pointed his torch across the room. It was a large airless space with no windows. Stacked against the far wall was a collection of paintings and three small statues.

Removing one of his two mobile phones from his rucksack, he set the camera app to video mode. The app recorded and immediately transmitted what he was pointing at. When he arrived at the stack of paintings, the recording continued. After the first seven pictures, he came across an interesting Munnings painting. On the frame it stated the name, '"Brown Surprise", by Sir Alfred Munnings'. Two pictures later, he found what he'd been specifically asked to search for and record. It was an abstract picture of a woman dressed in a green dress. He removed a second torch, a specialist ultraviolet torch, from his pocket and turned the picture over so he was now looking at the back of the canvas. Pointing the ultraviolet beam at the canvas, he could immediately identify the word 'original'.

Twenty minutes later, he'd completed all his tasks. As he retraced his steps, he relocked the doors and reset both burglar alarm systems. He was now walking along Solidarności Avenue, again, hiding in the shadows.

Chapter 35

The following morning, Oscar arrived at Mathis's home. He explained he wanted him to telephone the 'Boucher Gallery' in Guadeloupe. He needed to know if the gallery still had any records of Mathis purchasing the new frame. Mathis couldn't really see the point of the exercise, but, as Oscar was trying every avenue possible to improve the provenance, he agreed.

Oscar gave Mathis the telephone number and a list of questions to ask. When the call was answered, Mathis spoke in French. He was put through to a person with access to the gallery's records, and Mathis went through all the questions Oscar had given him. Oscar didn't speak French, so sat patiently whilst the conversation occurred. He just hoped Mathis was getting all the right answers. When the call ended, he eagerly waited for Mathis to speak.

"The good news is," said Mathis, now facing his colleague, "they do have a record of my purchase. It was dated 12th November 1990. Unfortunately, they didn't have any more information. They didn't keep a record of the painting's name, just my name, the make and size of the frame."

Oscar leaned back in his seat and sighed. "Okay, well that's something. At least we've got another date for the provenance, 12th November 1990. It might help Bruce, but I'm not sure how."

When Oscar returned home, he immediately emailed Bruce with Mathis's findings. Also, as he hadn't yet received a reply from Ellie, he decided to send her a chase-up email. This might be our last hope, he thought.

In England, Ellie had been in touch with Elizabeth Dubois again. Unfortunately, Elizabeth didn't have any more useful information about the painting. However, she had mentioned the name Claude Aubert. He had been Joan Mitchell's accountant and a friend in France. He might, she suggested, still have records of Joan's paintings about that time.

It was a long shot, pondered Ellie, but better than nothing.

Elizabeth looked through her old diaries and records and found Claude's business address in the 1992 diary. Ellie hoped he was still working at these premises.

Back in her office, Ellie accessed the internet and googled the French accountant's name and address. The result confirmed the company was still in business and at the address Elizabeth had given to her. She made a note of the telephone number and an email address, and started to type a message in French.

The following morning, Ellie spotted the company's reply. She read the brief report and made notes in English. In summary, the accountants confirmed they still had all the records of Claude Aubert's dealings with Joan Mitchell. However, they also reported that Claude had died five years ago. Ellie emailed Oscar with her report plus an invoice.

When Oscar read Ellie's report, he smiled and thought they were getting somewhere. He immediately emailed Bruce Campbell with a copy of Ellie's report.

Later that afternoon, Oscar received a telephone call from Bruce. "Hey, Oscar, how you doing? Thanks for the extra information."

"Hi, Bruce." Oscar waited excitedly for Bruce to say more.

"Got my colleague, who's Canadian French, to speak to those accountants. They've confirmed they knew about Joan's paintings and all her sales. They've also got a record that a painting called 'Sunflowers', was given to Mathis Laurent, as a parting gift, in 1990."

A big smile suddenly appeared on Oscar's face. "Wow, Bruce. That's got to be great news!"

"Yep. We're moving on nicely. I've also got a couple of guys who are really interested in buying. Sticking point is the price, but I'm working on that. Also my boss knows Harry Clarke's boss at the Foundation. Apparently, they're both members of the same golf club. After I gave my boss a copy of the Foundation's report and all this extra information, he said he'd speak to him. Fingers crossed, buddy."

Oscar took a deep intake of breath. "Bruce, I can see why Ian Caxton rates you so highly. You're really coming up trumps!"

Oscar heard Bruce's booming laughter down the line. "You tell my old buddy, I'm still the great guy he remembers."

Oscar laughed.

"Anyway," continued Bruce, "we're not there yet. Very close though. Will be in touch. Ciao!"

Bruce ended the call. Oscar placed his mobile down on his desk and sighed.

"Sounds like you're getting somewhere, finally," announced May. She was sitting at her desk opposite Oscar.

Oscar looked over his computer screen to his wife and smiled. "We're nearly there, May. So, so nearly there."

Chapter 36

Ian was sitting on the 11.35am train from Esher, travelling towards London Waterloo. George had telephoned the previous day, advocating another meeting. He'd said he had some very interesting news and suggested they meet at the 'Victory' pub.

Standing high above the hustle and bustle of London's famous Waterloo train station, the 'Victory' is a popular venue for train travellers. George said he particularly liked the great craft beers.

When Ian walked into the main bar, he noticed it was light and the decor modern. High ceilings and timber floors, plus the walls were adorned with an eclectic collection of old framed pictures and large windows. There was a buzz of chatter from the clientele sitting in groups eating and drinking. One particular group of four young women were dressed in smart office attire. They seemed to be celebrating something. Ian could hear their laughter from the other side of the room.

"Hi, Ian." George appeared beside him. "There's a quiet table over there. I want you to meet someone."

Ian looked to where George was pointing. A middle-aged man, with greying hair and wearing a smart dark blue suit, was sitting next to a wooden table containing two pints of beer.

"Let me get you a drink first, and then I'll introduce you to Gerry. He's with the Met… and he's got a lot to tell you. So, just be careful."

Ian looked at George with an alarmed expression.

Moments later, Ian placed his pint of beer next to the others and George made the introduction. "Ian Caxton, meet Detective Inspector Gerry Hudson."

Hudson stood up and gave Ian a half-hearted nod and a brief smile. He held out his hand and stared directly into Ian's eyes. "I've been hearing lots about you, Mr. Caxton. Been treading on our toes."

Ian tentatively shook the policeman's hand and looked at George. He was seeking an explanation, but George didn't say anything, he just gave Ian a nervous smile.

"Let's sit down, gentlemen," suggested the detective.

Ian looked at George again and then back at the policeman. He didn't say anything, but did sit down.

"Mr. Jonathan Northgate. What do you know about this character?" asked the detective, who, whilst still staring at Ian, picked up his glass and took a sip of his beer.

"Look. I'm not sure what this is all about, or what George has said to you, but…" Ian's sentence was interrupted.

The policeman leaned forward and, with a more serious expression on his face, said, "You could be in a lot of trouble, Mr. Caxton. George here has said nothing, except that I should speak to you. Now, we can either have a nice civilised chat in these pleasant surroundings or… if you prefer, I could ask you both to accompany me to the police station."

"Maybe I need to speak to my solicitor," responded Ian. He was anxious and wondered where this conversation was going.

The detective raised his eyebrows and gave Ian a more relaxed smile. "Ian, do you really want a formal interview with the police? We could discuss some other issues… at the same time."

"Okay," responded Ian. He tried to relax. "Can you be a little more specific?"

The detective leaned back in his seat and smiled again. "That's better, Ian. Not a good idea to get on the wrong side of the police. Our records go back a long way."

Ian stared at the detective and then looked across at George, who was sipping his beer and deliberately avoiding eye contact.

"Now then, Ian, if we're going to keep this conversation friendly, let's keep it to first names. I'm Gerry."

Ian stared at the policeman, but said nothing… and he had no intention of doing so until he knew what the meeting was all about.

"Let me explain," continued Gerry, "and you can fill in the gaps when you're ready. As I said, our records go back a very long time. Back to when your activities with a certain Russian gentleman, named Andrei Petrov, were in full flow. Recall that person?"

Ian sat quietly, trying not to give any bodily response. However, he could feel himself sweating and his heart pounding.

"I'm sure you do, having inherited his wonderful apartment in Monaco. Anyway, we're not interested in those activities… today. Could be tomorrow, though. It's Mr. Northgate who's our focus of interest… and his colleagues in the art industry."

Ian looked at George for comment, or a lead.

"I've not said anything, Ian," responded George. "However, it appears the police have been interested in our activities for quite a while."

"That's correct, George. Right buggers you've been too," said Gerry, picking up his glass and taking another sip. He looked across at George. "This is a nice pint. I'll have to come here again." Then, refocussing on the main point of the meeting, he turned his attention back to Ian. "Question one... Ian. How long have you known about Mr. Northgate's activities stealing paintings from your former employer?"

Ian was quiet for a few seconds and then took a deep breath. "Is this all off the record?"

Gerry briefly laughed. "Anything you say to me today, Ian, is unofficial. However, whatever you do tell me will determine what I include on the record."

Ian was a little confused with this comment, but bought some time by taking a large gulp of his beer. He was thinking of George's earlier comment, 'Just be careful'. He looked the detective directly in his eyes and then divulged a summary of what had happened following Penny's initial revelations. He was careful to exclude, completely, Penny's involvement and areas where he felt he might compromise himself.

He just hoped he could trust this devious policeman.

Chapter 37

About 30 minutes later, Detective Inspector Gerry Hudson left the pub. He'd made it crystal clear to both Ian and George that they should cease their investigations forthwith. However, there was one modification. The Inspector still wanted Ian to travel to Dubai, as he'd planned, to find out whether the original painting of 'The Green Dress' had arrived safely, or, more likely, been replaced with a copy.

"George, that was a shitty thing to do. Why didn't you warn me?" asked Ian, following the departure of the detective.

"Sorry, Ian. I've known Gerry for over 30 years. We worked together ages ago in the Met. He's always been a devious bastard, but a great cop. Don't worry, he's not looking to stitch you up."

"But he knew a lot about my dealings in the past. Andrei Petrov. That's a long time ago. We didn't always work within the law."

"Look, Gerry, as far as I can gather, is after Northgate and his colleagues. He's working with other European and American police forces too. They've been following this group for over three years. They've had surveillance teams in Moscow, Poland, New York, France and Belgium. It appears our involvement has caused them a few issues."

"I have one, and only one, reason for my involvement and that's to get my revenge on Northgate. The rest… well, I'm quite happy for the police to get on with their job."

"Okay, so we know how we stand. Despite what Gerry says, he's honest and just wants to put these criminals away behind bars for a long time… and if that includes Northgate, well, that achieves your ambition too, doesn't it?"

Ian drank the last of his beer. He needed another pint. "This conversation isn't over yet. I'll get us two more pints."

Ian was still annoyed when he walked to the bar and ordered two more pints of beer. Whilst the barman pumped the beer into two fresh glasses, Ian looked back at George, who was writing something in his notebook. He was still annoyed with his colleague, and when Ian returned with the beers, George quickly placed his notebook back into his briefcase.

Ian placed George's glass on the table in front of him. "Thanks," said George. "Look, Ian, I'm on your side, but remember, you're only one of my clients. I have to work with people like Gerry all the time. That's where I get a lot of my information from. For example, did you know your painting is currently in Warsaw?"

Ian's surprised expression told George he didn't.

"No, I know you don't. Gerry told me a couple of days ago, but I already knew. Remember the bug in the frame? That's why you're paying me, Ian, and that's why I work with Gerry and his colleagues. 'You scratch my back and I'll scratch yours', as the saying goes."

Ian sipped his beer. He realised he was in way over his head. This was an international crime investigation, the sort of thing he'd always tried to avoid. "Okay, George, I take your point. It's just that I'd have preferred to be kept in the loop and not surprised and challenged by the police like this."

"I'd hoped we could stay in control and, at the right time, give the police all the information we discover and get Northgate sent down for many years, but two weeks ago, Gerry challenged me and asked me what the hell I was doing. I didn't know, till then, that the police were already following Northgate, Cotton Enterprises and a number of similar organisations across the world. Northgate, I've been told, has been involved since the early days in New York. He's not been arrested because they want to get everyone at once, including the main bosses. It's a massive set-up, Ian, and made a lot harder when they were headquartered in Moscow. However, now they're in Poland, apparently, it's going to be a lot easier."

"What I don't understand is why Northgate's involved at all. When I was in New York, I knew he came from a reasonably wealthy family and had married into money. So, what's in it for him? Adventure, challenge, greed… stupidity?"

"All I've established is there was an incident when he was at university. I don't know what, but it would appear he got in with the wrong crowd. There were drugs involved and something happened… someone died. I'm not totally sure of the facts, but the result was bribery… for a long time."

Ian took a deep breath and thought back to his time in New York. He tried to think of any example where this situation was apparent, but he couldn't. "He tried to get me the sack, George, but I can't think of any incident where he stole or arranged for paintings to be copied and swapped. Maybe I wasn't looking closely enough."

"The key thing, Ian, is we now have to work with the police. Go over to Dubai and check out your painting. It's going to be a good copy; we both know that. Give the police all the information they want and then stand aside. Just watch what happens from the sidelines!"

Chapter 38

Four days after Oscar's last conversation with Bruce, he received another call.

The American telephoned to tell Oscar the good news. "Hey, Oscar, old buddy, things are really hotting up in the 'Big Apple'. Following my boss's chat with Donald Hardy, he's Harry Clarke's boss, it looks certain the Foundation is going to give Mathis's painting the green light. That extra information about the frame helped with the provenance. The accountant's information, too. I've got two possible buyers talking about an offer of around 18 million dollars for a private sale. But that figure's based on the Foundation's agreement to include the picture in the next edition of the catalogue raisonné. Even without that, one buyer's still prepared to offer ten mill. He, like us, thinks the painting's authentic and is prepared to put his money where his mouth is."

"Wow, Bruce. What great news. Mathis is going to be over the moon! Do you think 18 million will be the best offer, or would an auction get a bigger price?"

"Difficult to say. Joany's painting valuations have cooled a bit recently. Still in vogue, but not the top prices of recent years. You might get 20 mill at auction, given proper marketing, but that all comes with extra costs."

"Yes." Oscar was pondering the situation. "I need to speak to Mathis, see what he wants to do."

"Okay, buddy, let me know asap. We need a quick decision."

An hour later, Oscar was sitting with Matthis in his lounge. He'd just finished summarising Bruce's information.

"What do you think?" asked Oscar. He couldn't hide the excitement in his voice.

Mathis stared at the blank wall where Joan Mitchell's painting had once resided. "A lot to consider, Oscar."

"I know, but do you still want to sell?"

Mathis took a deep intake of breath. "I guess the answer to that is 'yes'. To tell you the truth, Oscar, I really need the money."

"Okay, so what do you think, an auction or a private buyer?"

"I don't mind. Probably a private buyer. I don't want to be greedy. Ten million, never mind 18 million, would make me financially secure. Then, of course, there's your commission and Bruce's costs, but I'll still have a lot to live on… and have a great quality of life."

Oscar smiled. "Yes, you will… and we'll all be winners as well!"

"Might even go back to France for a holiday and visit some of my old haunts. Time passes so quickly. You know, Oscar, you've worked really hard and deserve your reward. I couldn't have got this far without all your help."

"Thanks. I enjoyed the ride. I'll get back to Bruce and tell him your decision. Let's hope he can get the Foundation to change their mind and succeed with the 18 mill."

"And the copy of the picture for my blank wall that Bruce promised."

Oscar smiled. "I'll remind him."

When Oscar returned to his villa, he immediately drafted

an email to Bruce, telling him of Mathis's decision. Once completed, he excitedly pressed the 'send' button and stared at the screen. He rubbed his hands together and had a huge smile on his face.

Twenty minutes later, May returned to the villa. When she entered the kitchen, she spotted Oscar placing a bottle of champagne in the refrigerator. Smiling, she enquired, "Has Mathis agreed to sell?"

Oscar gave her a summary of his conversation with Bruce and then the follow-up with Mathis.

"Oh, Oscar, that's wonderful news." She placed her briefcase on the floor and rushed over to give him a congratulatory kiss. "It beats my good news."

"Two lots of good news in one day! So, what's yours?"

May moved back one step and faced Oscar. "I had a meeting at the Shell Gallery. Wesley and I have finalised the deal with David in Hong Kong. Those Hennrick Brown watercolours. We sold them for one and a half million dollars!"

"In that case, maybe I'd better put two bottles in the fridge! Well done, you."

Chapter 39

Immediately after breakfast, Ian entered his office and sat down behind his desk. He still hadn't heard from Joey Sanderson. The previous afternoon, Detective Inspector Hudson had telephoned enquiring whether he'd received any news. Ian was still anxious and wanted to get out of the police's hair. Too many opportunities for them to revisit his past... especially his activities with Andrei. He was still in shock that the detective even knew of his involvement with Andrei!

Ian switched on his computer and hoped he'd find a message from Joey. He didn't want to contact him himself. It might suggest he was panicking.

Five new emails had appeared in his inbox, but none were from Joey. He did, however, spot one from Oscar, who told him the good news about Mathis's painting and Bruce's brilliant work. Ian quickly sent a congratulatory reply and a promise he'd speak to him again shortly.

Standing up, he was just about to rejoin Emma in the kitchen when his computer made a 'ping' sound, indicating a new email. He casually looked at the screen, thinking it would probably be just junk email. However, to his delight, it was the email from Joey Sanderson!

Returning to his seat, he eagerly opened and read the

message. It was good news! He heaved a deep sigh of relief and went to the kitchen to find Emma. When he spotted her washing the breakfast crockery at the sink, he exclaimed, "Let's get packed, we're off to Dubai!"

Two days later, they were flying over Europe, heading for the United Emirates… Dubai. Ian had spotted two available business class seats on the Emirates daily flight. He'd booked them immediately.

Because of the spaciousness of the business class seating, Ian and Emma were not sitting side by side, but one behind the other. Both had window seats, 10A and 11A with direct access to the aisle. Ian had undone his seat belt and was standing next to Emma's seat. "Everything okay?" he enquired, leaning on the small storage unit containing a selection of small bottles and canned drinks.

"Mmm, it's nice and comfortable. I can stretch my legs out without any bother. I thought it might be a little cramped, but I've got lots of room."

"Good. Look, when we get to Dubai, the Emirates chauffeur service will take us straight to our hotel. I need to see Joey before he closes up for the day, so if you don't mind, I'll leave you to investigate the hotel's facilities. It'll still be light enough to take a swim or sunbathe if you want."

"Sunbathing in late November sounds wonderful. That's my plan."

"Excellent. I shouldn't be too long. Once I've seen the painting and emailed my report to the police in London, I can relax and join you for a well-earned holiday."

"Excuse me, sir," said the attractive stewardess. She was standing next to Ian and holding a tray containing Emma's ordered meal.

Ian went back to his seat, sipped his whisky and waited for his own meal to arrive.

Four hours later, the captain announced the plane would

shortly be commencing its descent. Ian looked out of the window. All he could see was a bright blue sky, no clouds and a lovely azure-coloured Arabian Gulf. As the plane descended, it began banking to the right. Ian saw some land, mainly desert, before it turned again and quickly crossed the coast at Fujairah, and over the Gulf of Oman. Finally levelling off, the plane then headed west and back across more desert towards Dubai. Ian continued to stare through the window. He was surprised at the existence of small clusters of communities, houses and some industrial buildings, surrounded in the distance by more sand and a few hills. Roads were few, and what there were looked more like dirt tracks.

As the plane dropped lower, more populated areas came into view. Roads were now much wider and tarmacked. In the distance, he could see skyscrapers and, towering above them all, the famous Burj Khalifa, the world's tallest structure.

Two minutes later, the plane landed on the runway and, with a roar from the engine's reverse thrust, it slowed down. The Caxtons had arrived in the city of Dubai.

Now it was time for Ian to see what his £1.1 million had purchased!

Chapter 40

In Antigua, Oscar was still waiting for Bruce to tell him what Mathis's painting had finally sold for. Also, he'd still not received confirmation that the Foundation had agreed the picture would be included in their next catalogue raisonné. Bruce's last words were 'it looks certain the Foundation is going to give Mathis's painting the green light'. But, these words were not a statement that the Foundation had definitely updated their earlier decision, just Bruce's assertion that 'it looks certain'. Not the same thing.

The more he thought back about the telephone call, the more he believed Bruce's enthusiasm could have been misplaced. He was pacing around his office when May walked in.

"Are you still worried about Mathis's painting?" asked May. She could see Oscar was now more anxious than he had been just 24 hours ago.

"I don't know whether what Bruce has told me is fact or just his enthusiasm."

"But you told me he definitely had two possible buyers."

"I know. 'Possible' buyers. They might have backed out. I'd hoped Bruce would have telephoned or… emailed, by now. Told me if the painting has been sold."

"All the worrying in the world won't change anything.

Isn't there something else you could be getting on with instead?"

Oscar chewed on his top lip. He couldn't concentrate on anything else for the time being. He needed to know the score!

As Oscar hadn't responded, May decided to change the subject. "Have you spoken with Ian recently? Are they all still coming to visit in January? It's only a few weeks away."

"Not about January, no. Ian sent an email saying he and Emma were leaving for a few days in Dubai. Something about a painting he's bought. I'll speak to him when they get back."

"I'm going to make a cup…" May stopped talking when Oscar's mobile phone started to ring.

Oscar quickly grabbed the mobile and noticed Bruce's number. "It's him!" he announced.

May smiled. At last, she thought.

"Hi Bruce," answered Oscar. He closed his eyes in hope and anticipation.

"Hey, Oscar. Great news, buddy," bellowed Bruce, with his usual powerful tone. "I sold Mathis's painting for 19 and a half mill! The Foundation are playing ball and they've confirmed, in writing, that the picture's going to appear in their next publication of the Joan Mitchell catalogue raisonné. How's that then, buddy!?"

"That's fabulous news, Bruce. Wow, Mathis is going to be thrilled… and I am too! That's absolutely brilliant!"

"Yeah well, I was able to play the two buyers against each other. A sort of private auction. Once the Foundation gave me written confirmation, the offers skyrocketed from eight mill."

"You've done a fantastic job, Bruce."

Bruce laughed. "All part of the service. By the way, tell Mathis I've arranged a copy of the painting, he'll probably receive it early in the new year."

"Okay. Thanks… he'll be pleased."

"I'll email the contract details and Sotheby's invoice to you later this morning. The quicker you get them signed and back to me, the sooner everyone's going to get paid."

"I'll go over to Mathis's house this afternoon and get everything signed and returned later today."

"Great, buddy. Must go. Been great fun dealing with you two guys. Next time you're in New York, look me up."

"Thanks for everything, Bruce. For me, it's been a nightmare! But we're finally there… thanks to you."

Bruce laughed again and said, "Bye, buddy," and he was gone.

Oscar switched off his phone, stood up and shouted out loud, "Yes!!"

May returned to the office with two mugs of coffee and a smile on her face. "I gather Bruce gave you some good news."

Oscar gave May a big kiss and then a summary of his conversation.

"Nineteen and a half million! Wow, Mathis is going to be pleased."

"Pleased!? He should be ecstatic. As soon as I've received Bruce's email, I'm going straight over. The sooner I get him to sign, the sooner we'll all get paid!"

Chapter 41

The taxi stopped outside Joey Sanderson's gallery. It was a much bigger premises than Ian had imagined. Certainly bigger than the gallery he remembered Joey owning in Hong Kong. After paying the fare, he looked at the building's modern four-storey facade, especially the six large display windows on the ground floor. He walked over and peered at the paintings being exhibited in each window. Mostly colourful abstracts with pricey labels. He could see why Joey had done very well for himself.

As Ian walked towards the entrance door, it automatically opened and he stepped into a climate-controlled atmosphere. About ten degrees cooler than the 30°C outside. He peered around the large, modern display area. Despite the strong sunshine, most of the pictures on display were individually illuminated by subtle spotlights. The smoothly polished grey concrete floor was impregnated with attractive small fragments of dark blue marble.

A smartly dressed young woman, in a white blouse and short green skirt, approached. "Can I help you, sir? My name is Gillian," she announced, in a clear English voice. She had a welcoming smile.

Ian smiled back. "Hello, Gillian. I'd like to see Mr. Sanderson, please. My name is Ian Caxton."

"I'll tell Mr. Sanderson you're here. I won't be a minute." Gillian walked back towards her desk and picked up a telephone. After about 20 seconds, she returned. "Mr. Sanderson will see you now, Mr. Caxton. Please follow me."

Ian followed Gillian past more colourful pictures on display. Mostly modern abstracts, but Ian did notice one Vermeer and a Degas. After leaving the display area, they arrived opposite two elevators. Gillian pressed the red request button and the right-hand elevator doors opened. They both stepped inside and Gillian selected the fourth floor. Moments later, the doors opened to reveal a large reception area. A man, about 30 years of age, wearing a smart white thobe, stepped towards them. "Ah, Mr. Caxton, welcome. My name is Bakir, Mr. Sanderson's PA." They shook hands. "Come this way."

At this point, Gillian departed back into the elevator.

The two men walked towards Bakir's desk, where Bakir pointed to a small flashing red light on his phone. "Mr. Sanderson is still on a call. He knows you've arrived. We've received your painting from Sotheby's. It's in Mr. Sanderson's office."

"That's what I'm here to see. By the way, thank you for purchasing it for me at the auction."

"That was not a problem. I knew the limit you had set. It was fun spending other people's money!" Bakir laughed, and Ian smiled.

"Ian Caxton!" announced a voice from the far side of the room. A fit-looking 50-something man came strolling across the carpeted floor. He had a big smile on his face and held out his hand.

Ian smiled back and both men warmly shook each other's hands. "Hello, Joey. Long time no see, as they say... you look great!"

"It's this wonderful climate, Ian, and our wealthy clients,

makes me feel ten years younger. You've met Bakir, I see, so, come into my office. We've got lots to talk about."

Bakir returned to his desk and Ian followed Joey into his office. Ian was surprised how large it was. It was almost as big as the reception area. The modern light oak furniture and large desk almost seemed lost! A bank of windows, the length of one wall, looked down onto a square where a fountain was slowly cascading water over a statue of a horse and into a small pool. Surrounding the square were similar-sized modern buildings, whilst in the distance, Ian could see the top of the Burj Khalifa.

On the far side of the office, Ian spotted an easel displaying what looked like his painting.

Both men sat down. Joey picked up his phone and told Bakir he didn't want to be disturbed, except with the delivery of freshly brewed coffee.

After replacing the phone, Joey opened the conversation. "I hope you've got plenty of time, Ian, because, as well as talking about yours and Karim's paintings, I want to hear everything about your life since Hong Kong."

Ian smiled and said he had plenty of time.

For well over an hour, only briefly being interrupted by the arrival of coffee and biscuits, both men talked about their lives since Hong Kong. Eventually, they started to talk about the pictures.

"I've looked at your painting, Ian, and, to be honest, it looks the way I'd expect the original to."

Ian smiled and got up from his seat. "There's one definite way to find out." He walked over to the painting, briefly looked at it and lifted it from the easel. After carrying it back to Joey's desk, he laid it face downwards.

Joey stood up and watched inquisitively, and when Ian removed what looked like a small torch from his jacket pocket, Joey asked, "What's that for?"

"You'll see... or maybe you won't. Depending on what I find."

Ian switched on the torch and a violet-coloured beam immediately shone over the rear of the canvas. Nothing unusual appeared. Ian switched off the light, smiled and looked at Joey.

"Am I supposed to understand what you've just achieved?"

"There's no 'original'."

Joey looked at Ian with a confused expression. He was none the wiser.

"Just before the auction, I arranged for the authenticated picture to have the word 'original' written in invisible ink on the back of the canvas. As you saw, it's not here."

Now it was Joey's turn to smile. "Sneaky. So you know, for certain, this picture is a copy, not the original."

Ian nodded. "Yes. As I expected, the original has been stolen. I was told a few days ago that it's probably residing in Poland."

Joey briefly laughed. "You're kidding. Poland?"

Ian nodded again.

"Just a minute. So, you spent 1.1 million pounds on an original, an authenticated painting, but knew you'd only receive this... a fake!?"

"I wasn't absolutely sure, but, yes, that's about the sum of it."

Joey sighed and shook his head from side to side. "I don't understand. Ah! Just a minute. I get it now! You deliberately wanted to set a trap... but come on, Ian. That's over one million pounds down the drain."

"Not yet. I still own the original, and I intend to get it back."

"I hope you know what you're doing." Joey had a questioning look on his face.

"I hope so too. Now about Karim's Munnings painting. Has he had the results of the analysis?"

"Not yet. However, based on your assumption, I'm sure we already know what the answer's likely to be. I'll let you know."

Chapter 42

Ian arrived back at the hotel just after 8pm. Emma had showered and changed her clothes. Now she was ready for dinner. Ian said he needed to send a brief email and would be ready in ten minutes.

Twenty minutes later, Ian had sent his email to Inspector Hudson, showered and put on a fresh set of clothes. "Right, I'm ready," he announced, when he entered the suite's lounge area.

"At last! Anyway, I've been productive and found a nice fish restaurant, five minutes walk away from here. I've also booked us a table for 8.45."

Ian looked at his watch. "Great, we'll be there in perfect time."

"Then you can tell me how your meeting with your colleague went."

"I'll do that whilst we eat," said Ian, walking towards the door. "By the way, you'll be pleased to know that you'll be meeting Joey, and his wife, tomorrow evening. He's invited us to their home for dinner."

Emma picked up her handbag and walked towards Ian. "Thank you for informing me now. It's usually the last minute when you remember!"

During their fish meal, Ian felt more relaxed than he had

been for a number of weeks. He knew he'd finished with the Northgate saga, it was now up to the police to finish the job. However, he still felt a little cheated; he really wanted to be directly responsible for seeing Northgate convicted. Still, the police had warned him off and he couldn't afford to step on their toes anymore.

He hadn't told Emma about Detective Inspector Hudson's intervention and warning. He just told her he'd now got enough information to pass on to the police, hence his email to them earlier.

"Do you think the police will arrest Northgate?" asked Emma. Having finished her starter of scallops, she was waiting for her main course.

Ian sipped his Chablis and replied. "I hope so. George gave them some extra information. We'll have to wait and see."

"You seem much more relaxed now. Is that it? You've finished all your investigations?"

"I don't see what else I can do. I just hope the police do their job."

"Penny's not going to be involved, I hope?"

"I've never mentioned her name to anyone. She's completely in the clear."

"Good. Is your colleague, Joey, involved?"

"No. His only involvement was via his PA, Bakir. All Bakir did was buy the painting on my behalf at the auction. It was a deliberate ploy of mine to make sure the painting was sent to Dubai."

"So, why the dinner tomorrow night?"

"Joey was a great colleague in Hong Kong. He and Oscar were my best pals there. We had a long chat earlier and he suggested we keep in touch. Nothing more sinister than that. I thought it was a great idea."

Emma smiled, but before she could ask any more

questions, a waiter arrived delivering her seabass and Ian's grilled red snapper.

The following morning, Ian checked his email inbox. There was a response from DI Gerry Hudson. His message simply said, 'Thanks.'

Ian smiled. He hoped it would be the last he heard from that particular policeman.

Checking his other new entries, he saw an email from Oscar. He opened it and read the contents. At the same moment, Emma appeared from the bedroom. She was wearing a long white cotton bathrobe.

"I've just received an email from Oscar," said Ian, looking across at his wife. "He's reminding us we've not confirmed the dates when we're going to stay with them in Antigua."

"I thought we'd agreed to those some weeks ago. Didn't you tell him?"

"I'll have to check. I know we're going in January."

"And only a few weeks away. Robert will be home next week, then the Christmas period will really fly by. Have you booked our flights to Antigua?"

"Er, no. Sorry, Emma. I've been a bit busy. I'll do that as soon as we get home."

The meal with the Sandersons was a success for Ian and Joey. They had a great time catching up and reminding each other of funny, and more serious, happenings in Hong Kong. Both were bachelors at the time, so some subjects were definitely 'off limits'!

Joey's wife, Sara, and Emma struggled initially to find common areas of interest. However, once the subject of children was raised, it started to demolish nervous barriers. By the end of the evening, they'd found lots of other subjects to discuss and laugh about.

For the next two days, Emma and Ian had a relaxing time. Emma topped up her suntan and Ian read more about the culture and recent developments in Dubai.

On day three, however, Ian received a phone call from Joey. Joey told him that Karim had been to see him. He was angry and showed Joey the report on his Munnings painting. In summary, it was a good copy, definitely not the original. He was going to speak to his lawyer and get him to 'sue the hell out of Sotheby's'!

Ian asked Joey if he could calm Karim and get him to temporarily hold fire, as the police were already investigating. "Tell him, I'll guarantee and cover the cost of his painting."

Ian immediately emailed Detective Inspector Hudson and told him about Karim's painting.

On the final morning, Ian and Emma were disappointed to be going back to England. It was December 4th and Ian had already seen the weather forecast for London, 'Sleet and cold winds. Temperatures between –2 and 2 degrees centigrade!' He was certainly not impressed. Still, another month, he thought, and then we'll be back in the warm sunshine.

In the meantime, he wondered when the authorities would finally make the decision to raid the art-copying organisation. He was desperate to see his nemesis and arch-enemy, Northgate, unceremoniously thrown into jail!

Chapter 43

On the 2nd January, Ian, Emma and Robert boarded a Virgin Atlantic flight, bound for Antigua. Having accepted Oscar and May's kind invitation, all three were excited to be leaving the cold and depressing English weather. Originally, they'd been invited for Christmas, but both Ian and Emma's parents had already been invited for the Christmas and New Year periods. The 2nd January was the earliest they could do, and with Robert due back at school in just over two weeks time, they intended to make the most of every precious minute of the lovely warm Antiguan sunshine and the wonderful hospitality of their hosts.

Ian had still not heard from the police, or, indeed, seen in the media any announcement of mass arrests in Europe. He was even beginning to wonder whether it was going to happen at all. What's the problem? Why the delay? Surely the police had enough evidence. Was Northgate going to escape, scot-free? He couldn't bear the thought.

"Excuse me, sir. Could you take your seat, please... and fasten your seat belt? The plane will be taxiing in a few moments," said the stewardess, now standing next to him.

Both Emma and Robert smiled as Ian was being ticked off. Even flying Upper Class, you had to abide by the safety rules.

Ian sat down, clicked his belt and finished the last of his complimentary glass of champagne. Even though it was only eleven o'clock in the morning, Ian couldn't resist a glass of champagne. It was all part of the experience, he said. Part of the anticipation of the flight ahead and the holiday still to come.

As the plane was slowly being pushed back from the gate, Ian looked out of the cabin window, back towards the terminal building. He counted eight aeroplanes waiting for their passengers to board. The heavy dark grey sky had been threatening all morning, and Ian spotted a few white flakes of snow drifting down on the chilly breeze. He couldn't wait to get away, before it became any thicker. Although he'd heard it could take several hours of light snow to generate ten centimetres on the ground, he didn't want to hang around to see if this theory was correct.

Fortunately, it was only ten minutes later that the Airbus A350 hurtled down the runway and lifted off. Almost immediately, Ian's view was completely blocked by the low clouds. He leaned back and closed his eyes. He didn't want to sleep, just rest his eyes and think about the warm sunshine in Antigua, just nine hours away.

At just after 4pm local time, the Virgin Atlantic flight landed at V. C. Bird International Airport on the island of Antigua.

Once the plane had come to a stop at Gate 5, the pilot switched off both the engines and the seat belt sign. Robert was impatient and immediately jumped up. Emma told him to sit back down as there would be a few more minutes before the passengers would be allowed to disembark. Robert grumbled and pointed to other passengers standing up and retrieving bags from the overhead lockers. However, it was another seven minutes before the plane's doors were finally opened.

Oscar and May were waiting in 'Arrivals'. They'd just spotted the update on the arrivals board indicating Ian's flight had landed. They were eagerly watching the exit doors. Three other flights had also landed, so there was a constant stream of passengers exiting.

Oscar knew, from experience, that getting through passport control could take anything from a few minutes to up to an hour! In fact it was another 35 minutes before Oscar saw Ian and family pushing two trolleys through the exit doors. He nudged May and waved. Ian said something to Emma and waved back.

"Welcome back to Antigua!" announced Oscar to Ian and Emma. And then looking at Robert, he smiled and said, "My, you've grown into a tall young man."

Robert smiled, but felt a little embarrassed. He wasn't sure what to say, as he couldn't remember meeting this man before.

The four adults then smiled and hugged each other.

Oscar took charge of Emma's trolley and walked with Ian towards the main exit. The two women chatted and followed close behind. Robert was slower, and, at the back, he was gazing at the building's modern white metal and glass structure.

When they arrived at the rear of a large 4x4 parked in the car park, Ian immediately asked, "Where's your Jeep?"

"That's at home. This is May's car," responded Oscar as he pressed his key fob and the boot lid slowly began to rise. "We wouldn't have got the five of us, plus all your luggage, in my car."

Whilst the women and Robert climbed onto the rear seats, Ian and Oscar loaded the cases and then climbed into the front seats.

Just over 25 minutes later, they arrived at Oscar's villa. This was the first time Ian and Emma had been back since the extension had been built. "This looks really good," said Ian, leaning forward and peering through the windscreen. "The villa must have doubled in size."

Oscar glanced in his rearview mirror at his wife and teasingly said, "It was all May's idea. We had to build a large extension to house all her clothes!"

"That's not true," announced May, a little disgruntled. "We've also built a wonderful guest bedroom and a large office."

Emma smiled, she recognised similar bickerings to those she had with Ian. "It looks wonderful. I can't wait to see inside."

"Yes," said Ian, wanting to change the subject, "and I want to hear all about Mathis's painting and your experience dealing with Bruce Campbell."

Chapter 44

It was just after 6.15pm and Ian and Oscar were walking along the beach: a stretch of wonderful powdery white sand immediately beyond the villa's garden. The sun had disappeared and a weak red sunset began to materialise over the horizon. Ian had left Emma and Robert to settle in. However, he wanted to chat with Oscar and stretch his legs.

"Bruce was a great help with selling Mathis's painting, then?" asked Ian, gently kicking at the sand as they ambled along.

"He was brilliant, Ian. We couldn't have achieved that result without his, and his boss's, intervention. It was a tough fight with the Foundation, but eventually they agreed to the painting's provenance."

Oscar then summarised the issues and challenges they'd overcome.

"So, all's well that ends well."

"Yep. Thanks to you for putting me in touch with Bruce."

"I knew he'd be helpful. He was an excellent colleague in New York, and we worked well together. I learned a lot from him."

The light level was slowly decreasing, the sunset had faded and the moon had started to shine on the now inky-black sea. Oscar suggested they turn back.

Ian took a deep intake of breath, kicked off his sandals and began paddling in the edge of the sea. At first it felt refreshingly chilly, but after a few strides, his feet adjusted to the temperature. "You know, Oscar, you've come a long way since Hong Kong. Successful business, lovely wife… and now living in paradise!"

Oscar smiled. "Yes, I've got a lot to be thankful for. You, and a lot of other people, believed in me, helped me get to this point. You've been a great pal."

Ian stopped walking and slapped his friend on the shoulder. Staring out across the sea, Ian's expression began to change. "I've got a big problem, Oscar."

Oscar stopped walking and stared up at his friend. He was alarmed and waited for Ian to continue.

Ian started walking again and summarised the Northgate events and the painting thefts. He didn't mention Penny or Viktor's involvement, although he told him about Joey, George and the detective, plus his £1.1 million investment and the £3.3 million guarantee he'd given to Karim for his Munnings' painting. At the end of his summary, they arrived back in the villa's garden, but neither were ready to go inside. They sat on two patio chairs and chatted some more.

About 15 minutes later, May arrived carrying a small tray containing two glasses of gin and tonic. "We thought you boys would like these. We've already started."

Both said, "Thank you," and reached up to take a glass.

"Dinner will be ready in about 20 minutes," responded May, who turned around and walked back towards the kitchen.

"Cheers, Oscar." Ian raised his glass. "And thanks for the invitation."

Oscar raised his own glass and clinked Ian's. "Cheers, to you. It's great you, Emma and Robert are here. Now, Mr. Caxton, it's my turn to try to help you!"

Ian sipped his drink and then looked across at Oscar. "What do you mean?"

"Well, as I see it, you're now totally dependent on the police authorities. They've not done anything so far, other than monitoring the situation. You have two ambitions: one, to get your revenge on Northgate, and two, make sure you don't lose 4.4 million pounds."

"Three ambitions, actually. I don't want the police to investigate my past anymore either. Hudson intimated he may take that sort of action if I didn't leave everything alone."

"Mmm, okay." Oscar wiped his forehead with his right hand, whilst he thought a little more. "That makes it a bit more tricky."

"I know. That's really the nub of the bigger problem."

Chapter 45

On the first full day of their holiday, Emma suggested she would prefer to relax, enjoy the villa's patio and swim in the sea. Oscar and May postponed their usual early morning swim until later in the morning, when they would join in with their guests' activities.

Robert couldn't get enough of the lovely warm sea, and Ian and Oscar took turns to keep an eye on him. It was only when Ian spotted red sunburn marks on Robert's shoulders that he told him to return to the shade on the villa's patio.

Although Emma had insisted they all apply lots of suntan lotion, and regularly top it up, with Robert in and out of the water, it quickly got washed off.

The rest of the day was dominated by meal times. Oscar's neighbours, Garfield and Ella, had invited them all around for a barbeque in the late afternoon. It was a lovely social get-together, and Ella and Emma had a lot to catch up on. The last time they'd spoken to each other was at Oscar and May's wedding.

Garfield and Ella hadn't met Robert before, so they spent time chatting with him too. Robert felt a bit like a spare part amongst all the adults, but when Emma agreed he could have just one weak spritzer, he was a lot happier.

The next day, they all went into St. John's. May wanted

to show Emma the main shops and visit Wesley at the Shell Gallery. Wesley had also arranged for Oscar and his guests to take a tour of the famous Sir Vivian Richards cricket stadium. However, as the new stadium was located in St George, Oscar dropped May and Emma off at the shopping centre first before driving Ian and Robert the seven kilometres to the cricket ground.

When they arrived at the stadium, a good friend of Wesley's, Jimmy Walsh, was waiting to show them around. Jimmy had been a steward at both this and the old stadium for the past 30 years. What he didn't know about Antiguan and West Indies cricket was not worth knowing. A cricketer himself, in his early days, he showed promise, but a serious knee injury sadly put paid to any potential career. In his youth, he had bowled in the nets to a young Viv Richards, and was keen to tell anybody listening that he had clean bowled the great man… twice!

Robert was enjoying his own cricket at school. He was opening batsman for the under 13s team and fascinated with everything Jimmy had to say. They visited both the home and away changing rooms, the large Andy Roberts and Curtly Ambrose stands, plus a brief walk around the wicket area.

Jimmy told them that this new stadium was opened in 2007 and had a capacity of 10,000 people. However, with extra temporary seating this limit could easily increase to nearly 20,000. Unfortunately, from the start, the stadium had been plagued with controversy. Fans preferred the old stadium and the state of the outfield caused constant concerns. Despite being relaid after the 2008 Australia Test, the 2009 Test against England was abandoned after just ten balls! The bowler's run ups were deemed too dangerous.

At the conclusion of the tour, Robert was presented with an Antiguan cricket team cap, which he said was "really cool". He couldn't wait to get back to school to show it to all his cricketing pals.

During dinner, later that evening, Oscar suggested that tomorrow, he and May would take them all to visit the famous Shirley Heights. He explained that the best time to see the wonderful views was to visit late afternoon and enjoy a picnic.

"What's at Shirley Heights?" asked Emma. The trip sounded promising.

"Originally named after Sir Thomas Shirley, the former Governor of the Leeward Islands, it's an old restored military lookout and gun battery," said Oscar, who, as well as telling them about the history of the site, also wanted them to see and admire the wonderful view. "The Lookout is on a high point. It's about 160 metres above the sea and gives a superb view of both English and Falmouth Harbours. One of the best views in Antigua. May and I have had picnics there many times. Often there's a spectacular sunset and English Harbour is all lit up. Nelson's Dockyard is also just below us. This area was a big military complex back in the 18th century, mainly to protect the island's valuable sugar produce, but it was also an important Caribbean Dockyard for the British."

"Sounds really good," said Ian looking at Emma. She nodded and smiled back. Even Robert looked interested.

"We studied Nelson at school," interrupted Robert, "but I don't remember him being in Antigua. I know about the battles and his victories at the Nile and Trafalgar, where he was killed."

"I don't know much about him being here either," replied Oscar, scratching his chin. "I think it might have been a lot earlier in his career."

Robert thought maybe that was the case. He would google it and find out.

"It all sounds excellent, Oscar," said Ian, sipping the last of his wine. "I think we'd better get a good night's sleep."

Chapter 46

The following morning, everyone was up early. Even Robert had arrived for breakfast before 9.30. He wanted to make sure he had plenty of time for swimming before they all travelled to Shirley Heights.

Following a leisurely breakfast, they walked the short distance to the beach and swam in the calm Caribbean Sea. Although it was still early morning, the sky was cloudless, which meant the hot sun felt extra strong.

After swimming and enjoying the warm water, Oscar, May and Emma were sitting in the shade of two palm trees. They were content to watch the other two playing in the sea. However, it wasn't long before May said she needed to prepare a light lunch and organise food for the picnic. Emma volunteered to help, and Oscar knew he needed to get some food out of the freezer.

Ten minutes later, Ian was sitting under the same palm trees and watching Robert swimming. After a few moments, Robert joined him and shook his wet hair all over his father.

"Hey!" shouted Ian, standing up.

Robert laughed and ran away.

"I'm going back to the villa. I want you back in ten minutes, max," said Ian, wiping his face and chest with a towel.

"Okay," responded Robert and ran back into the water.

When Ian arrived back at the villa, he found a hive of activity in the kitchen. "Do you need any help?"

May pointed to a cool bag. "It would be great if you could get some ice blocks out of the freezer and put them in that bag. We'll put two bottles of white wine in there later."

The hive of activity continued until Emma asked, "Where's Robert?"

"I left him playing in the sea. I told him, 'ten minutes, max'."

Emma looked at the kitchen clock. "You've been back here 15 minutes. Go and tell him to come in and have a shower, lunch isn't going to be long."

Ian put the knife down. He'd been chopping up some of the green salad. He wandered out onto the patio, and then the short distance to the beach. On first inspection he couldn't see Robert swimming, but suddenly became alarmed when he saw his son, face down, spreadeagled on the sand!

"Oh, my God!" he exclaimed, and ran quickly to where Robert lay. His back was red raw and his temperature sky high… but he was breathing, just!

Ian tried and failed to wake him up. Although Robert was tall, he was slim, and when Ian tried to lift him, it was a struggle. Suddenly he heard Oscar's voice, shouting as he ran across the beach to join him. "Is he okay? Let me give you a hand."

The two men lifted Robert and hurriedly carried him back to the villa. As they approached the patio, Oscar shouted, "May! Call an ambulance… quickly."

Emma appeared at the patio door, and seeing Robert being carried by Ian and Oscar, put her hands up to her mouth and screamed! "Is he okay? Please, tell me he's alright!"

"Lay him down on that sunlounger, the one in the shade,"

ordered Oscar, steering Ian and Robert in that direction. Once they'd laid him down, Oscar ran off and pulled a hose around from the side of the villa. When he was next to the lounger, he switched on a jet of cool water. "Looks like sunstroke. We need to keep him cool until the ambulance arrives."

"Good God, Ian. What happened?" pleaded Emma, bending down to inspect her son. She was oblivious to the water spraying her as well.

"I just found him, face down, lying on the beach."

"Ian," said Oscar, pointing the jet of water along Robert's whole torso, "can you ask May to get some towels and soak them in cold water? Bring them here… quickly."

A minute later, both Ian and May appeared with handfuls of cold wet towels. Oscar temporarily switched off the hose and, with Emma's help, spread them all over Robert's body.

"The ambulance should be here in a few minutes. I told them a boy had nearly drowned."

"It's sunstroke, May," said Oscar, placing the last towel over Robert's feet. He then turned the hose back on. "We've got to keep him cool until they arrive."

Emma brushed Robert's light brown hair. "He's got to be okay, please God."

In the distance, they heard the siren of an approaching ambulance. Oscar passed the hose to Ian and ran around to the front of the villa.

Suddenly, Robert moved his head and vomited, before collapsing back on the lounger.

"Oh my God," announced Emma. She put her hands over her eyes.

With his unused hand, Ian leaned over and put his arm round Emma's shoulders. "He's going to be okay, Emma. He wasn't in the sun for long."

"You shouldn't have left him!"

"He was fine when I left. I told him, only ten minutes."

A running Oscar reappeared, followed by two paramedics carrying a stretcher. "I've told them it's probably sunstroke."

Everyone stepped back to allow the paramedics to get closer to Robert. They checked his pulse, temperature and breathing.

The elder of the two looked up and said, "We need to get him to hospital urgently. Tim here will ring the hospital and tell them to prepare for a sunstroke emergency."

Ian and Oscar held the stretcher whilst the paramedics lifted Robert, face down, onto it. They then quickly wheeled the stretcher around the side of the villa towards the rear of the ambulance.

Oscar looked at Ian. "You and Emma go with them, I'll follow behind in May's car."

Emma had already disappeared with Robert, and Ian quickly caught up. Once the stretcher was loaded into the back of the ambulance, Ian and Emma jumped on board.

Oscar and May climbed into May's car and followed the ambulance.

Chapter 47

Ian, Emma, Oscar and May sat in a small windowless room, kept cool by the air conditioning. They were anxiously waiting for someone to update them on Robert's condition.

Earlier, when the ambulance had arrived at the St. John's hospital, several nurses and a doctor were waiting. They quickly pushed Robert through several doors and down a long corridor. Ian and Emma tried to follow, but a nurse persuaded them to sit in the waiting room whilst the doctor gave Robert a thorough examination. They were told that as soon as the doctor had evaluated Robert's condition, he would explain the situation.

That was 25 minutes ago.

Nobody said anything. Ian paced the floor and Emma nervously chewed her bottom lip.

Ian suddenly sat down and looked at Oscar. "Thanks for all your help. You seemed to know exactly what needed to be done."

"Sunstroke is a common problem in the tropics, particularly with tourists. I've seen a number of incidents, both here and in Hong Kong, so I just applied the knowledge I gained from seeing them."

"Anyway, Oscar," said Emma, taking a deep breath, "we're really grateful."

May, sitting next to Emma, gave her arm a comforting squeeze.

Moments later, the door opened and two women dressed in white lab coats entered. Everyone stood up.

"Mr. and Mrs. Caxton?"

"That's us," said Ian, pointing to his wife.

"Hello. I'm Doctor Jacobs and my colleague here is Nurse Ambrose. I've just examined your son and have to say he's been very lucky. Keeping Robert cool, as you did, probably saved his life. Without prompt and adequate treatment, heatstroke can be fatal."

Emma felt herself beginning to panic and stared at the doctor. Her eyes were wide open.

"He's going to be alright though?" asked Ian, hopefully. He was terrified at the thought of the answer.

"He's young, and we don't think there's been any obvious organ damage, but we want to properly examine him to be sure. He's in Intensive Care."

"Oh my God!" announced Emma. She started to cry.

Ian gave her a comforting cuddle and a gentle kiss on the forehead.

"Can we see him, please?" Her voice was almost begging.

"I'm sorry, not at the moment. We've sedated him and put him on a drip to avoid further dehydration. He's also being connected up to other monitoring equipment. Possibly, you'll be able to see him tomorrow. We'll then have a better understanding of your son's condition."

Ian reluctantly nodded. He couldn't argue against the doctor's reasoning.

Doctor Jacobs asked, "Have you recently arrived in Antigua?"

"Yes," said Ian. "A couple of days ago."

The doctor sighed. "I thought that might be the case. People who aren't used to our hot weather are especially susceptible to heat-related illnesses. It can take several weeks for your body to adjust to the hot weather. The sun in the tropics is much stronger and more powerful than in the UK."

Ian nodded again. He was annoyed with himself for not insisting Robert come out of the sea when he'd walked back to Oscar's villa. "What time can we visit tomorrow?"

Doctor Jacobs looked down at her notes attached to a clipboard. "Probably mid-afternoon," she said, looking across at the nurse, who nodded. "Hopefully, by then, we'll have most of the tests completed. Now, have you got any more questions?"

Emma and Ian looked at each other but didn't know what to say. They were still in shock.

"No," said Ian, quietly. "Maybe we'll have some questions for you tomorrow."

The doctor gave a sympathetic smile. "Of course. It's all been a great shock. But Robert's in the best hands. We've seen these situations many times before."

Emma gave a gentle smile and, with tears welling up in her eyes again, said, "Please look after him. If there's any change, can someone please ring us?" She handed over a card with both Ian and Emma's mobile numbers.

Nurse Ambrose leaned forward and took the card. "We'll certainly do that. When you come in tomorrow, ask for me at reception. I'll be on duty until 8pm."

Oscar drove everyone home. There was little conversation in the car. Ian was still annoyed with himself, and Emma was still annoyed with him. However, she began to think about all the hours Robert had been exposed to the sun and swimming in the sea during the last two days. His burnt shoulders should have been a warning sign. Now it was too late. She just hoped and prayed that the hospital wouldn't find any damage to his organs.

They arrived back at the villa and found the kitchen like a bombsite. Abandoned and half-prepared food was littered all over the kitchen island. May and Oscar started to tidy it up. Most was salvageable, but nobody was hungry, so they started to place all the food in the fridge.

Emma insisted she wanted to help; it might take her mind off thinking of Robert for a few minutes. Oscar stepped aside and walked out onto the patio, where he found Ian sitting on a chair, with his hands covering his face. He lifted up an empty chair, placed it next to Ian and sat down.

"He's going to be okay, Ian," said Oscar, with a comforting voice. "He's in the best place."

Ian sat up, removed his hands from his face and took a deep intake of breath. "If only I'd insisted he came back to the villa with me."

"You can't blame yourself. We all should have made sure he was alright. I know how strong the sun can be in the middle of the day. I should have said something."

Ian leaned across and laid his hand on Oscar's shoulders. "We're his parents, Oscar. He's our responsibility. It's not your fault. I just pray everything will be much better tomorrow."

Chapter 48

The following afternoon, Oscar drove Ian and Emma back to St. John's hospital. When he stopped in the car park, he said he'd wait in his car. Ian suggested they would get a taxi back to the villa, but Oscar insisted Ian should ring him when they were ready to leave.

Ian and Emma walked across the car park towards a pair of double glass doors. A large blue sign stating 'Reception' was positioned on the wall next to the doors.

"I'm really worried, Ian," said Emma, as they walked slowly, side by side. "I hardly slept last night, and when I did, I had horrible nightmares."

"I know. I couldn't sleep either," said Ian, pushing one of the entrance doors open for Emma.

The reception area wasn't very busy. It wasn't the A & E wing like yesterday, so when they walked across to the reception desk, there wasn't a queue in front of them.

A young woman receptionist smiled as they approached and asked how she could help.

Emma decided to take charge and said, "We were told to ask for Nurse Ambrose. We're here to see our son, Robert Caxton."

The receptionist looked down at her desk and flicked through some papers. "Ah, yes, Robert." She looked up and smiled again. "I'll just ring through. Please, take a seat."

Ian and Emma both smiled back and sat down on the two seats closest to the reception desk. They looked around the room. It was bright, clean and quiet. A woman nearby made eye contact with Ian and smiled. Ian nodded and smiled back.

"I've never liked hospitals," said Ian, turning his attention back to Emma.

"I don't think anyone actually likes them, but we'd be in a mess without them."

"Mrs. Caxton," the receptionist called.

Emma jumped up and quickly walked back to the desk.

"The nurse will be with you in about five minutes."

"Thank you," responded Emma, and returned to her seat next to Ian.

Three minutes later, Nurse Ambrose walked through a pair of doors at the end of the room to join them. Both Emma and Ian stood up.

"Hello. We've got some good news," said the nurse, shaking their hands. "Come with me."

Ian and Emma were relieved and had smiles on their faces as they followed the nurse through the double doors and along a corridor. The nurse pushed open a door displaying the name 'Senior Nurse J Ambrose' for Ian and Emma to enter. After they'd sat down, the nurse closed the door and sat down behind her desk. She reached across for a file and pulled it closer.

"Robert's doing very well," said the nurse, opening up the file. "Initial tests show there's not been any organ damage. However, we're still awaiting two more results."

Emma was relieved and took a big intake of breath.

"The main harm," continued the nurse, "is to his back and the rear of his legs. Excessive sunburn has caused a lot of blistering, but we've applied special medication, which should relieve the pain and discomfort. He was also seriously dehydrated, but that's nearly back to normal now. He should be out of Intensive Care once we're happy with the two outstanding results."

"That's great news," said Ian, looking at Emma.

"Can we see him now?" Emma asked, desperate to see her son.

"Once he's out of Intensive Care. Remember, Robert's still being monitored and watched because, when he's awake, he's been complaining of a headache. Also, his mind is still a little confused. That's not unusual, but we don't want him more stressed. We'll tell Robert you've visited, and once he's out of Intensive Care, and on a ward, there'll be no problem in visiting him properly."

Emma leaned forward and asked, "How long is he going to be in hospital?"

"That's difficult to say. It depends partly on the outstanding results and how soon we can move him into a ward."

Ian stared at the nurse and asked, "Will there be any lasting damage?"

"It's hard to say at this stage. As I said earlier, his organs, so far, look okay. However, there might be some skin scarring, particularly across his shoulders, but that would be the worst-case scenario. He's young, so his skin could recover completely, especially if it's not subjected to more excessively hot sunshine."

"I think we've all learned an important lesson there," said Ian, with a serious look on his face.

Nurse Ambrose rose up from her chair, which was a strong hint for Ian and Emma to do the same. "I'll telephone you in the morning and let you know how things are… and, hopefully, be able to tell you when Robert's going to be moved into a ward."

Ian and Emma were shown back to the reception area, where Ian thanked the nurse for all the attention Robert was receiving.

Emma smiled and also thanked her. She just wanted to see, and make sure, that Robert was okay. Another 24 hours, at least, could she really wait that long?

Chapter 49

Ten minutes after Ian had made his telephone call, Oscar stopped his car near the entrance to reception. Ian and Emma promptly climbed in.

"How's our little cricketer then?" asked Oscar, selecting first gear and accelerating the car away.

"He's a lot better, thanks," said Ian, looking across at Emma for her agreement, but she was staring out of the window. "He's still in Intensive Care, but they don't think any of his organs have been affected. They're now waiting on the results of two more tests."

Oscar stopped at the car park's exit and checked for oncoming traffic. The road was clear, so he eased the car onto the main road. "Any idea how long he's going to be in hospital?"

Emma said, "No. He's got serious burns on his back, shoulders and the rear of his legs."

"Ouch! It must be really painful."

"They've been giving him painkillers and applying plenty of medication," responded Ian. "Worst-case scenario, according to the nurse, is he could have a few scars."

Emma was quiet again and resumed staring out of the window.

May heard her car being parked in the driveway and immediately rushed outside. Spotting Emma, she walked over and gave her a hug. Emma hugged her back and started to cry.

"Fancy a beer?" Oscar asked Ian, as he shut and locked the driver's door.

"What a great idea. Thanks… and also thanks for the taxi service."

"No problem. Come on, I'll get the ladies something to drink too."

The rest of the afternoon and evening was spent mostly sitting on the patio. May had prepared a buffet prawn and crab salad and everybody helped themselves.

Discussions were low key, they couldn't even plan days out. This was not how each of them had expected to be spending their holiday. Even Ian declined more alcohol after just one can of beer.

Emma was especially quiet, and Ian kept thinking about how the holiday had been completely turned upside down. He was even wondering how they would get Robert back to England… and when! At least flying Upper Class meant Robert's seat could easily be converted into a bed.

Next morning, Oscar and May were awake early and, at 6.15, decided to get back to their usual routine of an early dip in the sea. Oscar checked outside Ian and Emma's room, but there was no sign of movement.

"It's all quiet in the guest bedroom," announced Oscar, as he entered the kitchen. May was already waiting. "I'll leave a note." He picked up a piece of paper and a pen and wrote his note, leaving it prominently on the kitchen island. "Okay, let's go. We'll probably be back before they stir, anyway."

Just over an hour later, Oscar and May returned to the

villa. The first thing Oscar spotted was his note, undisturbed on the island.

"I'll just go for a quick shower," said May, and headed off down the corridor. Oscar started preparing for breakfast. Whilst waiting for the kettle to boil, he decided to look at his computer. He didn't have a television, so obtained all the local and world's news via the internet. Firstly he checked his emails, but nothing was urgent or especially important. He then accessed one of the two websites he used for his world news. It was a Hong Kong-based website. Both he and May wanted to read and keep up with what was going on in their old home. For a change, all seemed to be quiet. He quickly scanned through a few reports but had recently lost trust in the information being provided and wondered how much the Chinese authorities were censoring broadcasting and publishing now.

The second website was the BBC world service. When he read the headlines, his eyes were immediately wide open in shock. The headline read, 'Huge Art Fraud Gang Arrested.' Slowly reading the rest of the article, it was all about the gang Ian had told him about. Wow, he thought, and continued to read. Arrests made in Poland, the USA, Europe and the UK. No names were mentioned, but many stolen paintings and sculptures had been recovered.

"What are you reading?" asked May. She'd just returned to the kitchen.

Oscar whispered, "Is Ian awake?"

"I heard some noises coming from their room, why?"

Oscar continued, "This report's about the gang Ian told me about. There's been mass arrests worldwide!"

"So why are you whispering? Surely, Ian will want to know."

"I know. But at this minute? When they're both still worried sick about Robert?"

"Mmm. Good point. But he's going to find out anyway. He's got his mobile phone."

"I was wondering if I should keep the news from him, at least until after the hospital phone call this morning."

May thought for a moment. "Okay, let's see what the hospital has to say first."

Chapter 50

Ian entered the kitchen about an hour after Oscar and May had returned from their swim. He said both he and Emma had slept much better than the previous night.

"Good," responded Oscar. He was pleased that Ian had obviously not seen the news on his mobile. "Where's Emma?"

"She's just finishing getting dressed."

May placed four glasses on the island, along with a jug of orange juice. "Do you know what time the hospital's going to phone?"

Ian tapped his back pocket. "I've got my phone here. They just said sometime this morning. I guess they'll have to wait until the doctor's seen Robert."

The kitchen island was now fully prepared for breakfast, so May sat down on one of the stools. Oscar finished preparing a cafetière of coffee and placed it on the island.

Two minutes later, Emma arrived and they all joined May and sat on the bar stools.

Conversation was light. Everyone was still feeling tense, waiting for the call. Emma couldn't properly concentrate and Ian kept checking his phone for an email or text message. However, for the next 30 minutes, nothing happened except for brief chats, eating and drinking. Oscar and May didn't know what to say. Oscar was pleased he hadn't mentioned the news just yet. He guessed he wouldn't be able to get Ian's full attention, anyway. Not until they'd finally received good news from the hospital.

At ten o'clock, Emma and May were sitting in the shade on the patio, whilst Oscar and Ian sat on the boundary wall, chatting and staring out to sea. It was another hot morning, there wasn't a cloud in the sky. A breeze had just started, but it was only moving the warm air, not cooling the temperature.

May was finding it difficult to fully engage with Emma. She knew this wouldn't happen until Emma had received some good news from the hospital. Nevertheless, May started to explain about some work she was doing with Wesley at the Shell Gallery. Emma nodded at the right places, but didn't properly interact. Suddenly, May was interrupted when, on the small table in front of her, Emma's phone started to ring. Oscar and Ian heard it, so they walked over to hear if it was the hospital. Ian had assumed it would be him they'd phone.

Emma didn't recognise the number and answered with a cautious, "Hello?"

"Is that Mrs. Caxton, Emma? Nurse Ambrose here."

Emma recognised the voice. "Hello. Thanks for calling. I hope you're going to tell us some good news?"

"Yes, Emma. I am. Robert has been moved to a ward. The last two tests were negative, so we don't need to keep him in Intensive Care any longer."

Emma closed her eyes and gave a sigh of relief. "So, can we come and visit him?"

Ian tried to lean closer to hear the conversation.

"Yes. However, you need to know he might still be a little confused. The dehydration has affected his mental state, but that's slowly improving. His burns are improving, too, and the medication we're applying has reduced the red colour of his skin."

"That's wonderful news. What time can we arrive?"

"We need to tidy him up a little, but four o'clock should be fine. He's in Ward 7."

"We'll be there. Is there anything we should bring?"

"Not at the moment. He'll eventually need his clothes, but not for a few days. I won't be here when you arrive, so ask for my assistant, Nurse Griffiths."

"Yes, I will. Thanks again for all your kind help."

The two women said their goodbyes, and Emma switched off the call.

"Sounds like he's on the mend," said Ian, standing back up straight. "What time can we see him?"

"Four o'clock. He's in Ward 7. We've got to ask for Nurse Griffiths."

Oscar and May were smiling and said how pleased they were with the news. Oscar pondered on telling Ian about the BBC report, but decided to delay it, just a bit longer.

At four o'clock, Ian and Emma were sitting in a different waiting room at the hospital. They'd been told Nurse Griffiths was currently dealing with a patient, but she knew they were waiting. Every minute that passed, Emma became more impatient. Finally, she stood up and paced around the small room.

"Robert's not their only patient," said Ian, watching her walking up and down the room. "Come and sit down… and try to relax. They know we're here."

Emma ignored him and carried on walking. "Maybe something's happened. A relapse… or something!"

"No it hasn't. They would have told us by now. You're going to make yourself ill. How's that going to help Robert when he sees you?"

Emma knew Ian was right and sat down.

"Good," said Ian, reaching over and holding her hand. "I'm sure they..."

Ian was interrupted when the door opened and a woman in a nurse's uniform walked in. "Mr. and Mrs. Caxton?"

Emma immediately shot up, nodded and said, "Yes."

Ian also stood up, but more slowly.

The nurse moved forward and shook both Ian and Emma's hand. "Hello, I'm Nurse Griffiths. I understand from my colleague you're here to see your son, Robert."

Again Emma expelled an anxious, "Yes!"

"Fine. Now, before we go to the ward, there are a couple of things you need to be aware of."

Oh God, thought Emma, he has had a relapse!

The nurse continued. "You might find him a little drowsy. That's because Robert's been given a sedative, to try to calm and relax him. His mind tends to wander and occasionally he feels frightened. This is just a passing phase, and we should see improvements over the next few days."

Ian was listening carefully and nodded, showing he understood. Emma was more alarmed.

"Also, Robert's still being monitored and has a drip feed attached to his nose. Please don't be alarmed; the drip is just making sure we keep his fluids topped up."

Nurse Griffiths looked at both Ian and Emma's faces. Once satisfied, she resumed, "Right, let's go and see your son."

Ian and Emma looked at each other. Ian could see she was still anxious, so he gave her a reassuring hug. They followed the nurse out of the room and down a corridor.

Chapter 51

It was 5.45pm when Ian telephoned Oscar. He arrived 15 minutes later. May was also in the car. Once Ian and Emma had climbed onto the back seat, Oscar and May turned around and waited for the update.

"Is he okay?" asked Oscar, but the answer was already written on Emma's face. She had a relieved smile.

Ian was smiling too and replied, "He's progressing well. Still being monitored and linked up to a drip, but the nurse explained that this was normal practice in his circumstances. He's still a little confused and his mind tends to drift, but they say that's normal too."

"Phew," said a relieved Oscar, and turned back to start up the car's engine.

May pushed her hand across towards Emma and squeezed her hand. "I bet he was pleased to see you."

Emma tried to smile and nodded her head. Tears began to well up in her eyes.

May continued to hold Emma's hand. "You've had a tough time, but now you know he's on the mend."

Emma squeezed May's hand and said, "He looked so pathetic, May. I just wanted to give him a hug, but with all the wires and tubes, it wasn't possible. At least I know he's over the worst."

Oscar drove them back towards the villa. There, he'd decided, he was going to tell Ian about the other interesting news of the day.

A few minutes later, Ian's mobile rang.

Ian looked at the caller's number and raised his eyebrows in surprise. "It's Penny!" he announced, and then answered the call. "Hi, Penny. You're up late. Lovely to hear from you."

"Hi, Ian. Finally got you. I've called several times, but keep getting no reply. Anyway, I've got you now. Have you heard the news?"

"News? What news? Is it good news, or bad?" Ian had a wry smile on his face.

"It's Jonathan."

"Northgate? Please tell me he's resigned."

Penny laughed. "Nope. He's been sacked!"

It was Ian's turn to laugh. "Sacked! You're kidding?"

Oscar looked across at May and raised his eyebrows. Now Ian knows.

"Seriously, Ian. In fact, the police have arrested him."

"Arrested! Oh, wow. The news gets better all the time."

"Rumour at Sotheby's is that Security have been watching and monitoring him for at least the last 12 months. They'd informed the police, some months ago, about his suspicious activity and behaviour."

"So they knew all along? Before we got involved?"

"It appears so. Still, you've finally got your wish."

Ian laughed again. "Wonderful!. There's a lot more I can tell you, but we're currently staying with Oscar and May in Antigua. I'll speak to you when we get back home."

"I'll also let you know if and when I know any more."

"Thanks, Penny. Wonderful news. Speak to you soon. Bye."

"Goodbye, Ian."

Ian switched off the call. "Wow! Did you hear all that? Northgate's been arrested! Two wonderful pieces of news in one day. I want to celebrate!"

Oscar smiled to himself. Well, that solved his dilemma. "Champagne all round?"

"Not for me, Oscar," answered Emma, speaking more seriously. She was staring out of the side window. "Not until Robert's out of hospital."

"Yes, you're right, Emma." Ian removed the smile from his face. "Robert coming out of hospital will be the time for us to celebrate properly."

Although the champagne didn't flow that evening, both Ian and Emma were more relaxed and a lot happier than they'd been just 24 hours earlier. Oscar didn't let on that he'd known about the arrests earlier that day, but he did show Ian the BBC website report of the mass arrests.

After finishing reading the article, Ian sat back in his chair. He and Oscar were sitting in the office. "Wow!" he said, and sipped his white wine. "I knew a few bits and bobs about what the police were doing… but… this is a massive coup."

Oscar nodded. "Sounds like your colleague Northgate was just the tip of the iceberg."

"I'd never call Northgate a colleague. A nemesis, certainly. Definitely an enemy. There must be a lot of red faces at Sotheby's."

Oscar smiled at his friend's enjoyment of the situation. "Sotheby's are in an embarrassing moment."

"That doesn't please me, Oscar. There are a lot of good people still working there. Bit of a storm in a teacup for the company. It'll survive. It's had more difficult situations to deal with in the past."

"Maybe they'll want you back?"

Ian laughed. "No chance! My life's moved on so much

from my last days in London. I went back there from Hong Kong. Mind, that wasn't really my choice. The future is my choice, and it'll never include the thought of working back at Sotheby's."

After sipping his wine, Oscar teasingly smiled and patted Ian's shoulder. "Never say never!"

Ian smiled and shook his head.

"What now then? Now that your nemesis has been arrested?"

"Now? All I want now, Oscar, is to see Northgate hanged, drawn and quartered!"

Chapter 52

Over the next week, Ian and Emma visited Robert every day. On each visit, they could see a definite improvement. Doctor Jacobs and Nurse Ambrose kept reporting positively on his recovery. Even when Oscar and May visited, they saw he was almost back to his old self. His shoulders and the back of his legs were now a pinky red, and not so raw. The cooling creams were obviously doing their job.

It was on the eighth day after Robert's admission to the hospital that Doctor Jacobs suggested to Emma that she should bring in some light and baggy clothes plus a wide-brimmed hat. Plans were set for Robert to be discharged the next afternoon.

Emma was almost counting the minutes. She just wanted her son back, fit and healthy, again.

Finally, at 3.30 on the ninth day, Robert was sitting in a wheelchair and being pushed down the corridor. He was heading for the hospital's exit. For the last three days, he'd been walking for short spells, longer each day and shadowed by a trainee nurse. The same nurse was now pushing the wheelchair. Ian and Emma were walking at his side.

Emotional goodbyes had been exchanged by Emma and the nursing staff. Ian shook both Doctor Jacobs and Nurse

Ambrose's hands, and thanked them for their wonderful care and professionalism.

In his short-sleeve shirt pocket, Ian had placed the list of all the do's and don'ts, with regard to Robert's next few days of continued treatments. He'd promised that every order would be obeyed, and Robert, whilst continuing to improve his walking, would be fully protected from the sun. After all, Ian thought, we fly home in three days' time... back to a British winter.

Parked close to the exit doors, Oscar and May were waiting patiently in May's car.

When they saw Robert being wheeled out of the building, they looked at each other, somewhat surprised. Oscar quickly jumped out of the driver's seat and opened both the back doors. When the group arrived at the side of the car, the nurse assisted Robert to stand up, then Ian helped him climb onto the back seat. A rubber cushion was gently eased to the bottom of Robert's back, helping him keep his shoulders and legs away from the seat. Finally, his seat belt was clicked into place.

Ian and Emma slipped in on either side of Robert, and Oscar started the engine. Twenty minutes later, they arrived back at the villa. Robert insisted he wanted to get out of the car on his own and walk into the villa. Ian reluctantly agreed but shadowed him all the way to the kitchen. Next to the patio doors was a small armchair, which Robert eased himself into. The four adults stared at him anxiously.

Robert looked up, and when he saw four worried faces watching him, he gave a short laugh. "I'm not a cripple. Can you give me some space... please?"

Ian slowly shook his head and looked at Emma. She was still staring intently at her son. "Look," Emma said suddenly, "you've been in hospital for over a week. You were seriously ill and could have died. Show a bit of respect. We've all been worried sick."

Robert bowed his head. "Yes, sorry, Mum… Dad. I know it was all my fault. I just want to get fit and normal again."

Ian pulled the sheet of paper out of his top pocket and waved it in front of his son. "These are the instructions Doctor Jacobs has given me. You're going to follow every one… religiously. Okay?"

"Yes, Dad. Sorry."

May tapped Oscar gently on the shoulder and then nodded her head towards the door. It was her way of saying they should leave Robert to his parents.

During the rest of the afternoon and early evening, the tension between Robert and his parents gradually eased. Robert knew he'd caused a lot of stress to his parents and accepted he needed to change his attitude. The best way to do that, he thought, was to get back on their side and not be a nuisance.

That evening, Robert said he didn't want any dinner, as he felt too tired and exhausted. Ian helped him get ready for bed, it was just after 7.30. By 7.45, he was fast asleep.

Oscar, meanwhile, had secretly placed two bottles of champagne in the fridge. He hoped that now Robert was out of hospital, Ian and Emma might want to celebrate.

At eight o'clock, the four adults sat down to a lobster and salad dinner. Oscar looked at Emma and tried to gauge her mood. She was certainly smiling more and seemed more relaxed. "Are you ready for the champagne now, Emma?"

Emma looked at Ian and smiled. Then, looking at Oscar, her smile became much wider and she nodded her head. "That would be lovely, Oscar. Thank you."

Oscar went over to the fridge and removed one of the chilled bottles. At the same time, May collected four crystal champagne glasses. Everyone then watched as Oscar cautiously removed the cork. The resulting 'pop' made May jump, which caused sniggers from the others.

After Oscar had filled all four glasses, he made a toast. "To two special friends, cheers!" They all clinked their glasses and then Emma stood up, holding her glass out in front of her. "Oscar, May. It's not been the holiday we'd all planned, but just being in your wonderful company is a pleasure in itself. Thank you for your understanding and patience during a difficult time... and thank you, Oscar, for the taxi service. You must both come and stay with us... and I guarantee you one thing. Nobody's likely to be taken to hospital due to sunstroke in January in the UK! Cheers!"

Emma sat down and all four clinked their glasses again. Ian leaned over and kissed her on the cheek. "Well said. That was great." For the first time in nine days, Ian could see the old sparkle back in Emma's eyes.

Chapter 53

The following morning, Oscar and May were up early and sneaked off for their early morning swim. When they returned, nobody had stirred from either the guest, or Robert's, bedroom.

"I'm going for a shower," said May, departing along the corridor.

Oscar made himself a mug of coffee and looked at his computer. A few emails, he noticed. Two needed a reply. Twenty minutes later, he accessed the BBC website. He wanted to see if there'd been any more news or updates about the art fraud arrests. Unfortunately, there was no more news. Okay, he thought, no message for Ian.

"Morning, Oscar."

Oscar looked over his laptop screen and was startled to see young Robert standing in front of him. His hair was matted and uncombed and he was wearing a blue tee shirt and underpants. "Hi. How are you feeling?"

"Pretty good, thanks. Any chance of a glass of water?"

"Of course. Sit down and I'll get you one."

Robert sat down on one of the bar stools and, after placing his left elbow on the island, he leaned his head on his raised hand.

Oscar filled a glass from the tap and placed it in front of him.

"Thanks," said Robert, still half asleep. "Mum and Dad up yet?"

"No. Probably having a lay-in. I don't think they've had much sleep this week."

Robert nodded. "Yea, my fault. Look, Oscar, I'm really sorry. I didn't realise… or think."

"It's okay. I know you wanted to enjoy our wonderful warm sea, but the sun's pretty powerful after about ten o'clock here in the tropics. May and me, we go for a swim at about six o'clock."

"I'm never awake at that time. It's the middle of the night!"

Oscar smiled. "Yes, well, that suits us. Do you want anything to eat?"

"I'm hungry, but I'll wait for everyone else."

Oscar nodded and tried to listen for any noise coming from the guest bedroom, but it was still quiet. "You know, your parents were really worried about you."

Robert nodded again. "I know. It was pretty stupid what I did, but I've learned a lesson. This is the first time I've been to the tropics; I'll know better next time."

"Not just the tropics. The sun's pretty powerful everywhere… if you're exposed to it for too long."

Robert sipped his water. "I didn't know that… another lesson I've learned."

They both sat quietly for a few moments. Oscar wasn't very experienced when it came to talking to kids. He closed his computer down.

Robert stared at his glass. "You're my godfather, right?"

Oscar nodded his head. He wondered where this conversation was going. "Yes. Why do you ask?"

"It's just a bit strange. I don't remember you from the past, but you've always sent me a birthday card."

Oscar smiled. "The last time I saw you was… probably before you started school."

Robert pondered on that statement. "You've known my dad for a long time."

Again Oscar nodded. "Before he was married to your mum. I was his best man at their wedding."

Robert scratched his ear and leaned his head back on his raised hand. "Do you know a lot about art?"

"Some. Nobody knows it all. It's a big subject."

"Dad knows a lot. He's made lots of money too. That's what I want to do. I want to be as rich as he is."

"Who's your favourite artist?"

"That's easy, Canaletto. Dad took me to some of the galleries in London. Modern art, I think it's rubbish, but Canaletto… and Turner, are my favourites. Who's your favourite?"

"Okay. I guess I don't really have a favourite. My business is all about buying and selling pictures and paintings… making a profit. My favourite is the one that I can make the most profit from."

"Dad… and sometimes, Mum, do the same. There must be a lot of money in trading. I want to make a lot of money."

"There's a lot to learn first. You need to specialise in a certain area and understand the different artists and the periods they lived in. It's hard work and nobody has been an overnight success."

"That's what Dad says."

"We both agree on that then. It's definitely hard work."

Robert nodded again, finished drinking his water and pushed the empty glass towards Oscar. "Thanks. I'd better get dressed. Nice talking to you, Oscar. You're cool." Robert carefully stepped down from the stool and gingerly ambled back towards his bedroom.

Oscar watched until Robert had disappeared. He then listened until he'd heard the bedroom door close. He rubbed his chin and smiled to himself. What was that all about?

Chapter 54

During the last two days of their holiday, Ian and Emma decided to remain close to the villa and help Robert with his recuperation. His energy levels were almost back to normal and with gentle massage and cream applications, the burning sensation had almost disappeared. His skin was still pinkish red on the more damaged areas, but his walking strength had increased significantly. Ian was determined Robert would be as comfortable as possible during the ten-hour flight back to the UK.

On the final morning, all four adults were up early. Robert was still fast asleep. Oscar had suggested, before the sun became too strong, that he and Ian should have a stroll along the beach. He was curious to know what Ian's plans were now that his long-time nemesis, Jonathan Northgate, would soon be out of his life.

After they'd stepped onto the quiet and deserted beach, both men removed their sandals. The sand was warm and soft between their toes. Ian decided he'd like a last paddle in the Caribbean Sea, so Oscar suggested they walk towards the old lighthouse and back, close to the hotel where he and May were married.

As they strolled along the water's edge, Ian looked out to sea. The orange glow of the sun was slowly rising above the horizon. "You know, Oscar, I'm going to miss this beach and Antigua's lovely warm climate. It must feel like you're permanently on holiday."

Oscar smiled and kicked gently at the water. "Yes, it does have its benefits, but I've still got to earn a living. There's less activity here compared to Hong Kong. That's both good and bad. Mind, May still keeps in touch with colleagues in Hong Kong and China. The internet's a great benefit."

"Selling the Joan Mitchell painting in New York, that must have improved your bank balance."

"That was brilliant," said Oscar, smiling and looking up at Ian. "Thanks again for your help. Yes, it would be great if I could unearth one of those successes every now and then. We definitely wouldn't have succeeded without Bruce Campbell and Sotheby's involvement. Often, it's who you know, rather than what you know."

For a few moments they both walked in silence. Oscar could see Ian was in deep thought. He wondered whether he was thinking about Northgate or his future. He knew from previous conversations that Ian wasn't completely satisfied with life and would like to try something new, but Emma was less keen. She was the one who wanted stability… and for them to continue living in their lovely home in Esher.

After a couple of seconds, Oscar broke the silence and asked, "When you get back to England, what are your plans?"

Ian stopped walking and gave a big sigh. "You know, Oscar, I don't really know. The Northgate situation has taken up quite a bit of my time recently. Now, hopefully, that's coming to an end. So, seriously, I don't know. I've still got to recover my Oliver Squires painting. I paid over a million pounds for that, so I need to get it back."

Oscar smiled at his friend. But made no comment.

Ian wondered what Oscar was thinking. "Why? Have you got a suggestion?"

Oscar began to laugh and said, "Never say never!"

"No, Oscar, Sotheby's is out of the question. Never definitely means never in my book. It's a fresh challenge I'm looking for, not an old one."

Oscar looked at his watch. "We better get back. May will have prepared breakfast… and you never know, even Robert might have emerged."

They turned around and headed back the way they'd come. Ian looked at the large building on his left-hand side. "Hey! That's the hotel where you and May were married. That was a wonderful day. No regrets?"

"No, Ian, definitely no regrets. May's wonderful. She gave up everything in Hong Kong to be here with me. We work well together and have a great life. I wouldn't go back to Hong Kong now… not even for a holiday. May's colleagues say it's all changed, primarily due to the Chinese government's influence… and certainly, the changes haven't been for the better."

"It's such a shame," responded Ian, thinking back to his time working for Sotheby's in Hong Kong. "We had a great time. There was always a buzz, the excitement… a great challenge. Mind, we were both single in those days, so maybe we look back through rose-tinted glasses."

"You don't miss that life?"

"Yes and no. It was great then, but my life's so different now. I try not to dwell on the past, except, say, with you, for the odd reminisce. Tomorrow and the next day, that's what I look forward to. I'm a curious person, Oscar… and I need a new challenge!"

"Never say never, Ian!"

Chapter 55

Nine hours after Ian and Oscar had walked off the beach, both families stood in the departure terminal of the V. C. Bird International Airport, saying their goodbyes. Ian had checked in all the hold luggage and was holding three boarding passes. He shook Oscar's hand. "Sorry, Oscar, it wasn't the holiday we'd all planned, but it was still great to be here and enjoy both yours and May's lovely company. Thanks."

"Things happen. It just means you'll have to come back... and soon. It was great to see you, Ian. Good luck with your new challenge... whatever it is."

Both ladies hugged and Emma said, "You must come and see us in England. We're only ten hours away."

"I'd like that," replied May with an emotional smile. "I've only been to England once... and that was on a school exchange trip."

Emma laughed, and they hugged again.

Robert stood quietly, not knowing what to say. Oscar gently tapped him on the shoulder and held out his hand. "Well, young man, it was great to see you again, after all these years. Keep in touch. I want to know how you're progressing towards achieving your ambition."

Robert smiled and shook Oscar's hand. "I'm so sorry I upset everyone's holiday."

Oscar leaned forward and gave him a very gentle hug. He was well aware that Robert's skin might still be tender and whispered into his ear, "The past you cannot change, the future's in your own hands. Go with your ambition."

When the embrace had finished, Robert smiled and nodded. "I will. Thanks."

Studying Oscar's face, Ian asked, "What's this, 'ambition'?"

Oscar grinned and tapped the side of his nose. "An understanding between a godfather and godson."

Emma and Ian looked at each other and then at Robert.

Robert gazed back and shrugged. He had a relaxed expression on his face and said, "Oscar's cool!"

"Right," said Emma, picking up her cabin bag. "We'd better head for passport control. I've just noticed the time."

Final goodbyes, hugs and handshakes were made, then Oscar and May were left standing on their own.

Oscar took a deep breath and stared at May. "That was a shame. We didn't show them much of the island."

May grabbed Oscar's hand and gave it a squeeze. "There's always next time."

They walked slowly across the concourse towards the exit. "I guess so," said Oscar. "Incidentally, Ian was telling me about a possible new challenge. He's always been a bit restless, regularly looking for the next career move, the next opportunity or challenge. Even young Robert is showing similar traits. Ian's a great friend, May, but I wish he'd just settle down and be thankful… of where he is… and what he's already achieved."

"Some people never settle down. It's not in their nature. They never retire, because they know they'd be bored. Maybe Ian's a bit like that."

Oscar pondered on May's comment as he pushed open one of the large glass double doors. Outside and away from the terminal's air conditioning, the hot and sultry atmosphere hit them. "You could be right," replied Oscar, "but somehow, I think it's an excuse. He told me once that his Russian colleague, Andrei, was a workaholic. He never had time to benefit from his vast wealth, until it was almost too late. Ian said he didn't want that to happen to him and his family. He wanted them to be able to enjoy their money whilst they could. No, I think it's more to do with Emma. She was against Ian's involvement with Andrei right from the start. She's more the stability in his life. Not so daring and adventurous."

May suddenly stopped walking and looked at Oscar with an accusing face. "Are you saying Emma's holding Ian back?"

"Not really. As I say, she's his stability. Makes him think deeply and more seriously about any venture Ian's plotting."

"What's wrong with that?"

"Nothing. I'm just saying Ian's more of a 'gung-ho' character, 'go for it' type of guy. He was in Hong Kong... and he had a lot of success. Most things seem to work out for him... in the end. He's always been lucky. Why can't he see that? Because, one day, that good luck just might run out!"

Chapter 56

On the first full day back from the holiday, Ian caught up with all his emails and outstanding correspondence. Emma, meanwhile, was sorting out the clothes Robert would be taking with him tomorrow, when he'd be returning to school. Robert continued with his leg and back exercises. He was determined to be fully fit for the forthcoming indoor cricket practice. The sun damage to his body was healing well, and mentally, he felt completely recovered. Nevertheless, Emma kept asking him if he was sure, because she could always ring the school and tell them he'd be returning a day later. Robert, however, was adamant. He still felt guilty for fouling up the holiday and wanted to get out of his parents' hair... and as soon as possible.

The following morning, after packing Robert's bags into the boot of Emma's car, Ian gave Robert a brief hug and reminded him to make sure he telephoned his mother at the end of the week. Robert nodded and then climbed in the car.

Ian kissed Emma and wished them both a safe journey. He then waved and waited for them to disappear before returning to the house. He needed to get ready to catch the 11.13 train to London, for his meeting with Penny. The previous evening he'd telephoned her and suggested lunch at their usual restaurant, close to Sotheby's. Penny said she would be free after about 1.15. Ian wanted to find out more about the Northgate situation and tell her about his involvement with a certain Detective Inspector Hudson.

On the train, Ian tried to contact George Bailey but only got George's answerphone. He left a message saying he was back in the UK and would like a meeting to discuss the events that had happened whilst he'd been away.

Ian arrived at the restaurant just after one o'clock. He'd made a reservation for 1.15. The maître d' said his table was not quite ready, but if he waited at the bar, he'd call him when it was available.

Ian knew he was early, so wandered over to the bar and ordered a glass of Chablis.

Five minutes later, Ian felt a tap on his shoulder. Turning around, he saw the smiling face of Penny. They hugged and Ian kissed her on both cheeks. "You're looking great," he said.

"Thank you. You're looking well too… and a nice suntan. Did you have a great holiday?"

"I'll tell you about that over lunch. Now, firstly, let me get you a drink. What would you like?"

"What have you got there?" Penny pointed to Ian's glass.

Ian picked up his glass. "It's Chablis. Do you want one?"

"Mmm. Okay. I don't think one drink will harm my work this afternoon."

Whilst Ian was ordering Penny's drink, the maître d' arrived and informed him his table was ready. He also said he'd arrange for the lady's glass of wine to be delivered there.

Ian and Penny followed the maître d' to a quiet table, set in a small secluded alcove. They removed their coats and sat down.

"Now, your holiday, Ian. I sense there was a problem."

However, before he replied, a waiter delivered Penny's drink and two luncheon menus.

"Cheers," said Ian, and raised his glass.

Penny did the same and took a sip, waiting for Ian to speak.

Ian summarised the events leading up to and including Robert's stay in hospital.

Penny stared with surprise. "Oh dear. Robert's okay now, I hope?"

"He seems to be. He was certainly keen to get back to school this morning. Emma said she was going to speak to his form teacher."

Penny smiled. "Good. I guess you weren't able to do any sightseeing?"

"No, but Oscar and May's hospitality made up for it. They've got a lovely life in Antigua."

"You sound jealous," said Penny, picking up her glass and peering at him over the rim.

Ian sighed. "Maybe… a little bit. The weather there is wonderful. Much better than our cold and horrible wet climate."

Penny briefly laughed and then said, "They have hurricanes."

"Even so."

"Can I suggest we order our food, and then I'll update you about Jonathan Northgate."

Ten minutes later, they'd ordered their meals and Penny started to speak. "Well, it all came as a shock. Vic and I were watching the evening news on TV when they announced all the arrests in Europe and America. The newsreader said the police had been following the gang's activity for quite some time but weren't able to act and make arrests until all the various police forces were ready. I know now that Jonathan was arrested at his apartment."

The words 'Jonathan' and 'arrested' made Ian smile.

"It appears you were also right about Sotheby's security

team, because they'd been watching him separately... and working closely with the police. Once these details got to the Chairman, Jonathan was immediately sacked."

"Excellent news! So, what's been happening since?"

"Tony Clover, you know him?"

Ian nodded. "Of course."

"Well, he's been temporarily appointed. As for Jonathan, he's been released on bail. Rumour is, he's had to hand in his passport. That's about it... I think."

Ian leaned back in his seat and folded his arms. "It could be quite some time before he comes to trial, bearing in mind all the different countries involved. Plus... Northgate can afford the best lawyers."

Penny spotted two waiters heading in their direction, carrying their meals.

Once the plates had been positioned on the table and the waiters had left, Ian leaned forward and, lowering his voice, said, "Now it's my turn. I've also been followed and watched for quite some time... by the police!"

"What!?" exclaimed Penny, with a worried look on her face. Leaning forward herself, she whispered, "I hope you're not going to tell me they've been watching me too!"

"No. No worries there. Your name's never been mentioned. Certainly not by me. It's me they were following, because of my activity with Northgate. Apparently, I was treading on their toes... upsetting their surveillance."

"How did you find out... and what are they going to do?"

"It all happened just before the holiday. I'd arranged a meeting with my private investigator, only this time we were joined by a Detective Inspector Hudson from the Met."

"Oh goodness! What did he say?"

"It was a mix of threats about my past and a warning to stop monitoring Northgate. However, I did mention my Oliver Squires painting and the Munnings that went to

Dubai. Incidentally, I've since found out that both the originals were definitely stolen by Northgate and delivered to the gang in Charlton Street. The owners were delivered copies."

"So, you've received a copy of 'The Green Dress'. Vic told me the original sold for over a million pounds! Are you going to get the original back?"

"That's my intention. However, I might be too late. The gang in Poland may have already sold it via their black market connections."

"If you don't recover it, you'll be over a million pounds out of pocket. Oh, Ian."

"I know, but it was always a risk. I needed to get solid proof on Northgate. When he finishes up in prison, it will have been worth every penny!"

Chapter 57

Just after 3.30pm that same afternoon, Ian received a telephone call. He was on the train travelling home after the meeting with Penny. Glancing at his mobile, he recognised the caller. It was George Bailey. "Hi, George. Thanks for calling back. I'd like a meeting. When are you free?"

George ignored Ian's questions and responded with a serious tone to his voice. "Ian, you need to know that our friend in the Met would like to speak to you again."

Ian closed his eyes and let out a deep sigh. He had hoped he'd heard the last from that particular man. "Okay. Do you know why?"

"No. Just said he wanted to speak with you. I told him you were on holiday."

"Did it sound urgent?"

"No. He only said he wanted a meeting. Where are you?"

"I'm back in the UK... heading home on a train. Where does he want to meet?"

"Look, I'll text you his mobile number and you can contact him yourself. We'll have our meeting after that."

"Okay," replied Ian, a little reluctantly. "Is there anything more I should know? I've heard about Northgate and the gang's arrests."

"That's about it. Our friend wasn't very forthcoming,

although I found out from another source that some of the stolen paintings have been recovered in Poland."

"Thanks, George. You don't know if one of them was mine, do you?"

"Sorry, Ian. My source didn't say any more, although my app says your painting is still in Warsaw."

"Okay. Send me the text and I'll speak to him. I'll let you know if I need a good lawyer!"

"Good luck!"

"Thanks, again. I'll be in touch."

After switching off his phone, Ian leaned back in his seat and stared out of the window. He pondered on the probable reason for the detective's request. Maybe he just wanted to thank me. Mmm, probably not. Or, probe into my past, again? Hopefully not.

Ian felt unnerved. Did the police think he was involved with the gang!? If so, what evidence did they have? Well, there was only one way to find out!

Ian accessed his text messages, noted the detective's number and telephoned it. The number was engaged. He wasn't sure whether he was pleased or disappointed.

When Ian arrived home, the house was quiet. Emma obviously hadn't returned from taking Robert back to school. He walked into his office and, whilst standing next to his desk, telephoned the detective's number again. This time it was answered. "Detective Inspector Hudson."

"Hello, it's Ian Caxton," said Ian, trying not to sound nervous. "I gather you wanted to speak to me."

"Yes, Mr. Caxton. I may have some good news!"

Ian sat down on his chair. He was a little shocked. "Good news!?" he queried. This was certainly a different approach that the policeman was taking.

"Yes, we've received a list of paintings and a number of photographs. About 40 paintings in all. They were all recovered in Poland. I was wondering if two might relate to those paintings you emailed me about?"

"Maybe." Ian couldn't think of anything else to say. He was wondering when the policeman's approach would change. He needed to stay on his guard.

"You live in Esher, I understand?"

"Yes," said Ian, hesitantly. He certainly didn't want the police calling on him at his home.

"I have a meeting at Kingston Police Station on Friday. How are you fixed?"

"You want me to meet you there?"

"That's the idea. About two o'clock would be good. Do you know where it is?"

Ian shifted uneasily in his seat. "Err, no, but I'll find it."

"Good. It's in the High Street. Just ask for me at reception. They'll know where I am."

"Fine."

"Thanks."

Ian switched off the call and placed his mobile back in his jacket pocket. He stared across at Emma's empty desk and took a big intake of breath. "Wow," he said out loud and then briefly laughed. "Maybe I don't need a solicitor after all!"

A few minutes later, Ian opened up his computer and downloaded a street map of Kingston upon Thames. He wondered how far the police station was from the railway station. It was pretty close. He thought the train would probably be an easier and less stressful option than taking his car.

Emma arrived home about 40 minutes later. She told Ian about her conversation with Robert's form master. He'd sympathised with Emma's concern and promised he'd keep a close eye on Robert over the next few days.

When Emma had finished, Ian told her about his telephone conversation with Detective Inspector Hudson.

"That sounds promising," said Emma. "Do you think they've got your painting?"

"I'm not sure. I agree it appears promising. However, I'm still wary of the detective's motives. Last time he made a number of threats, now it's the 'good cop' approach. You know, Emma, I don't trust this man."

Chapter 58

On Friday, Ian caught the 12.42 train from Esher. He was still apprehensive about the forthcoming meeting and wanted to give himself plenty of time. There wasn't a direct train service to Kingston, only one change, but he didn't want to be late.

As Ian exited the railway station, he pulled up the collar of his overcoat. He'd still not fully acclimatised back to the cold and damp British winter weather, plus he was still very apprehensive. Which cop would he meet this time? 'Good cop' or 'bad cop'?

He followed the directions shown to him by Google maps and soon spotted the three-storey, brick-and-concrete building, probably 1970s design, he guessed. It was next to a bridge crossing the Hogsmill River.

Pushing on the large glass door, Ian walked nervously into a dour but functional reception area. Several posters warning of burglaries, car thefts and muggings were pinned to otherwise bare walls. The reception area was quiet with only a middle-aged uniformed policeman standing behind the reception desk and writing in a large notebook.

The policeman glanced up when Ian entered, but continued writing until he decided he'd finished. He then looked up and, speaking in a surly tone, asked, "Yes?"

"I have an appointment with Detective Inspector Hudson," said Ian, a little dismissively. He wasn't going to be intimidated by this surly policeman and let him believe he had the upper hand.

"Name?" said the policeman, looking back at his note-book, his ballpoint pen poised.

Ian stared at the top of the policeman's bald head until he eventually looked up. "Ian Caxton," he replied.

The policeman picked up his phone and tapped several numbers. "Ian Caxton, at reception, sir... Yes... fine." He replaced the handset back on his desk and, looking back at Ian, waved in the direction of a vacant plastic chair. "Sit there."

Ian continued to stand still. This obnoxious sod, he thought, could explain properly.

The policeman stared back and said, "Someone will collect you shortly... sir."

Ian smiled and said, courteously, "Thank you," and walked across to a plastic chair and sat down.

The policeman went back to writing in his notebook.

Meanwhile, Ian, disinterestedly, stared at the poster on the wall next to him. He smiled when he read the heading, 'Have you been mugged?' He wondered if the police still investigated these types of crimes nowadays?

"Mr. Caxton?"

Ian turned and looked up into the face of a uniformed policewoman. Standing up and smiling, Ian said, "Yes."

"Please come with me, sir. The Inspector's waiting for you."

Ian followed her through two doors and down a bland corridor until she stopped at an open door, where she tapped and walked in. "Mr. Caxton, sir."

"Good. Thank you, Lisa," announced a voice that Ian immediately recognised. "Send him in."

Ian stepped through the doorway and smiled at Lisa as she passed and walked away.

"Mr. Caxton," said the detective, walking from behind his desk towards Ian. He was holding out his hand. "Good of you to come."

Ian hesitantly shook hands and was invited to sit down. The detective returned to his own chair behind his desk.

"Firstly," said the detective, leaning back, trying to convey a relaxed mood, "I want to thank you for your emails. They were extremely useful to my colleagues in Poland. The word 'original' invisibly written on the back of your painting was a great help."

Ian smiled, but sat quietly. He was waiting for the psychology used by the detective to change.

"I think I mentioned, when I spoke to you on the phone, that about 40 original paintings were recovered from the gang's premises in Poland."

Ian nodded and continued to gaze at the detective.

"I'm also pleased to say we've recovered an additional 25 from the property you visited in Charlton Street."

Ian raised his eyebrows in surprise. He wondered whether this was going to be good news after all.

The detective stood up and walked over to a nearby desk, from which he collected two brown cardboard files that he passed to Ian. "Have a look at those. Tell me if your painting's listed there."

Ian placed the files on his lap and opened the first folder. It contained a number of A4 size photographs. He examined each picture carefully, realising some of the paintings would be quite valuable. Each picture had a number affixed to the top right-hand corner. When he came to picture number 8, he smiled, as he knew he wouldn't have to pay out on his guarantee to Karim. "This photograph, number 8, is the Munnings painting I told you about."

The detective wrote some details on his notepad. "Good. Any others you recognise?"

"I recognise some of the artists," said Ian, continuing to turn over each photograph. When he came to number 17, he grinned and looked up at the detective. Pointing to the picture, he announced, "This one is mine. Number 17."

The detective wrote some more notes. "Okay. Any more?"

Ian continued to flick through the rest of the collection. When he turned over the final photograph, number 65, he said, "I don't recognise any of the others. However, I'm reasonably certain two are by Van Gogh and three by Monet."

"Have a look at the other folder."

Ian placed the first file on the edge of the detective's desk and opened the second. This file simply contained a sheet of A4 size paper revealing a long spreadsheet with a listing of numbers 1 to 65. Only five items had been populated with the name of an artist and the title of the picture. Number 17 stated, 'The Green Dress'. Oliver Squires.

Ian closed the folder and placed it back on the detective's desk. "Sorry, I don't know any others. Most of the photos show modern abstracts… They're not my forte."

The detective leaned forward and placed a ballpoint pen on the folder. "Can you write down the names of the artists you think you do know?"

Ian picked up the pen and wrote the names of the artists against numbers 4, 16, 33, 39 and 51. "You'll need to check, but I'm reasonably certain. I recognise their style. However, I don't know the titles." He returned the folder to the desk.

"We'll get there in the end. Problem is, most of the owners don't know their paintings are missing. They've received copies thinking they were the originals. Especially those bought via auction at Sotheby's."

Ian nodded. "Sotheby's will know the correct owner, but

it'll take time to sort it all out. In the meantime, what about my painting? When am I likely to get it back?"

The detective gave Ian a wry smile. "Ah, there, Mr. Caxton, we may have a problem."

Ian looked at the detective suspiciously. "A problem? Why? Surely, we both know 'The Green Dress' is my property. I bought it fair and square at Sotheby's auction."

"Nobody's doubting that. However, your painting currently resides in Warsaw… Poland."

"I'm aware of that, so, I repeat, why is that a problem?" Ian was becoming agitated.

"All 40 paintings recovered are now in the hands of the Warsaw police. They need to be sure each painting will go back to its rightful owner. Politics and diplomacy also come into play."

Ian shook his head and rubbed his chin in frustration. "So, what happens now?"

"To tell you the truth, I don't know. I've never been involved with a case like this before."

Chapter 59

After leaving the meeting, Ian slowly walked back towards the train station. He was pondering on his difficulty and realised he needed to speak to someone... high up in authority. But who? Should it be his local MP, the Foreign Office? Who?

A few moments later, he thought of Viktor and his police contact in the Met's Art and Antiques Unit. Would he be able to help? Then there was George Bailey. Yes, maybe it would be best to speak with George first.

When Ian arrived home, he walked straight into the office and told Emma about his meeting and the problems of recovering his painting.

"So, the police detective couldn't help?"

"Couldn't or wouldn't. I still don't trust him, Emma."

"What are you going to do now? I don't think you can just fly to Warsaw and claim your painting back."

Ian sat down on the edge of Emma's desk. "No. There's obviously too much politics involved. Pity it wasn't one of the pictures in Charlton Street. Maybe that would have been easier to recover."

After a pause, Ian continued, "I need to discuss the matter with George before I decide on anything. He may have some suggestions."

Emma stood up and put a sympathetic hand on Ian's shoulder. "A lot of aggravation just to get your revenge on Northgate, Ian."

"One way or another, Emma, it's going to be worth it. I've been waiting since I worked in New York to do just that."

After finishing his discussions with Emma, Ian picked up his mobile and telephoned George Bailey. "Hi, George. We need to meet up. I've got a lot to tell you and I need to pick your brain!"

After a little to-ing and fro-ing about dates and times, a meeting was agreed for four days' time. It was back to the pub, located high above the hustle and bustle of London's Waterloo train station, the 'Victory'. However, this time, George promised, there would only be the two of them. Definitely, no Detective Inspector Gerry Hudson.

When Ian told Emma about these arrangements, she said she'd like to join him as she'd not been shopping in London for ages… and she needed some new clothes!

Ian thought about the already full three wardrobes upstairs!

They caught the 11.35am train from Esher. Whilst Ian was deep in thought and apprehensive about what George may say, or not, about recovering his painting, Emma was excited about her shopping trip. She'd even suggested Ian could help her carry her new purchases home.

Although it had been some years since Ian had commuted for work, as the train approached Waterloo station, he stood up and was eager to disembark.

Emma stared up at Ian's urgency. "We're not there yet."

Ian suddenly realised he didn't need to be the first off the train anymore. He smiled at Emma and sat down. "Force of habit, I guess. I was miles away, thinking about my meeting with George. When the train slowed down, I just automatically stood up."

Emma smiled back. "Fancy commuting again do you?"

"There's no way I'm going to do that, ever. It was always the worst part of working in London."

"Sotheby's may want to speak to you again… now that Northgate's gone."

"That's what Oscar said. My answer's the same as I told him. There's no chance I'd be interested. I turned it down once, and I won't even consider it again. I'm looking for something different going forward."

After alighting from the train and passing the ticket collector, they said their goodbyes with a brief kiss. Emma walked towards the taxi queue and Ian headed for the 'Victory' pub.

Ian followed the now familiar route and entered the main bar. He remembered the high ceilings, timber floors and eclectic collection of old framed pictures. Whilst last time there was a buzz of chatter, this time the bar was surprisingly quiet. He even wondered if the pub was closed until he spotted George walking towards him.

"Hello, Ian," announced George, holding out his hand to greet him.

Ian smiled and shook George's hand. "The pub's really quiet today. No police, I see."

George ignored Ian's comment and steered him towards the bar. "What do you want to drink?"

"I can't remember what I had last time, but it was a nice beer."

"Probably the 'Bishop's Tipple'. That's what I'm drinking."

"Okay," said Ian, and whilst George ordered his beer, he scanned the rest of the room. He could see a few more people eating and drinking. They'd been hidden from his earlier view by tall wooden partitions.

"Here you are." George gave Ian his glass of beer and pointed to where he'd been sitting.

Once they'd sat down, George asked, "So, how was your meeting with Gerry?"

After sipping his beer, Ian gave a summary of his meeting with the Detective Inspector. He concluded by emphasising that he still didn't trust the man.

"At least you know for definite where your painting is."

"Mmm, I know. But that doesn't help me. Any ideas how I can get it back from the police in Poland?"

George thought for a few moments. "No. Not really. Didn't Gerry offer any names or suggestions at the Met?"

"No… and I also got the impression he was enjoying my predicament."

George smiled. "You really don't like him, do you?"

"I just don't trust him. Especially after threatening me about my relationship with Andrei. I don't know what he knows."

"Okay. Look, leave it with me. I still know a couple of guys in the Met's Art and Antiques Unit. I'll give one of them a buzz."

Chapter 60

Jonathan Northgate stood in his lounge, staring through the floor-to-ceiling window. His view was dominated by more of the skyscraper Docklands apartments, similar to the block he resided in. Between two of the buildings, he could just glimpse the River Thames. Even so, it wasn't the view that commanded his attention, he was worrying about his present wretched predicament.

His lawyers had managed to keep him out of jail, at least for the time being, although the stringent bail conditions only gave him temporary freedom. To achieve his release, he had to lodge one million pounds as a guarantee to attend his forthcoming appearance in court. Other orders included handing over his passport and not being allowed to leave London unless he'd obtained prior permission from the police.

Turning around, he walked into the middle of the room and stared dejectedly at the bare walls. The police had removed all of his pictures. Unfortunately for him, one painting had been destined for delivery to the 'organisation'. The others he'd honestly acquired. However, the pictures were the least of his worries. Although he was resigned to being convicted for the thefts and knew he would have to spend a few years in prison, he could take that; what he definitely wanted to keep hidden was the murder he'd committed when he was a teenager in New York. He'd paid the blackmailer's demands for all these years and felt he'd already suffered sufficient punishment.

Besides the potential sentence of imprisonment, he knew this was not the only problem he faced. After he'd telephoned his wife in America and explained the situation, she'd made it absolutely clear that their marriage was over. She was going to file for a divorce immediately. When the call had ended, he'd burst into tears. He was devastated, but not totally surprised with his wife's response. His recent relationship with her and her family had become increasingly strained following his career move to London. Now, he reasoned, there was no job, no career, an alienated wife and probably future estranged relationships with his children. Definitely a bleak future, unless his legal team could argue a good case on his behalf. However, he was not optimistic. The legal process and wranglings in the UK were different to America. There was no plea bargaining here. No politicians or judges his lawyers could try to bribe.

No, he was on his own.

Okay, he considered, if I don't have a future myself, then I'm going to make sure other people don't have one either. Starting with eliminating my blackmailer in New York, I'll have one last chance to succeed with the ambition I failed to achieve all those years ago.

He dropped down on the sofa and closed his eyes. Gradually, a smile appeared on his face and he said out loud, "Ian Caxton, I'm also coming to get you!"

Chapter 61

Ian was in his office when he received a telephone call from George Bailey. "Hello, Ian."

"Hi, George. I hope you're phoning to tell me some good news. I need some."

George briefly laughed and said, "Mind reader. Yes, well, partly good news. The Met have been in touch with the police authorities in Poland. They said each picture will be released once they're satisfied it will go back to its rightful owner. That's the good news, Ian. The bad news is concerning their definition of the word 'satisfied'."

"Okay. I understand that, but surely they must be satisfied with the ownership of my painting?"

"Yes, they are, partly. They know all about the word 'original', and have confirmed that 'The Green Dress', does have this word written in invisible ink on the back of the canvas. What they now need is a copy of the purchase paperwork and confirmation from Sotheby's that they sold the picture to you."

"I don't see that as a problem. I can talk to Sotheby's."

"The paperwork then needs to go to Detective Sergeant Andrew Baker at the Met Art and Antiques Unit. He's the contact for the UK owners' restitution."

Ian thought for a moment and then asked, "And that's it? I'll get my painting back?"

"As far as I can gather, yes. By the way, your colleague Karim will have to talk to Dubai's equivalent of the Met's Art and Antiques Unit."

"Okay. I'll let him know. I'll also speak to Sotheby's immediately after this phone call."

"Good luck. Let me know the outcome."

"Thanks, George, I will."

After Ian finished his call, he immediately telephoned Penny's extension at Sotheby's.

Penny answered after two rings. "Penny Kuznetsov."

"Hi, Penny. Ian."

"Oh, hi, Ian. Lovely to hear from you."

"I'm looking for a favour."

"Mmm. It might cost you!"

Ian laughed and then explained why he wanted a letter from Sotheby's confirming his purchase of the painting.

"That's not a problem. Do you want it emailed or posted?"

Ian thought before he responded, "Both would be great."

"I'll make sure it's done today. By the way, I've got some more news. Not on this phone though. Can I ring you on my mobile at lunchtime?"

"Intriguing. Yes, that should be fine. Ring my mobile."

"Will do. Look, Ian, I've got to go. Speak to you later."

"Bye, Penny."

Ian had one more person to contact. He opened his computer and composed an email to Joey Sanderson in Dubai. He wanted his colleague to inform Karim that his Munnings painting had been found, but to recover it he needed to speak with the Dubai police and ask them to liaise with their equivalent in Warsaw.

After pressing the 'send' button, Ian leaned back in his chair and took a deep breath. He was satisfied that Karim could contact Sotheby's and make all the noise and complaints he wanted. At least Ian was personally off the hook as far as his £3.3 million guarantee was concerned.

The only person still not off the hook was Jonathan Northgate!

Chapter 62

Ian was in the kitchen helping Emma unpack the supermarket shopping when his mobile phone rang. He recognised Penny's number. "Hi, Penny."

"Sorry I couldn't speak to you earlier, but I had Tony Clover hovering near my desk."

"How are you getting on with him? Must be a breath of fresh air after Northgate."

"He's certainly different… Let's just say it's still a work in progress."

Ian laughed. "Good luck. Anyway, you said you had some more news. About Northgate, I assume."

"Mmm, partly. The latest rumour is that as part of Jonathan's bail conditions, he's had to lodge one million pounds as a guarantee. Also, he's handed over his passport and isn't allowed to leave London."

"I'm not surprised. He's lucky not to be in prison already. Any idea when his case will be heard?"

"No. Nobody seems to know whether he'll be tried on his own or as part of the gang."

"Good point. If it's part of the group, it'll take ages before it comes to court. Meanwhile, Northgate will be free as a bird."

"As free as a caged bird, Ian. Remember he's not allowed to leave London."

"Okay. But he should be sitting in a cell in Wandsworth."

Penny smiled. "There's also another rumour."

"Not any facts?"

"Well, you may know the answer to this one. It's about you."

"Me!" exclaimed Ian, which made Emma look across in his direction.

"Apparently, you're the odds-on favourite to return as CEO."

Ian made a large and frustrated sigh. "Is that so? Well, here's a fact: I'm not! I haven't spoken to the Chairman since... well, in a long time. Anyway, I'm not interested. I turned it down once before and I'll turn it down again."

Penny briefly laughed. "Still odds-on in my book."

"Well, don't lose your money on a bad bet. I'm not coming back!"

"It would be great to be working with you again, Ian. Sotheby's have missed you."

Ian sneered, "Sounds like the Chairman's asked you to sound me out."

"As if. Maybe you should think about it. These thefts have caused a serious embarrassment for Sotheby's."

"Embarrassments don't last forever. Tony and the Chairman will soon sort it out. Anyway, enough about Sotheby's, how's Vic? I've not spoken to him for some time."

"Changing the subject now, are you? Well, Vic's fine. He's still working with Alexander and part time with the CLAE. He seems a lot happier and contented now."

"That's good. Can you tell him I'd like to speak to him?"

Penny was about to ask Ian why, but she suddenly noticed the time. "Sorry, Ian. I've just looked at my watch. I've got a meeting in ten minutes, I'd better go."

After the call ended, Emma walked over to Ian. "You sounded a bit agitated talking to Penny."

Ian placed his phone back on the kitchen island and smiled. "Apparently, the Sotheby's staff are suggesting I'm odds-on favourite to replace Northgate."

"Ah, I see," said Emma, smiling. "Maybe the Chairman will contact you after all. Have you changed your mind?"

"My answer's the same as it was when I turned it down last time. I'm much happier now than when I was commuting. The last few years have been really good. Also, as a family, we've got far more freedom. Don't you agree?"

"Oh, yes. I can still remember when I was a partner at Murray, Caxton and Tyner; we hardly saw each other. Then Robert came along. It's so much better now."

"However, I sense you have a 'but'. You think I should consider it?"

"No, not a but exactly. I was thinking about you. When we stayed with Oscar and May, you said you were looking for a new challenge. Could this be it?"

Ian's face looked more serious. "Firstly, I've not spoken to the Chairman and have no intention of approaching him. Secondly, yes, I do want a new challenge, but not at Sotheby's. Maybe not even in the art world, I don't know. I don't want to rush into anything quickly. I'll know when the time comes... but it definitely won't be at Sotheby's!"

Chapter 63

Jonathan Northgate knew he needed to move quickly. He still didn't know when his trial would begin, or where. If it was Poland, he could be transferred very soon. That would definitely scupper his plans. His solicitor had told him it was most unlikely, but he wouldn't promise it couldn't happen.

Jonathan assumed his computer, phone and apartment were probably bugged, but he hadn't found anything untoward when he'd investigated. Nevertheless, he couldn't afford to take any chances. After all, he wasn't a security expert.

Firstly, he bought a refurbished laptop and a simple calls-only mobile phone from a small repair and technology shop in the East End. He then purchased a £100 pay-as-you-go card. No account details were required, and no calls could be traced back to him. Besides, he'd only be keeping the phone for a few days. Finally, after setting up a new Google account with a user id made up of a selection of random characters, he was ready to start.

The following day, he took his laptop and mobile to a café in the West End. Still not trusting his existing devices, he decided to leave them all in the apartment. He wanted to keep all prying eyes and ears away from his objectives.

Using the café's free wifi, he emailed a colleague in New

York. He kept the message brief but asked his colleague to ring him on the quoted new mobile number.

Forty minutes later, Jonathan was sitting on a bench in a nearby park. He was watching two mothers helping their young children feed swans and ducks swimming next to the edge of the lake. Although they were about 20 metres away, when his phone rang, Jonathan stood up, answered the call and walked away.

Jonathan told his colleague his instructions. He promised two million dollars once the contact was completed, half up front.

The deal was agreed and the call ended. Jonathan had written down the colleague's bank account details and was walking towards the nearby Underground station. He needed to make the initial transfer. His own account was in a fictitious name, and the bank's head office was in the Cayman Islands. All the money deposited in this account he'd acquired from payments by the organisation and other secret deposits. Other than the bank, nobody was privileged to the account details, not even his wife. This was his personal nest egg account and he'd not even made one withdrawal since the account had been set up during the early part of his career. A business client in New York had helped him set up the account in exchange for a small original Andy Warhol watercolour.

An hour later, the transfer of one million dollars was made. It would reach his colleague's account via a convoluted route through accounts both in Switzerland and the Bahamas.

All he needed to do now was wait for the announcement of the death of Senator Arnold Hamilton!

Each day, Jonathan examined the online edition of the *New York Times*. However, it wasn't until day three that the article he was waiting for finally appeared. It was headed, 'Senator Arnold Hamilton – boating tragedy!'

Jonathan smiled. Two jobs to do now, pay another million pounds and… organise the demise of one Ian Caxton.

Chapter 64

Ian scanned his purchase invoice for 'The Green Dress' into his computer. He'd also received a copy of the sales document from Penny. It fully confirmed Ian Caxton as the purchaser at auction. All he needed now was the email address of Detective Sergeant Andrew Baker at the Met's Art and Antiques Unit. He hoped Viktor might know his contact details. He picked up his mobile and phoned him.

"Vic? Hi. It's Ian."

"Hi, Ian. Great to hear from you. Penny said you wanted to speak to me."

"Yes. Remember you said that you had a contact at the Met's Art and Antiques Unit?"

"Yes, nice guy. Andy Baker."

"Would that be Detective Sergeant Andrew Baker?"

"That's him. Why do you want to know?"

Ian summarised the situation with his painting and the Polish police, ending with the reason for his call. Did Vic have the policeman's email address?

"Penny told me about some of your problems… all to get your revenge on Northgate. I hope it's going to be worth it, Ian. Anyway, give me a minute and I'll check in my email address book."

Ian heard Viktor put his phone down and rustle pages

in the background. "Here we are." He dictated the email address and Ian wrote it down.

"Thanks, Vic. I'm hoping the Polish police will accept all my paperwork and I'll finally get my painting back. I've still not actually seen it!"

"I thought it looked pretty good at the auction. I know you're not really into abstracts, but if you want to sell it, I might already know of a buyer."

"I certainly don't want to keep it. If you can get me one and a half million, you'll have a deal. However, first things first. I've got to get it back to England. Let's hope your police colleague will be successful."

"Don't worry. He'll come up trumps."

When Ian finished the call, he opened up his computer and typed his email. Twenty minutes later, he'd finished the covering email and attached a copy of both the purchasing invoice and sales document. After double checking everything, he pressed the 'send' button.

Moments later, the email had arrived in Detective Sergeant Andrew Baker's inbox.

The following morning, Ian was in the garden when he heard Emma calling. She walked across the patio holding the phone out in front of her. "It's Detective Sergeant Baker. He wants to speak to you."

"Thanks," said Ian, taking the handset. "Hello, Ian Caxton speaking."

"Good morning, Mr. Caxton. Sergeant Baker from the Metropolitan Police. I thought I'd ring you to talk about your email."

"I'm pleased it arrived."

"Yes. I gather from George Bailey that you already know your painting's with the Warsaw police."

"He's spoken to you?"

"Yes. George and I used to work together. Look, Mr. Caxton, I just wanted to update you on the current position."

"Thanks."

"I've sent copies of your email and attachments to Warsaw. As far as I can see, your paperwork looked fine. Unfortunately, the situation is somewhat fluid. It's not just a straightforward police procedure. Political diplomacy and bureaucracy is involved too."

"All I want to know is, when will I get my painting back?"

"The short answer, Mr. Caxton, is, I don't know. Our Chief Constable is in direct contact with the Foreign Secretary, and the Foreign Office is in discussions with their counterparts in Poland."

Ian sighed.

The detective could hear Ian's sigh of frustration. "I'm sorry, but, as I say, it's not just a police matter."

"No. Well, thanks."

"As soon as I hear anything more, I'll let you know."

They both said their goodbyes and Ian switched off the connection.

Emma, who had been standing next to Ian, had heard most of the conversation. "Not very helpful was it? Nevertheless, it was good of the policeman to ring you."

"I was hoping it was going to be much better news. He sounded as frustrated as I feel."

"Once politicians become involved…"

"Quite."

Emma sympathetically patted Ian's shoulder. "I'll make us a pot of coffee."

247

Chapter 65

Jonathan Northgate knew of one of the key members of the 'organisation' who hadn't been arrested: Bernie Laker, one of the two top bosses. He owned a terraced house near Hyde Park, in Warwick Mews. Jonathan had been there a few times before and he now needed to speak to Bernie urgently.

After exiting Green Park Underground station, Jonathan walked for a short distance along Piccadilly. He was reasonably sure he wasn't being followed, but just in case, he chose to walk away from the shortest route to Warwick Mews. When he arrived opposite The Ritz London hotel, he turned left along Berkeley Street. Stopping outside a Barclays Bank, he stared through the window and then back along the route he'd just taken. Two women were approaching, engaged in chatter, but a few metres before reaching him, they stopped and entered the next-door premises, Starbucks coffee shop.

Jonathan turned into Mayfair Place and headed towards the tall concrete columns forming part of the attractive facade of Devonshire House.

At the end of the street, he turned left into Stratton Street, and whilst heading back towards Piccadilly, he approached a different entrance to Green Park Underground station. There he stopped inside the entrance and waited.

After a few moments, he moved back out into Stratton Street. Satisfied that nobody was waiting for him, he headed towards Piccadilly and followed the shortest route to his destination.

Ten minutes later, Jonathan arrived at the turning into Warwick Mews. He proceeded along the blue cobble road surface until he arrived opposite a white-painted three-storey building. He looked both ways along the Mews before stepping into an open porch area. Directly in front of him was a white-painted door, and to his left, fixed to the wall, was a large number 5 and a video intercom system. Jonathan pressed the button three times, then a further twice and stood back, staring at the camera.

After a few moments a male voice announced, "Yes?"

Jonathan leaned forward to speak into the mike. "It's Northgate. I need to speak to you."

There was silence for a few moments. Jonathan knew Bernie would be checking the video screen and his two other CCTV cameras scanning activities along the Mews.

Suddenly, the voice announced, "I've got nothing to speak to you about."

"I need to speak to you. You owe me."

"I owe you nothing."

"I've told the police nothing."

Jonathan waited for a reply. He was becoming more anxious.

"Wait there."

Jonathan stood back and waited for the door to open.

Moments later, the door moved slowly but was held to a narrow gap by a security chain. "You shouldn't be here. What do you want?"

"Do you really want me to talk to you out here... where passersby can hear?"

Jonathan watched as the door closed and heard the chain

being undone. The door reopened. A smartly dressed man in his sixties stared round the edge of the door. He checked the area behind Jonathan and, when satisfied, opened the door wider and waved him in.

Jonathan stepped through the doorway and into a luxurious hall. It was furnished with a large antique oak cupboard, oak floor tiles, expensive Glasshouse Navy wallpaper and a spectacular candle-style crystal chandelier hanging from the high ceiling.

"In here," ordered Laker, and he led Jonathan towards a small study. It too reflected the wealth of the owner. Displayed on one of the walls were three original abstract paintings supplied by Jonathan. "What do you want?"

"I need your help."

"You'd better sit down." Bernie Laker pointed to a leather button-studded armchair. He, meanwhile, walked behind his desk to sit down on a large luxury brown leather executive chair. "Well?"

"I need someone to organise an… accident!"

Laker raised his eyebrows but said nothing.

"I want my revenge on someone… but only after I've been sent to prison."

"I see." Laker leaned forward to his normal sitting position and looked directly at Jonathan. He knew he was out on bail. "I don't need to know who or why, but do you want this person killed or just maimed? And, how much are you willing to pay?"

"Seriously injured, minimum. Killing would be a benefit. As for money, I can offer one million pounds, but I want you to guarantee it will be done."

Laker laughed. "What if I just take your money and let you rot in prison?"

"Then the police will be told of everyone involved in the organisation. And I do mean everyone."

Chapter 66

Two days later, Ian answered the landline in his office. "Ian Caxton,"

"Hello, Mr. Caxton. Detective Sergeant Baker from the Metropolitan Police."

Ian was hoping this was finally going to be good news. "Hello."

"I thought I'd let you know ten paintings have just been released by the Warsaw police and they're on their way to the UK right now. Yours is amongst them."

"Oh, excellent!"

"Well, yes. That's the good news. However, I'm sorry to tell you I still don't know when your picture will be formally released. As I told you before, the Foreign Office is involved."

"What does that mean?"

"Bureaucracy, I'm afraid, but the ten paintings should be here at the Met sometime in the next few days. At the moment, that's all I can tell you. I'll let you know more when I know more myself. Sorry."

"Okay. Anyway, thanks for phoning."

"Hopefully, next time, I'll have better news. Goodbye, Mr. Caxton."

"Thanks again. Goodbye."

Ian replaced the phone on its base and gave a deep sigh.

Emma looked across from her desk and asked, "Still no good news?"

Ian summarised the detective's message and briefly laughed. "This painting's a nightmare! I feel fated never to see it. I've spent all this money on something I've still never seen."

Emma smiled. "At least it helped to get Jonathan Northgate arrested."

"But he's not locked up! That was my objective."

"He's only out on bail and bound to plead guilty."

Ian, frustratedly, shook his head. "I won't believe anything until he's locked in prison. How did he get bail in the first place?"

"Obviously he can afford the best lawyers."

"Mmm. Paid for by his ill-gotten gains. There's something wrong there."

"Patience, Ian," said Emma, standing up. "Come on, let's get some lunch."

During lunch, Emma took the opportunity to remind Ian they hadn't been back to the apartment in Monaco for quite some time. "It's April next month, and the weather will be lovely in Monaco."

"You're right. Our trip to Antigua seems like a long time ago. Should I see what flights are available?"

"Robert will be home at Easter, but I think we ought to go before then. He finds the apartment 'a bit boring', using his words. Besides, I think he still wants to go on the school trip to Rome with his friends. It should be a good experience for him."

"Hopefully, even a little educational too!"

"He seems to have recovered well from his sunstroke, so he should be fit enough to join in on the programme of visits to all the old Roman historical sites."

"Okay. I'll look for flights for the end of this month. Maybe by then, the Met police will have recovered my painting. I've promised Vic first refusal. He says he's already lined up a buyer."

The next day, Ian received another telephone call from Detective Baker. This time, the detective told him his painting had been delivered to the Met and he could collect it whenever he wanted. A happy and relieved Ian agreed to collect it on Friday.

Ian's next telephone call was to Viktor. "Ian, hi. Recognised your number."

"Some good news, Vic. My painting's finally arrived back in the UK."

"That's great, Ian. What are you going to do now?"

"That's why I'm phoning. The picture's at the Met. Your buddy Detective Baker has it. Do you want to come with me to collect it? Also, have you still got that buyer you told me about?"

"Yes, to both. The buyer's really keen. Can I take it to him afterwards? He's agreed to pay your price... plus my commission."

Ian smiled at Viktor's last few words. "I told Detective Baker I'd collect it on Friday at noon. Is that okay?"

"That's fine with me. I'll ring my client now and see if he's available Friday afternoon. He lives in Mayfair, not too far away."

"I'm looking forward to finally seeing what I've bought... even if it will be just for a few minutes."

It was a day of telephone calls for Ian, because the next call he received was from an exhilarated George Bailey. "Ian, hi. Have you heard the news?"

"Hi, George. What news is this? You sound excited."

"It's Northgate; he's been found murdered!"

Chapter 67

"What!?" exclaimed Ian. "Are you sure?"

George briefly laughed. "I've just been told by Gerry Hudson. He says the River Police found him in the Thames at low tide, early this morning. Shot three times through his head."

"Wow. I don't know what to say."

"You finally got your revenge, Ian."

Ian was suddenly alarmed. "Do the police think I was responsible?"

"No. No worries there. They have a good idea who was responsible and why."

"I'm not sure I want to know. Wow. Northgate dead. That was never in my plans at all. I just wanted to see him suffer in prison."

"I know, Ian. I can't say any more, as Gerry told me all this in confidence. However, the press will soon hear all about it."

Ian wiped away the fresh perspiration from his forehead. "This is all quite a shock, George. I really can't believe it."

"Believe it, Ian. It's definitely true. Look, I'll let you go now. Maybe you need a brandy."

"Okay. Thanks. Bye."

"Goodbye, Ian."

After Ian finished the call, he slowly walked from his office and into the garden. Emma was taking advantage of an unusually warm day to pull up some weeds.

"Emma," called Ian, walking across the patio.

Emma stood up to her full height and looked to where Ian was calling from. Seeing him almost collapse on the bench, she rushed over to join him. "Ian? Are you alright? Your face is white as a sheet! What's happened?"

"Northgate's been murdered!"

"What!? Oh, my goodness," she exclaimed, sitting down next to him.

"George just telephoned. The police found him in the Thames. Been shot three times, through his head."

"That's horrible." Emma wiped her dirty left hand and placed it gently on Ian's. "Hasn't he got a wife and young children?"

"Yes, but I don't know how old they are. They're all in America."

"I think you're still in shock. Come on. Let's get you into the house. I'll make some tea."

Later that afternoon, Ian had calmed down, almost recovered. He was sitting on a settee in the lounge, thinking. The shock of Northgate's death had eased, but now he was feeling guilty. Yes, he wanted his reprisal, but not at the expense of hearing that Northgate had been murdered. He was wondering whether he was partly responsible?

Emma walked in and sat down next to him. "How are you feeling? You've got some colour back in your cheeks."

Ian made a deep sigh and leaned forwards. "I don't feel in shock anymore, Emma. Just a bit guilty."

"Guilty? Why? You weren't responsible."

"But, my efforts to find evidence against him could have contributed."

"Look, Ian. There's no way you contributed to his murder.

Northgate was involved with a lot of dangerous people. He knew what he'd got himself into. He was a greedy fool. What's the saying? If you live by the sword, you die by the sword."

Ian tentatively smiled. "You're probably right."

"Anyway, Penny telephoned earlier. She'd heard the news. I told her you'd telephone her back when you felt better."

"Thanks. I'll give her a call now." Ian pushed himself out of his seat and straightened up.

"Sure you're okay?"

"Yes." He took a deep breath and started to walk towards the office. "I need to stretch my legs."

Emma followed close behind, but after he'd sat down behind his desk, she left him and went into the kitchen.

Ian telephoned Penny's mobile. After three rings, she answered. "Hello, Ian. I gather from Emma you've already heard the news about Jonathan. It's been quite a shock to us all."

"I know. His death was not part of my plans."

They were both quiet for a few moments, and then Penny said, "He's been a fool. Why did he ever get mixed up with such dangerous people?"

"I understand it's been going on for some time. Just after he started with Sotheby's in New York. I've also been told he's been blackmailed for a number of years."

"Oh, Ian. His poor wife and children. I wonder if his wife knew?"

"I doubt it. I wouldn't tell Emma something like that if I was in the same position."

"No. Still." After a short pause, Penny continued. "You know, Ian, I just wonder if Jonathan would still be alive if we hadn't interfered."

"I know. I was thinking the same thing. Emma says he was heading for trouble anyway. They're obviously very threatening people. Besides, the police and Sotheby's security team were already watching him before we got involved. It was just a matter of time."

"Do you think there'll be any ramifications for us?"

"The police know I wasn't involved in his murder, although they do know I was investigating him. They've got their own ideas as to who was responsible."

"So it's all over now is it? I mean for us?" asked Penny, but, deep down, she wasn't convinced it really was.

Ian wasn't convinced either, but wanted to protect Penny. "We don't know anybody else in that organisation. We're not a threat."

"I hope you're right."

Chapter 68

Viktor was standing on the pavement at Victoria Embankment, staring over a long, low wall at the mostly white, six-storey concrete building directly in front of him. He could just see the upper section of the ground-floor facade. It appeared to be constructed of a bank of tall glass windows. Above the windows was a sloping, wrap-around roof, extending out over most of the lower frontage. Proudly standing out on top of this roof, in large bold letters, was a sign stating 'New Scotland Yard'. This was the headquarters of the London Metropolitan Police.

Viktor hadn't been here before, although he knew three policemen who worked in the Art and Antiques Unit. Detective Sergeant Andrew Baker, he'd met on a number of occasions when he'd previously uncovered some stolen paintings.

Viktor turned around and looked up and down the road. No sign of Ian. His watch said 11.50. He knew he was early but expected Ian to still be on time. Now looking across the road, his eyes were drawn to the people on the far side of the Embankment. Some were strolling along the pavement whilst others just stood and stared at the views across the River Thames.

A minute later, a taxi pulled up. Ian jumped out and walked towards him.

"Hi, Vic," said Ian, shaking his colleague's hand. "Been waiting long?"

"About five minutes. I've never been here before."

"I had to visit Scotland Yard once. The police were hoping Sotheby's could identify a stolen painting. But that was some time ago."

"Can you remember how we get in? This wall seems to run the length of the building."

Ian smiled. "Yes, come on." They started to walk along the pavement towards another sign in the distance. It was slowly revolving and stated, 'New Scotland Yard'.

After climbing up a few steps and walking in front of the glass pavilion-like windows, they eventually arrived at the entrance. Ian pushed on the revolving door and they entered into a large and airy reception area.

Viktor immediately spotted Detective Sergeant Baker. He was chatting to a uniformed policeman next to the reception desk.

Viktor tapped Ian on the arm and pointed out the detective. "That's Andy."

Ian nodded, and they strolled towards him.

"Hello," said Viktor, now standing almost next to the detective.

"Vic. Hi. What are you doing here?"

The uniformed policeman walked away, and after Viktor and the detective shook hands, Viktor said, "Detective Sergeant Andrew Baker, meet Ian Caxton."

"Ah, Mr. Caxton, we finally meet." Ian and the detective shook hands. "I've got your painting. It's in the meeting room over there. Let's make sure nobody has nicked it again."

All three briefly laughed at the joke as they walked towards a light-oak-coloured door.

"I hope not," responded Ian, still smiling. "I've still not seen it for real."

259

Andy pushed open the door. The room was small but big enough to accommodate a pine table and six matching chairs. In the middle of the table lay a package wrapped in thick grey paper.

Andy pointed to the package. "In that case, you'd better check if this is really yours. I've not seen what's in it either. It arrived from Poland like that."

Ian read the label stuck on the outside cover, 'Oliver Squires, abstract painting. "The Green Dress". Owner Ian Caxton. UK'. Smiling, he proceeded to gently unwrap the outer paper covering. The parcel was well wrapped in several sturdy sheets and then further protected by two layers of plastic bubble wrap and hardboard.

Eventually, Ian slid the painting out from the last of its packaging and raised it up.

Viktor moved next to Ian to take a closer look. After a few moments, he said, "There doesn't appear to be any damage, and it definitely looks like the painting I saw at the auction."

"Mmm, it also looks like the copy I saw in Dubai. There's only one way to check for sure." Ian laid the painting face down and removed a small torch from his jacket pocket. When he pressed the top, a purple-coloured beam of light immediately shone on the canvas.

Viktor and Andy, with surprised looks on their faces, watched closely as Ian moved the beam across the blank canvas. After a moment, what Ian had been hoping for suddenly appeared. The word 'original' was written' in the top left-hand corner!

"Phew!" said Ian, switching off the beam.

"So, is it the original?" asked the detective. "Are you happy?"

Ian scratched his chin and then turned the painting to face upwards. "I'll need to get it definitively authenticated by the artist, but it appears to be the original Sotheby's sold at the auction."

"Okay. You can take it with you," said the detective. "But first you'll need to sign this release document." He picked up a pen and a sheet of paper from on top of a small cupboard behind him.

Ian read the document. When satisfied, he signed his name at the bottom.

Chapter 69

"Right, Vic, here you go," said Ian, handing over the package. They'd arrived back on the pavement. "Good luck with your sale."

"Thanks. I'm seeing my client at two o'clock, so I've got a bit of time. Are you sure you still want to sell?"

"It's no good to me. I only bought it to trap Northgate."

Viktor nodded, but then had a serious look on his face. "Ian, can we go and sit on that bench?" He pointed to a black-painted metal bench in front of them. "There's something I need to talk to you about."

Ian raised his eyebrows and followed Viktor to the bench, where they sat down.

Viktor laid the package carefully next to him and started to speak. "It's about Northgate and his murder. Penny's worried sick. I've tried to reassure her she's got nothing to worry about, but I can't seem to convince her."

"To be honest, Vic, I feel the same. I'm sure some people in the organisation Northgate was involved with knew of my initial investigation. I visited their premises in Charlton Street. But only you, Emma and I know of Penny's involvement. I've never mentioned her name to the police. That was deliberate on my part."

After a moment, Viktor nodded. "Well, that's something,

I guess. I'm not sure what else I can do. I'm worried because she's worried."

"Look, Vic, I'm sorry. I can speak to Penny if you want me to, but I'm not sure I can tell her anything more than I've just told you. I'm annoyed with myself for being so selfish, just to get my revenge on Northgate."

For a few moments both men sat quietly. Eventually, Viktor stood up and said, "I'd better get a taxi and take this painting to my client."

Ian also stood and placed his right hand on Viktor's shoulder. "I'm really sorry, Vic. I'm going to speak to a detective inspector who knows of my involvement and hear what he's got to suggest."

"Okay," replied Viktor, but he wasn't convinced this would be the end of the matter. "Do you want to share a cab?"

"No, thanks. I need to go back in there." Ian pointed back to the New Scotland Yard building they'd just exited.

Viktor flagged down an approaching taxi and jumped in. After telling the driver his client's address, he looked through the window towards where he'd left Ian. However, Ian was now striding back towards the large white building.

When Ian arrived back at the reception desk, he told the uniformed policewoman his name and asked if Detective Inspector Gerry Hudson was available.

The receptionist picked up her telephone and made a call.

Ian stood back and gazed around the room.

"Mr. Caxton," the receptionist called. "Inspector Hudson is in a meeting, sir, but he'll speak to you shortly. Can I suggest you take a seat over there?"

Ian looked to see where the woman was pointing and said, "Thank you." After walking across the reception area, he sat down and checked for messages on his mobile.

Fifteen minutes later, a different policewoman walked towards him. "Mr. Caxton?"

Ian stood up and smiled.

"Inspector Hudson will see you now. Please follow me."

Three minutes later, the policewoman knocked on a part-open office door. Hearing the "Come in" shout, she pushed the door fully open and announced Ian's name. As Ian stepped into the office, he glanced at the sign on the door saying, 'Detective Inspector Gerald Hudson'.

"Ah, Ian. Didn't think I'd be seeing you again so soon. Come in, sit down."

Ian strode over to a functional leather lookalike chair on wheels and sat down. "Thanks for seeing me. It's about Jonathan Northgate."

"Yes, I thought it probably was," responded the detective. He sat back and waited for Ian to continue.

Ian explained his concern following Northgate's murder and asked what the detective could suggest.

"I understand your distress, but officially, there's nothing really I can suggest." At this, Hudson stood up and walked over to close the door. He then returned to his seat. "Unofficially, and because you were helpful – eventually – in assisting us to capture most of the gang, I want to help you."

Ian smiled back.

"There are some of the gang who are still out there, hence the murder of Northgate. We mostly know who they are but don't yet have proof. I'm not sure if they're aware of your involvement, but my guess is they are. Whether that means your life's at risk, well, I don't know. Other than Northgate, we don't know of any other murders attached to them. They're certainly thieves and fraudsters but not necessarily murderers. We think Northgate's murder was carried out by a professional. Probably because Northgate knew too much, and maybe he'd threatened the wrong person with what he knew. We had him followed whilst he was out on bail, and three days before his murder, he was observed visiting one of the gang's known bosses. Three days later, he was shot in the head and dumped into the Thames. Read from that what you will."

Ian nodded but was unhappy with what he was hearing.

"My suggestion, Mr. Caxton, is watch your back and don't go down any dark alleyways. I think you should be okay, but don't hold me to that. This is the result of sticking your nose, uninvited, into ongoing police operations."

Ian sighed and rubbed his chin. "I just wanted to gather enough information and evidence to prove Northgate was a crook... and then hand all my findings over to you."

The detective smiled. "Backfired, didn't it?"

Ian looked down and stared at his hands on his lap. "Now I'm faced with the consequences."

The detective nodded. He then made a surprise suggestion. "Do you still want to help the police?"

Ian had a worried look on his face. He wasn't sure he wanted to answer yes, but...

Hudson stood up and leaned over his desk. "Fancy a beer?"

Chapter 70

Ten minutes after walking from New Scotland Yard, the two men arrived outside the 'White Hart' public house in Parliament Street.

Ian looked at the black-painted facade with its grand and ornate pillars. It looked old, but also appeared to be full of restored character.

"I'm told the food in here's really good," said the detective, pointing at a stand displaying the menu, "but I only pop in occasionally for a pint. It's a nice pint too."

Ian was still curious as to why the detective had brought him here... and, more importantly, what he was about to say.

They walked past six outside tables and through the entrance door. Ian had never been in this pub before and was impressed by the olde worlde feel, especially the renovated oak furnishing and fittings.

The detective ordered two pints of the special bitter. "Trust me, Ian. This is a great pint."

After paying and collecting the drinks, the detective pointed to an unoccupied table close to one of the windows.

Before sitting down, Ian took a sip of his beer, firstly to taste the brew and secondly to try to settle his nerves. "This is a nice pint," he eventually said.

"I knew you'd like it. Anyway, I've not brought you here just to enjoy the beer. I wanted to get away from the office to discuss my proposition."

Ian took another sip and waited to hear the details of the obviously unofficial plan.

"I mentioned in the office that we knew of at least three people who we think were involved with the theft and fraud of the paintings, but we have no actual proof."

Ian nodded.

"Right. Firstly, this is all confidential and no one, and I mean no one, should be told of this discussion."

Again Ian nodded. What else could he do? He remembered back to the earlier threat the detective had made about his own activities with Andrei. He accepted that he was probably trapped.

The detective looked around him to check no one else was in earshot. Once satisfied, he leaned forward and started to explain. "I mentioned Northgate visited one of the bosses of this organisation just before he was murdered. This obnoxious man's name is Bernie Laker, a wealthy, lowlife toerag. He's been involved in a number of dubious and illegal activities over the years, but it wasn't until your colleague Northgate arrived in England that he became more seriously involved with the paintings. He was approached by the American and Russian sections to link with Northgate and set up a fronting company called Cotton Enterprises. Remember visiting their premises in Charlton Street?"

"Yes, of course. How could I forget?"

"We've been watching Mr. Bernie Laker and his other activities for quite some time, but then information came to our knowledge about Northgate and Cotton Enterprises. Incidentally, Sotheby's security team were on the ball watching Northgate before us."

Ian could see all the pieces of the jigsaw beginning to fit together.

"You seem surprised, Ian. They'd been tipped off by Sotheby's New York's security team."

"And yet the idiot was still transferred and promoted."

"Maybe you should ask Sotheby's chairman about that. Anyway, what we now have is Mr. Bernie Laker and his colleagues roaming free, when they should be rotting in prison. I want to change that situation, Ian… and I need your help."

"Now I know what you've just told me, I suppose I don't have any choice?"

"I'm not a dictator, Ian. Maybe a kindly persuader. You help me get Bernie Laker, and his cohorts, convicted and sent to prison, then your life and your family's health will be much more secure."

Chapter 71

After leaving the 'White Hart', Ian walked alongside the detective back to the New Scotland Yard building. No words had been exchanged for the last five minutes. Ian had been pondering on the scheme outlined in the pub. When they reached the revolving New Scotland Yard sign, both stopped and faced each other.

"Think about it, Ian. I know I'm asking a lot, but you'll be helping both us and yourself."

Ian nodded. "Give me 24 hours. I'll telephone you tomorrow."

They shook hands and the detective gave Ian an encouraging smile before striding back to his office.

Ian slowly walked along the pavement, heading towards the Embankment Underground station. He had a lot to think about. The idea was definitely fraught with danger. He knew that, but did he have a choice? If the plan worked out, then any future threat from Bernie Laker and his cronies would probably be ended. However, was there really a threat now? Could he trust Hudson's words? After all, so far he'd not trusted him at all. Where was the evidence that Bernie Laker knew of Ian's involvement, or even existence? And then there was Hudson's dig, some weeks ago, about his involvement with Andrei. What did the police really know? Was that a more worrying situation than Bernie Laker?

As Ian entered the Underground station, his attention was drawn to a poster advertising career opportunities in Dubai and the UAE. It showed a young, smiling couple in swimwear on the beach in front of the famous ship-like Jumeirah Burj Al Arab five-star hotel. Ian smiled when he read the headline. 'Bored with your job? Looking for a fresh challenge? So were we. Come and join us. We're now living the dream!'

Ian thought back to his conversation with Oscar on the beach in Antigua, when his colleague teased him about the possibility of rejoining Sotheby's. He'd told Oscar, 'It's a fresh challenge I'm looking for, not an old one.' However, he certainly didn't envisage his 'fresh challenge' involving helping the police to capture a dangerous Mafia-like villain!

Ian took a deep breath and whispered to himself, "Be careful what you wish for!"

Later that same day, Ian and Emma were relaxing on the settee, enjoying an after-dinner coffee. Ian had decided not to tell Emma anything about Detective Hudson's proposal. He just mentioned he'd collected his painting from the police station and handed it to Viktor.

Emma was just about to ask a question when Ian's mobile rang.

Checking the caller's number, Ian announced, "Talk of the devil, it's Vic. Hello, Vic. Good news, I hope?"

"Hi, Ian. Yes. I've sold your painting. My client originally wanted to buy it at Sotheby's auction, but his flight was delayed from New York. He's a massive fan of Oliver Squires' work."

"Well done, you. All's well that ends well."

"I'll get the money transferred to your account later this week if that's okay?"

"Yes, Vic. That's fine. By the way, how's Penny?"

"Still a bit unhappy and confused with Northgate's death, but I think she's less worried about any possible personal implications."

"That's good. Tell her the police know I wasn't involved… and I've not mentioned her involvement to anyone."

"Will do. Bye, Ian."

After saying his own goodbye, Ian switched off the call.

"Sounds like you've had a profitable day," said Emma, sipping her coffee.

"Not really, probably broke even after all the hassle and costs of getting the painting back and our trip to Dubai. Still, Vic got his commission and the painting proved Northgate's involvement with the theft. That was the main purpose. Plus, Joey Sanderson gave me a few dirham for the copy painting."

"So, we're all finished with Northgate and the police… finally?"

Ian smiled, but decided still not to tell Emma the truth.

"Right, Mr. Caxton, we'd better start thinking about packing for Monaco."

Chapter 72

Detective Inspector Hudson was sitting in Chief Inspector Bradshaw's office explaining his plans. Bradshaw sat quietly and listened. He'd worked for the Met all his career and was part of the old school of policing: bobbies on the street, not stuck behind a computer.

Once Gerry had finished, Bradshaw leaned forward and spoke for the first time in a while. "Caxton is okay with this?"

"He needed a little bit of friendly persuasion, but yes, sir. He's on board."

"He's taking a risk. Laker's a dangerous character."

"My sources say Laker doesn't know of Caxton, or of his earlier involvement following Northgate's activities. He should be okay."

"We need to get Laker and his cronies all locked up. He's got away with far too much already. The Super keeps chewing my ear."

Hudson nodded. He knew his boss and the Superintendent didn't get on. Superintendent Robbins was a high-flyer and 20 years younger than Bradshaw. He was from the modern school of policing, by numbers and computers. A politician.

"What's the next step?"

"Caxton's already organised a short holiday with his wife to their apartment in Monaco."

"That's the apartment the Russian gave him?"

"Yes. He won't cancel the holiday, as he's not told his wife about Laker… and I don't blame him."

"No. We don't want more people than necessary knowing of your plans."

"He's back in the UK in ten days. By then we'll have everything set up."

"Keep me informed."

"Yes sir."

Ian and Emma arrived at their apartment in Monaco. It was early evening and both were pleased to be finally there. Their flight from London Heathrow had been delayed by two hours as a result of a backlog of flights. All were victims of the early morning fog.

After unpacking their clothes, Ian opened one of his pre-ordered bottles of Chablis from the fridge. Emma had already opened the doors leading out onto the balcony and was staring at all the activity down in the harbour. Ian joined her and handed over one of the two glasses.

"Isn't it wonderful to be back?" said Ian, standing next to Emma and leaning on the balcony's railings. "This is still a superb view."

"Cheers, Ian." Emma gently clinked her chilled glass against Ian's. "I never get bored of looking at this scene, especially when the harbour's lit up like this."

They watched as people strolled along the esplanade, stopping occasionally at restaurant entrances to check out the menus. Many of the moored ships had their navigation or masthead lights illuminated. It was a colourful and spectacular sight.

Emma took a deep intake of breath, savouring the different smells either originating from the sea's ozone or drifting up from the nearby restaurants. "I thought it might be cooler this evening, but it's still okay."

"Yes, and so much better than back home. How many times have we flown out here and been delayed at Heathrow by either fog, snow or rain?"

Emma smiled. "I know you hate the climate at home, but there are still a few positives you always overlook."

"Okay, I hated the climate in New York too. It was either freezing or scorching. Hong Kong was great in winter and spring, but summer was too hot, humid and airless. Here it's almost perfect."

Emma laughed. "You sound like Goldilocks!"

Ian began to smile. "Despite everything, Emma, we've been really lucky... and it's been mostly down to me meeting Andrei. I know you never trusted him, but we wouldn't have enjoyed this sort of lifestyle without him coming into our lives."

Emma stared at her glass and slowly pushed her finger around the rim. "I sometimes think Andrei's presence is still in this apartment. It's not that I feel it's haunted, just the suspicion he's never really left."

"You've never said that before. It doesn't scare you, does it?"

"No, not now. In the beginning I didn't want to be here. I just had a feeling that we were trespassing... being observed and judged. You know, Andrei constantly checking up on what we were doing to his apartment. That sort of thing."

"Isn't that funny? Because I've often said 'thank you' to him whilst I've been here. Somehow, I was hoping his spirit would be listening. Even after all this time, I still miss him, Emma. There are so many things I'd like to tell him and seek his advice on."

Emma turned her head and returned to watching the activity down in the harbour. Ian, however, started to contemplate his forthcoming involvement in the Detective Inspector's plans. He knew the idea was dangerous, and he was definitely worried about the eventual outcome. This was certainly a time when he'd have treasured hearing Andrei's words of wisdom on the matter.

Turning around, Ian unconsciously, started to gaze into the dimly lit lounge area. To his shock and surprise, standing in the middle of the room, he thought he could distinguish a vision of Andrei looking in his direction. The image had a serious expression on his face and was slowly shaking his head. Ian knew it was an apparition, but he looked so real.

The vision moved towards the glass doors and started to speak. "Ian. How many times did I tell you, never, ever get involved with either the Mafia or, even worse… the police!"

Chapter 73

Detective Hudson was telling five police officers their roles in the scheme to entrap Bernie Laker. Two were male plain-clothes detectives and two were in uniform. The fifth was a woman, and she was going to have an important role with Ian Caxton. Sergeant Jenny Archer was already known to Laker, she'd spent the last eight months working undercover and had befriended Jonathan Northgate. Her next job was to set up Ian's introduction to Laker.

After 20 minutes, the group was dismissed. However, Hudson asked Jenny to remain.

Once the rest of the group had disappeared, Hudson spoke. "Are you convinced Laker will bite on this one?"

Jenny was 28 years old, attractive and eager to progress in her career. She enjoyed the undercover role, and although she knew one false move could be her last, she nevertheless relished the challenge. "Laker's shrewd and very confident, sir. Whether he'll accept Caxton as Northgate's replacement, only time will tell."

Hudson nodded. "Yes, it's a gamble, but Caxton likes a challenge. You need to persuade him to make the extra effort. We missed Laker last time. I can't afford another slip up."

"I know, sir. When will I meet Mr. Caxton?"

"He's back from his holiday in three days. I'll ring him and set up a meeting for you."

"Thank you, sir. Can I ask why Mr. Caxton has been selected? He's not a policeman."

"I've watched Mr. Ian Caxton for a number of years. He used to work with a dodgy Russian art dealer, until he died. He was always borderline breaking the law, but one thing's for sure, he knows his way around the art market and knows an original painting when he sees it. He's far more knowledgeable than Laker."

"From the notes, sir, he sounds very wealthy. Why does he want to be involved?"

Hudson smiled and tapped his nose. "Well, that's a good question. Let's just say a little bit of friendly persuasion was needed."

Jenny wondered what the 'little bit of friendly persuasion' entailed, but decided to leave that question for another time. Maybe Mr. Caxton would be more forthcoming. "Yes, sir."

"Right, go and join the others and make sure everyone fully understands what they're responsible for."

Jenny smiled. She wasn't the eldest in the group, but she knew the Inspector wanted the others to be focussed on her role. After all, she was the one who had the most to lose.

After Jenny left Hudson's office, he wandered over to the window. It was cold and wet outside, but the Detective Inspector wasn't interested in the weather, he was thinking about the last hour. He went through the plan again in his mind. Finally, satisfied, he said to himself, "It now all depends on Archer and Caxton."

Chapter 74

The morning after Ian and Emma arrived back from Monaco, Ian was sitting in his office catching up on emails. Emma had gone to the supermarket for urgent groceries.

Just after ten o'clock, Ian received a call on his mobile. "Hello, Ian Caxton," he answered.

"Ian, I hope you had a good holiday."

Ian recognised the detective's voice immediately. He'd been nervously expecting him to get in contact. "Thank you, Detective Inspector Hudson. We had a great time. I'd have liked to stay a lot longer."

"Ah, Ian, but then you'd have missed all the fun… and the action. That's what I'm ringing about. I want you to meet our undercover policewoman. She's operating with Laker. Are you free tomorrow afternoon?"

"Where and when?"

"I don't need you to come to London. There's a Starbucks on the Weybridge road from Esher, do you know it?"

"I know of it, been past a few times, but never been in."

"Good. Can you be there at two o'clock?"

Ian took a deep breath. He still wasn't convinced he should be involved. "Are you sure you still need me?"

"Yes, very sure. The success of the whole exercise depends on your participation."

Ian had already reluctantly agreed to his inclusion, but he still wanted to remind the detective he wasn't happy with the situation. "How will I identify this policewoman?"

"She knows you, Ian. Don't worry, she won't be in uniform. And, Ian, don't tell anyone else. The fewer people who know, the better."

"No need to worry about that. It's not something I'd brag about, or even consider mentioning to my wife."

"Good. Two o'clock. Jenny will find you."

"Jenny?"

"Goodbye, Ian… and thanks."

Ian switched off the call and closed his eyes. What had he got himself into!? Moments later, he could see the same vision of Andrei staring back at him. He was still shaking his head in despair.

The following day, Ian arrived at the Starbucks coffeehouse at just before two o'clock. He parked his car next to a grey Audi and got out. The morning mist had disappeared and the sun was now shining. As Ian strolled across the car park, he could feel the warmth of the sun's rays on his face. Nevertheless, he still had the same nervous chill in the bottom of his stomach. After pulling one of the glass entrance doors, he stepped inside. Whilst he stood at the back of a short queue, he had time to examine some of the customers' faces. He had no idea what the policewoman looked like, so turned around and ordered a cappuccino. He then walked towards the till and waited whilst his coffee was prepared.

"I'll pay for that."

Ian looked behind him and saw a young woman with short dark brown hair. Her deep blue eyes briefly glanced at him before she handed over a £10 note to the cashier. She collected her change and pointed to the far corner of the room where a large mug of coffee was already sitting on the table. Ian collected his own mug and followed.

"Mr. Caxton," announced the young woman, once she'd sat down. After offering what she hoped was a reassuring smile, she held out her hand. "I'm Detective Sergeant Jenny Archer. I work with Detective Inspector Hudson."

Ian smiled back and shook her hand.

"I understand we're going to be working together. How do you feel about that?"

"I don't think my feelings come into it," said Ian, a little dismissively. "Your boss had a way of... let's say, persuading me."

Jenny raised her eyebrows slightly and grinned. "He's good at that. So, Mr. Caxton, can I call you Ian? Far less formal. You can call me Jenny."

Although Ian was still feeling tense and uneasy, he realised he was not being fair to this attractive young woman. She, at least, deserved to be spoken to in a more friendly manner. "Okay... Jenny."

Jenny smiled. "Look, Ian, I realise this is a difficult situation for you, but if we're going to be working together, I need to feel you're on my side, my partner. Laker's a nasty piece of work, and we need to demonstrate our unity. Otherwise, he'll instantly smell a rat... and that, Ian, will land us both in serious trouble. Remember what happened to your colleague, Jonathan Northgate?"

"Northgate was no colleague of mine. He was my enemy, my nemesis. I wanted to see him thrown in prison... not murdered."

"Northgate thought he could blackmail Laker, but he was a fool and he got what a fool deserves. By the way, did you know Northgate was offering one million pounds for you to be seriously injured?"

"What!" exclaimed Ian.

Jenny looked into the room to check whether anyone had heard Ian's outburst. She then nodded and told him to keep his voice down.

Ian stared intently at Jenny. He was breathing deeply. This was all much worse than he'd feared. Lowering his voice, he said, "How do you know that?"

"I was in the room when Laker told Lester Ford, one of his cohorts. To be honest, Ian, I don't know whether Laker took Northgate's statement seriously. All I do know is that it was Northgate who finished up dead and was dumped into the Thames."

Ian slowly shook his head. His heart was pounding.

"You can see now why we need to get these people locked up."

Ian knew he was 'between a rock and a hard place'. He realised the only way out of this nightmare was to work diligently with the police... Jenny. After all, his potential assassin could still be out there just waiting for the right opportunity.

For the next 20 minutes, Ian listened intently as Jenny spelled out the details of the police's plan, and, in particular, his role and involvement. The more he listened, the more his initial alarm was changing to anger. He was angry with Hudson, angry with Northgate and angry with everyone else involved in the sordid affair. But more than this, he was angry with himself. Not only had he put his own life at risk, but potentially Emma and Robert's futures too! He definitely had to do something about it!

Chapter 75

Jenny became involved with Laker's organisation after she'd befriended Jonathan Northgate. It all happened about eight months ago when the police had set up a trap for Northgate. Northgate's route to Charlton Street took him via a narrow passageway. It was only about 20 metres long. However, using it saved him a longer journey. He rarely met anyone else using this thoroughfare, but this time, it was early evening and he was attacked by two young policemen posing as yobbos. Their orders were not to hurt Northgate, just frighten him. As the yobbos pretended to try to steal the package he was carrying, Jenny had appeared at the thoroughfare's entrance. She'd shouted and called out loud for the police. The sound of Jenny's voice had frightened the yobbos off. Jenny ran to Northgate's assistance and asked if he was okay. She was deliberately dressed provocatively, in a short skirt and slightly low-cut blouse, deliberately to attract him. It worked, Northgate was hooked.

Next to the end of the passageway was a café, and Jenny suggested they have a coffee while he took time to recover from his ordeal. When Jenny had suggested they call the police, Northgate knew this was the last thing he wanted and made an excuse by saying he was okay. The yobbos hadn't stolen anything, and thanks to Jenny, he was feeling a lot better.

They continued to chat for a while, and then Northgate, to show his appreciation for Jenny's actions, invited her for dinner. Jenny smiled and agreed. However, Northgate said he firstly needed to deliver the package he'd been carrying. They both walked the short distance to Charlton Street, where Northgate handed over the parcel to Cotton Enterprises. From that moment on, their relationship blossomed, and occasionally, Jenny would deliver Northgate's parcels for him.

Three months later, Jenny met Laker for the first time. Northgate had been ordered to a dinner meeting at Laker's home in Warwick Mews. He wanted to discuss some changes in the organisation's plans. Jenny joined Northgate for the meeting, but when Laker saw her, he asked Northgate, "What the bloody hell is she doing here!?"

Northgate told him about Jenny's involvement and said she was also his partner. Laker bought the excuse and, during the meal, he slowly became attracted to her. Jenny knew she needed to get involved with Laker too. This she slowly did whilst, at the same time, continuing the relationship with Northgate.

Hudson was watching events from afar and had catch-up meetings with Jenny once a week. At the last meeting, he told her to be extra careful because the police raids on London, Poland and the USA were about to take place. She was told the date and time.

Unfortunately, somehow, Laker had been tipped off, and two days before the raid, he and Jenny disappeared to his villa in Portugal.

Of those arrested, nobody dared to mention Laker's name or involvement. Once the dust had settled, Laker and Jenny returned to the UK.

Chapter 76

Ten days after Northgate's death, Jenny needed to set Hudson's plan in motion. She had to suggest to Laker that he should meet Ian Caxton.

They were dining at Laker's favourite restaurant in London, the Murano, in Queen's Street, Mayfair. He particularly enjoyed the quiet, relaxed atmosphere and the à la carte Italian menu. Jenny had persuaded Hudson to agree to her buying an appealing and attractive new black dress. On expenses of course.

The main-course plates had just been taken away, and the second bottle of 2017 Gaja Barbaresco had arrived. The waiter topped up both glasses.

As the waiter walked away, Jenny leaned towards Laker and whispered, "Are you trying to get me drunk?"

Laker glanced at Jenny's now partly exposed cleavage and smiled. "Do I have to?"

Jenny smiled back, picked up her glass and gazed at Laker over the rim. "No. It's far too nice a wine to get drunk on."

Laker picked up his own glass and stared back at Jenny. He didn't respond.

What was he thinking about? wondered Jenny. Maybe this was the right moment to mention Ian Caxton. "Bernie?"

Bernie was still staring at Jenny. She felt uneasy and preferred it when he was speaking.

"Mmm?" was his unhelpful reply.

"Now that the police have broken up the organisation, have you got new plans?"

Laker put down his glass. "Why do you want to know?"

Jenny gave him one of her best smiles and leaned towards him again. It had the desired effect, Laker glanced at her cleavage. "I think I know of someone who might be able to replace Jonathan."

Laker didn't reply. He'd spotted the waiter bringing their desserts. Once the waiter had gone, Laker leaned forward himself and whispered. "Who?"

Picking up her spoon and toying with her panna cotta, Jenny said, "His name's Ian Caxton. He used to work for Sotheby's."

Laker raised his eyebrows in surprise. Ian Caxton, he thought. Wasn't that the guy Northgate wanted to have taken care of? "Used to work for Sotheby's, you say? How's he going to obtain the paintings?"

"He still has colleagues who work at Sotheby's."

"How do you know about Caxton?"

"Jonathan used to talk about him, mostly in a disparaging way. They once worked together in New York. Apparently, Ian's quite an art expert. I can try to speak to him if you want. Then you could at least talk to him, make your own decision."

Laker ignored his tiramisu and took a long drink of his wine. He was pondering Jenny's suggestion. "You say he's an expert?"

Jenny had just placed a small portion of panna cotta into her mouth, so nodded.

"What's his speciality?"

"I don't know. Jonathan didn't say. That's something you could ask him."

"What's he doing now? How does he earn a living?"

"I think he works for himself, buying and selling paintings."

"Is he married?"

"Jonathan mentioned he has a wife and a young son."

Laker smiled and nodded his head. "That's useful," he said, and placed a large piece of tiramisu into his mouth. He knew the chef used his mother's old family recipe and sat back whilst savouring both the taste and texture.

When Laker didn't say any more, Jenny became anxious. She didn't know what else to say.

After a few moments, Laker looked around the room, then leaned forward and whispered, "Okay. If you know this guy, set up a meeting… at my house."

Jenny smiled, but, deep down she gave a sigh of relief.

Laker, however, was just staring at her. He wondered whether this attractive woman was leading him into a trap.

Chapter 77

Detective Inspector Hudson and Chief Inspector Bradshaw sat in Superintendent Robbins's office. It was just after 7am and Hudson had a big smile on his face. Thirty minutes ago, he'd been told a long suspected killer, Frankie Harris, had been arrested. The police had earlier been tipped off that Harris was responsible for the murder of Jonathan Northgate. Harris was also known to have connections with one Bernie Laker.

A warrant for Harris's arrest and search of his home had been issued the previous day. At 2am that night, a team of eight policemen and two policewomen arrived at his Victorian house in Muswell Hill. Although Harris had tried to flee via the back door, he ran straight into three uniformed policemen.

Detective Sergeant Bates had entered through the front door, brandishing the search warrant to an angry and distressed Mrs. Harris. The two policewomen escorted Mrs. Harris into the lounge and sat her down on the settee. The rest of the team began searching the house.

Ten minutes later, Constable Jackson called out, "Sarge… I've found two handguns hidden in the back of a wardrobe."

"So, you're hoping one of these guns was responsible for killing Northgate?" asked the Superintendent. Despite being forced to arrive at his office well outside his usual hours of work, he was pleased to hear about the team's results.

Hudson thought this was a wonderful example of proper policing, so when he replied to the Super, he still had a smirk on his face. "More than hoping, sir. The bullets taken from Northgate's head were shot by a Glock 43X handgun. The two handguns taken from Harris's house were a SIG Sauer P365 and... a Glock 43X... sir! Just waiting for forensics to say whether the bullets match. When we know the result, we'll be interviewing Harris. We've left him stewing in a cell for the time being."

"Well done, Inspector. Keep me informed."

Hudson stood up and proudly said, "Yes, sir."

By ten o'clock the forensics department had delivered the results. There was an exact match.

At 10.30, Hudson and Bates were waiting in the interview room for Harris to arrive from his cell. Harris had already been read his rights, and when he was escorted into the room, he said nothing... and had no intentions of answering any questions... at least until his solicitor arrived.

Hudson smiled as Frankie Harris sat down opposite the two policemen. "Hello, Frankie, good to see you again."

Bates smiled and stared at Frankie, but left the initial questioning to his boss.

"You're in serious trouble this time, Frankie. Caught with a murder weapon in your home. How do you explain that?"

Harris didn't move a muscle. He just gazed nonchalantly back at the policemen.

"A Glock 43X handgun, complete with your fingerprints. Care to explain?"

Harris knew Hudson was trying to trick him. He always wore thin surgical rubber gloves when he carried out his work. Also, both guns were kept clean as a whistle. He remained silent.

"Seems, Sergeant, Frankie here has lost his tongue. Any thoughts as to how we can help him find it?"

"I can think of a few, sir, but they wouldn't be very pleasant."

"Okay, Frankie, serious now. Who paid you to kill Northgate?"

Harris leaned back forcing the front two legs of his chair off the floor. "I'm saying nothing until my solicitor arrives."

Chapter 78

Jenny arranged Ian's meeting with Laker for the following Tuesday evening at 6pm, three evenings since Laker and Jenny had dined at the Murano restaurant.

As Jenny and Ian entered Warwick Mews, Ian could feel the butterflies in his stomach. He was anxious to get his own involvement in the operation over and done with as quickly as possible… and… without any unfortunate consequences. Jenny had explained what was likely to be required of him at their previous meeting. He could handle that… he hoped!

"Are you okay?" asked Jenny, looking at Ian as they walked along the pavement.

"I'd prefer not to be here."

"We can't stop now, Laker will be watching us via his CCTV system."

"I'll be okay as long as we'll only be talking about paintings."

A few moments later, they stood opposite the white-painted front door. On their left, fixed to the brick wall, Ian noticed a large number 5 and a video intercom system. Jenny pressed the button and stood back, staring directly at the camera. They both heard the door click, but it remained closed.

Moments later, a male voice from inside announced, "The door's open."

Jenny stepped forward and turned the handle. After pushing the door fully open, she entered the large hall. Ian followed and closed the door.

Facing them, about three metres away, stood Laker. He had a shotgun in his hands. Both Jenny and Ian were immediately alarmed.

Jenny certainly wasn't expecting this sort of welcome. "Why the gun, Bernie? It's just the two of us, promise."

Laker pointed the gun towards his study. "In there."

Both Jenny and Ian hesitantly stepped into the study. Laker followed behind.

"What's this all about, Bernie?" asked Jenny. She'd never seen Laker like this before.

"Sit down."

They did as they were told, and Laker walked to the other side of his desk and sat down. He laid the gun on the desk directly in front of him. "An associate of mine was arrested yesterday, for the murder of your pal, Northgate. Know anything about it?"

Ian stared ahead, eyes wide open. He wondered what was going on.

Jenny slowly shook her head and wondered why her boss hadn't informed her. "Honestly, Bernie, I haven't got a clue what you're talking about."

Laker stared intensely at Jenny and then at Ian. Both seemed genuinely surprised with his information. "Mmm, okay. Can't be too careful in my line of business."

Both Jenny and Ian started to relax, but neither were comfortable with Laker's outburst... and the gun was still lying on the desk.

"I can leave, if you wish," said Ian, standing up.

"Sit down. I'll tell you when it's time for you to leave."

Ian slowly returned to his seat.

Laker stood up and walked over to stand next to three abstract paintings, hanging on the wall immediately behind Jenny. "Jenny says you're an expert, Mr. Caxton. What can you tell me about these paintings?"

Whilst still seated, Ian turned and looked at the pictures. "Abstract paintings aren't really my forte. My knowledge is more 18th and 19th century. Can I stand up and take a closer look?"

Laker stood back and waved him over.

Ian got up and walked over to the nearest picture. He leaned forward and scrutinised the painting more closely. It showed a small cloaked figure on a speeding white horse, racing across a grass and rock strewn meadow. The rider and horse were set to the right-hand side of the picture and the rider was wearing a blue cloak. The figures were neither dominating nor clearly defined. In the background, and on top of a grassy hill, were two copses of tall trees painted with autumn-coloured leaves. The trunks were depicted as having white bark. "This looks like a Kandinsky painting. It's not one of his best, but it does give an early idea of what his future work would be like. I think it's titled 'The Blue Rider'."

Laker briefly clapped his hands. "Very good, Mr. Caxton. It is indeed 'The Blue Rider', by Wassily Kandinsky. It's the original, painted in 1903."

Ian suddenly realised why he was being shown this painting. He thought he could remember it being sold at Sotheby's London auction when he was still working there.

For the next hour, Ian and Jenny were given a guided tour of other rooms where Laker had paintings on display. Most were either abstracts or expressionist pictures. Easy to copy. Two others were colourful pop art, but one in the lounge was a very pricey Picasso. Ian made a mental note of the ten pictures he'd been shown. He was convinced they'd all been stolen after a Sotheby's auction. He needed to ask Penny to check Sotheby's records.

When they returned to the study, Laker told them to sit down. As he walked back to his own seat, he said, "That's my collection, Mr. Caxton. They're the sort of paintings I would like you to deliver to me from Sotheby's. Can you do that?"

Ian shifted a little in his seat. This, he thought, is where it's going to get more tricky. "I've got a colleague who works there; he'll be able to acquire some similar pictures."

"Good. Jenny's probably told you about the organisation I used to be involved with."

Ian nodded.

"Well that's all finished. What I also need is an excellent copier. Any suggestions?"

"I certainly know two excellent copiers of abstract paintings, but they're both legit. Not sure they'd want to be involved in anything illegal. I'll have to speak to them and let you know."

"Fine. You do that."

"What's this all going to be worth for me? I'm not a charity."

Laker smiled. "Neither am I, Mr. Caxton. You get me a suitable copier and we can then talk about money."

Chapter 79

After the meeting with Laker had ended, Jenny and Ian were anxious to get out of the building as quickly as possible. The shotgun was still sitting on the study desk. Laker wanted Jenny to remain, but she was concerned about this new Laker she hadn't seen before, so made her excuses and left at the same time as Ian.

As they walked along Warwick Mews, Ian told Jenny that, after that experience, he was desperately in need of a drink. Jenny told him the 'Queen's Head' was only two streets away.

When they arrived at the lounge bar, Jenny decided she'd have a glass of cold chardonnay. Ian ordered a pint of best bitter.

After collecting their drinks, Ian pointed to an empty table. Once they'd sat down, he removed his mobile and said, "I need to make some notes of all the paintings we saw."

They both began to think about Laker's collection and were able to recall the titles of all ten pictures and the artist's names. Ian started to draft his list. "I'll send this list to a colleague at Sotheby's to check their records."

When Ian finished writing, he looked across at Jenny and asked, "What do you think's going to happen next? We didn't plan on needing a copier."

"No." Jenny was deep in thought. "He may just be playing for time. My guess is Laker's going to do a lot of thinking. Will he trust you? Will he be satisfied with your answers about how you'll be acquiring the paintings?"

"I didn't believe it myself. I was really out of my depth."

Jenny placed her glass back on the table. "You know, Ian, I'm not convinced Laker's going to carry on. He was certainly hesitant when I first suggested your name. The organisation in Poland has gone, and he must know the police will be watching his every move. That shotgun was a real surprise."

"It certainly wasn't what I was expecting. Being greeted by a host pointing a shotgun at me. I don't mind admitting, I was really scared."

"I've never seen Bernie so nervous... or tense."

"What's this all about Northgate's murderer being arrested? You never mentioned it."

Jenny scowled and picked up her drink. "That's because I didn't know anything about it myself! My boss never said a word."

Ian stared at his own drink and said, "Sorry, Jenny. I know he's your boss, but I've never trusted Hudson. Right from the start I thought I might be used as a scapegoat."

Jenny was quiet for a few moments, then asked, "What did you make of Laker's picture collection?"

"Something really bothers me there. I'm guessing they were all stolen from the rightful owners, most of them after a Sotheby's auction. I need to check that out. The problem is, Northgate hadn't been transferred to London when Laker said he'd acquired 'The Blue Rider', and probably some of the other pictures too. That means someone, before Northgate, was already stealing pictures from Sotheby's!"

Chapter 79

Two days after she and Ian had visited Warwick Mews, Jenny met with her boss in the café at Euston railway station. She gave him a summary of what happened.

Hudson listened intently, and when she'd finished, he pushed his empty tea mug away and leaned forward. "Sounds like Laker's getting a bit panicky. Obviously, us arresting Harris has touched a nerve."

"He told us he'd heard Northgate's murderer had been arrested, and thought I might be involved too. By the way, why didn't you let me know? I wasn't prepared."

"The shock on your face probably convinced Laker you weren't involved and were still on the level."

After a moment, Jenny nodded. That answer seemed to make some sense. "I don't think Laker's going to carry on stealing and copying paintings. The old organisation has been broken up and many people have been arrested. Our best hope is Sotheby's auction records... unless, of course, Frankie Harris decides to implicate him in the murder."

"Harris is being typical Harris. Says nothing... and hides behind his solicitor. We're working hard trying to find sufficient evidence for the CPS to prosecute. All we have at the moment is finding the murder weapon hidden in his wardrobe. No fingerprints... The gun's completely clean."

"Your plan seems to be falling apart, sir. Is there a plan B?"

Hudson looked sternly at Sergeant Archer. Cheeky bugger, he thought. But, deep down, he knew she was correct. He definitely needed a plan B, otherwise both his boss and the Super would be down on him like a ton of bricks! Suddenly, he had an idea. "We're going to raid Laker's home!"

The following morning, just after 6.30am, Warwick Mews was crawling with 12 members of the Met police force. Hudson and Sergeant Bates stood in the porch area of number 5, facing the white-painted door.

Hudson was about to bang on the door when Bates pointed to the video intercom system. Hudson pressed the button and they both stared at the camera.

There was no reply.

Hudson shouted into the mouthpiece and said if Laker didn't open the door, they would break it down.

Still no reply.

Hudson gave it a few more seconds, and then he and Bates stood back. He gave the order to use the battering ram. Two constables stepped forward and smashed the large 'enforcer' into the door. After three thumps, the door crashed into the hallway, activating the burglar alarm. The noise was so loud that neighbours began peering through their bedroom windows.

Despite the deafening noise, Hudson and Bates stepped over the threshold, but then Hudson turned around and shouted, "Someone switch that bloody alarm off."

A uniformed PC pushed past his boss and disappeared into the house. About a minute later, the noise stopped. Eight policemen now searched every room, but Hudson already knew they were too late. The house was empty.

Later that morning, Penny emailed Ian to tell him that all ten pictures on his list had been sold by Sotheby's at different auctions over the past 15 years.

Ian decided to inform Jenny immediately, but as he was in his office and with Emma sitting directly in front of him, he certainly didn't want her to hear his conversation. He picked up his mobile and walked out of the room. Emma was still engrossed on her computer.

As soon as Ian arrived in his garage, he telephoned Jenny's mobile number and told her the details of the message he'd received.

"Thanks, Ian, but it's too late."

"What do you mean? Now you can arrest Laker for receiving stolen goods."

"Laker's scarpered. The team broke into his house early this morning. Laker, his paintings and most of his possessions have gone. We've missed him again."

"What about the murderer? Has he said anything?"

"Nope. Frankie Harris is famous for playing dumb. Other than the gun being found on his premises, we've got nothing more to hold him on. CPS needs more evidence. My guess is he'll be released later today."

Ian pondered on the new situation. "Does that mean I'm no longer required?" he hoped.

"I don't know, Ian. My boss makes that decision."

That wasn't the answer Ian wanted. He needed to get Hudson off his back.

Whilst Ian was still thinking, Jenny's next comment hit him right in the centre of his solar plexus. "Ian, Detective Inspector Hudson is the least of your worries. We don't know if Northgate's one-million-pound bounty offer was ever taken seriously, or if it was, whether it was Frankie Harris, or someone else, who agreed to take on the contract."

Ian couldn't believe what he was hearing. This was a nightmare!

"Ian, please be careful."

Chapter 80

A few minutes later, Ian trudged back towards the house. His mind was in turmoil. He was angry and frightened. Was his life really at risk?

Passing by the bench on the patio, he decided to sit down. Despairingly, he stared across the lawn and wondered how he could get out of this mess. He didn't dare tell Emma; she would be furious and terrified. George may have a solution, but would he be able to establish whether his life was really at risk? The police didn't know for sure, at least that's what they were telling him. Would George have a better idea? Maybe he'd speak to him anyway.

Returning to the house, he found Emma still working on her computer.

Emma looked up. "Ah, there you are. I've been calling you."

"Sorry, Emma. I was in the garage. What did you want?"

Emma pressed some keys on her computer. "I've found this picture online. I wanted to hear your opinion."

Ian leaned over Emma's shoulder to see what she was pointing at. This was no time to be looking at possible pictures to buy. However, he couldn't let Emma know how anxious he was. "What have you found?"

Ian's eyelids suddenly shot up. He was staring at a Picasso painting he'd seen before... at 5 Warwick Mews!

"It must be a copy, Ian, but the article says it's the original. It's being offered for two and a half a million pounds. I've checked other similar Picasso sales, and they've sold for ten million and above. It doesn't make sense."

Still staring at the screen, Ian said slowly, "No it doesn't. Who's the seller?"

"Coleman Gallery in Winchester. I think we should go and see it."

For the first time that day, Ian finally smiled. "So do I."

The following day, Ian and Emma drove to Winchester and parked in Friarsgate car park. According to Ian's mobile, the Coleman Gallery was only a ten-minute walk.

After following the mobile's instructions, they arrived outside the gallery. It was a two-storey, brick-built terraced building with two large ground-floor windows displaying modern art paintings.

Ian was keen to get inside, so eagerly pushed on the entrance door. They both walked into a warm and welcoming atmosphere. Six paintings were exhibited on easels and more were hanging on the surrounding walls.

Emma spotted the Picasso picture on one of the easels. It was strategically placed under a soft and enhancing spotlight. She strolled across to view it more closely.

Meanwhile, Ian had seen another painting he recognised. Standing on an easel, behind the Picasso, was 'The Blue Rider', by Wassily Kandinsky. It was priced at £75,000. He took a closer look and immediately noticed the same minor scratch on the frame that he'd detected before. It was the same picture!

"Good morning, sir, madam. My name's Peter, can I help you?" A portly, middle-aged man in a black-and-white pin-striped suit had joined them. He was smiling as he adjusted his black-rimmed spectacles.

Ian pointed to 'The Blue Rider' picture. "This painting, I think I've seen it before. Have you had it long?"

"The Kandinsky. Lovely example of the man's work. A pioneer of abstract painting in Western art, you know. Funny enough, we've only had this painting on display for two days. I'm very confident it will sell very quickly."

Ian nodded and moved next to Emma. "My wife seems keen on this Picasso."

"It is lovely, isn't it? Many of Picasso's paintings sell for tens of millions of pounds." Peter leaned closer to them and whispered, "Between you and me, I think the owner's mispriced it. If I had two and a half million pounds, I would have snapped it up myself!"

Emma and Ian smiled.

Ian then asked, "Have you got a copy of the provenance?"

"We'll have it in the office, sir. Do you want me to get you a copy?"

"No, I just wondered who the last owner was."

"Well, actually, it's the current owner. We're selling it on his behalf. We've got ten of his pictures in all. This and 'The Blue Rider' are the only ones we've currently got on display."

Ian nodded. "What's your best price for this Picasso?"

Peter looked aghast. "As I said earlier, sir, I think it's underpriced as it is. I'm sure the owner won't want to reduce it any further; it's already a bargain."

Emma was enjoying listening to the conversation. However, she decided to intervene. "It really is a nice picture, Ian."

"Madam's right, sir... and a bargain!"

Ian stared at the painting again, and after a few moments, said, "We're in Winchester for the day. Let me think about it. We'll be back later."

At that, Ian and Emma left the gallery.

Two premises away from the gallery, Emma noticed a coffee shop. She suggested they stop for a drink.

After ordering two cappuccinos, they sat next to a corner table.

Emma was the first to speak. "Are you serious about the Picasso?"

"I would be in normal circumstances. After all, Peter's correct. It's a bargain at that price."

Emma was confused. "I know there's a 'but', coming up."

Ian nodded and said, "It's stolen!"

"What!" exclaimed Emma. She nearly spilt her coffee.

"And so's 'The Blue Rider'."

Emma shook her head. "How do you know?"

"When I went to the Met to collect my painting, I also spoke to Detective Inspector Hudson. The police and Sotheby's have now identified a number of the paintings stolen by Northgate."

"Wow. So, these two were on their list."

Ian nodded. He didn't want to say any more, one half truth was enough.

"What are you going to do now?"

"I need to make a telephone call!"

Chapter 81

Two days after Ian's telephone call to Detective Inspector Hudson, Ian heard his mobile phone ring. He was driving home, having just visited a client near Haslemere. He pressed the green 'answer' sign on the hands-free connection. "Ian Caxton."

"Ian. Hi, Gerry Hudson. I can hear you're in your car. Can you speak?"

"Yes, I'm hands free. I'll slow down."

"I won't talk details over the phone, but just wanted to say a big thanks."

Ian knew about the raid on the Coleman Gallery, the startled staff and the gallery providing the police with a local address for a Mr. Burton, aka, Bernie Laker.

"I'm just relieved it's all over." Or, at least, he hoped it was.

"Ian, I'm in Chobham at the moment. Are you nearby?"

"I'm on the A3. Chobham's about 30 minutes away."

"I'd like us to meet. I've got some news. Know the 'Red Lion' pub? It's on the Chobham to Woking road, the A3406."

"No, but I'll find it."

Forty minutes later, Ian pulled into the pub's car park. It was located at the side of a large brick building. A sign hanging over the entrance was displaying the famous heraldic red lion of Scotland.

It was nearly two o'clock, but as Ian approached the entrance door, he glanced at a notice stating the opening times. The pub was open all day.

The large tavern room was about half full. Most of the customers were occupying tables and eating meals.

"Ian!" a voice called from the bar area.

Ian spotted the detective and walked over. They shook hands.

"Got you a pint of Farmer's Gold. It's a lovely pint," said Hudson, handing Ian his drink.

"Just the one," said Ian, hesitantly. "Remember I'm driving. The police are hot on breathalysing around here."

Hudson smiled. "We don't want that, do we? Come on. Let's sit over there. Those people are just leaving."

Hudson walked briskly to secure the table whilst Ian ambled behind. He sat down next to the detective.

After taking a large gulp of his beer, Hudson said, "Lots of news to tell you, Ian."

Ian nodded.

"Laker, as you know, has been arrested. He's been singing like a bird, trying to buy a lower sentence. He also said that he never took Northgate's bounty seriously. He thought Northgate's outburst was just him letting off steam. He also said Northgate was all hot air and an idiot, anyway."

Ian briefly closed his eyes with relief. He then grinned at Laker's description of Northgate. "At least Laker's judgement of Northgate is sound."

Hudson smiled. "Laker's also given us a few more names involved in the organisation. They're being rounded up as I speak. CPS is likely to prosecute Laker just for receiving stolen goods. They'll probably agree to a lower sentence too."

Ian nodded and then sipped his beer.

"Now, Frankie Harris and Northgate's murder. That's still an ongoing issue. Laker states, categorically, that he didn't employ Harris, or anyone else, to murder Northgate. Meanwhile, Harris is sticking to his original story that the guns found in his wardrobe are neither registered nor owned by him. He's no idea how they got there. His wife affirms Harris was in bed with her on the night that Northgate was murdered."

"Mmm. Tricky."

"Yes. So, if Harris didn't murder Northgate, who did... and why? That's what we're working on now. We're not going to dismiss Harris's possible involvement, not yet. He's still in the frame, but we need a lot more evidence. Any thoughts yourself?"

"Me!?" exclaimed Ian, putting his drink back on the table after nearly dropping it.

"Thought you might know someone from Sotheby's with a grudge. Did Northgate have any enemies there... or in New York?"

Ian took a deep breath and started to think. "I wasn't working at Sotheby's in London when Northgate arrived. The only time I worked with him was in New York. That was a long time ago. I gather, from what you told me earlier, that he was mixed up with some shady characters back then, but honestly, I wasn't aware of anything he was up to when I was there."

"We've asked the New York police for their help. Just waiting for their reply."

There was silence whilst both men sipped their beers. Ian wondered if he was finally off the hook with Detective Hudson. "Are you finished with me now?"

"It would seem so, Ian... unless, of course, it was you who murdered Northgate?"

"Very funny. My only motive with Northgate, as you know, was to see him rotting in prison. I've never owned or even shot a gun in my life."

Hudson gave Ian a teasing smirk. "You could still have arranged it."

Ian was getting angry and anxious. He raised his voice. "Look, for the last time, I had nothing to do with Northgate's murder." He stood up and was about to leave.

"Sit down, Ian… please."

After a moment, Ian reluctantly resumed his seat.

Hudson lowered his own voice. "My philosophy, Ian, is, everyone is guilty until they can prove their innocence!"

"Fortunately, that's not how the law works and you know it. Innocent until the prosecution can establish guilt beyond all reasonable doubt!"

"You watch too many TV dramas."

Ian shook his head and looked away in frustration.

Hudson now spoke in a more friendly tone. "No, Ian, I'm reasonably sure you weren't involved, but somebody killed Northgate… and, guess what? I'm going to be the bloody copper who finally nails Mr. Jonathan Northgate's murderer!"

Chapter 82

Ian was back in his car, driving towards home. He was still angry with Hudson. Why wouldn't the bugger finally let him go? Okay, Hudson had stated he was 'reasonably sure' that he wasn't involved with the murder, but obviously, in Hudson's book, Ian still had to prove conclusively that it wasn't him who had arranged it. How in hell was he going to do that!?

After a few moments, he decided it was time to speak with George. As a former policeman and a colleague of Hudson's, he hoped the private detective might have a realistic suggestion.

Later that afternoon, when Ian had managed to speak to George, they'd agreed to meet in two days' time. George said he had an early morning appointment in Guildford, so he could stop off on his way back to London. Ian suggested he would meet George at Claygate railway station.

"I'll take you to 'The Royal Oak' pub," said Ian. He knew George liked his beer. "It's only a short drive from the station. We can talk there."

Ian arrived in Claygate, but was struggling to find a parking space. Then, whilst driving slowly along The Parade, he noticed a van pulling out from a space opposite the local fish and chip shop. He quickly reversed into the gap. After locking the car, he strode briskly towards the railway line he could see in the distance. George had texted which train he was catching and Ian had checked the timetable. The train was due to arrive at 12.16. He was ten minutes late.

At the end of The Parade, he turned left and saw the red brick station building. He easily spotted George; he was standing on his own next to the entrance. He rushed over and they shook hands.

"Sorry, George. I struggled to find a parking space."

George shrugged his shoulders. "No problem. I've only been here a couple of minutes."

The two men slowly walked back to Ian's car, and a few minutes later, Ian had parked in 'The Royal Oak' car park.

The pub was part of a national chain with little individual character. However, Ian chose it because it was the nearest pub to the station where he could park… and he knew George would like the beer. The bar wasn't very busy, and Ian had no problem being served. He ordered two pints of best bitter.

After they'd sat down and taken sips of their beers, Ian explained his predicament and his latest dealings with Detective Inspector Hudson.

When Ian had finished, George smiled. "Don't worry about Gerry, Ian. He hasn't got any serious evidence against you. It's just his style. Tries to make people feel uncomfortable."

"He certainly achieved that with me. Right from the start his threats angered me, and I've never trusted him. Now I loathe him even more."

George studied Ian and started to smile. "Anyway, I've got much better news for you. The police think they've caught Northgate's murderer!"

"What!?" exclaimed Ian, and then enthusiastically asked, "Who? When was this?"

"The Met spoke to the New York police, and their information was extremely helpful. In short, it appears Northgate arranged for the killing of a prominent US Senator a while back. There's some thought the Senator was Northgate's blackmailer."

Ian raised his eyebrows. "Wow."

"The Senator was known to be mixed up with a nasty group in New York. Prostitution, drugs, murder, people trafficking… you name it, they're involved. They've also got connections in a number of other cities too… including London."

"Ah!" Ian could see where this story was going. "So, this group decided to get their revenge on Northgate."

"Exactly. The New York police also suggested the Met might like to have a chat with a certain Lester Ford, an American living in London. And guess what, Jenny Archer said she'd briefly met him… at Laker's home!"

"What about the guns in Harris's house? How did this Lester Ford manage to hide them there?"

"The police don't know for sure, but their best guess is that Harris agreed to hide them for him. After all, both Harris and Ford are now known to have been in cahoots with Laker."

Ian laughed. "That's really great news, George, so I'm finally off the hook?"

"I thought you'd be pleased."

"Blasted Hudson."

"There's more news too."

"You're kidding! What's the next gem you're going to surprise me with?"

"Recognise the name, Peter Abbott?"

"Abbott? Mmm… I knew a Peter Abbott at Sotheby's. He retired about a year before I left. Didn't know him very well, though."

"Same person. He died about six months ago. In a car crash. Brakes failed."

Ian raised eyebrows again and stared intently at George.

"Sotheby's and the Met both think he was responsible for the theft of pictures from Sotheby's before Northgate came onto the scene in London."

"Next you'll tell me his car crash wasn't an accident. Another reprisal!?"

"Correct. It seems that way. The police aren't sure why Abbott needed to be eliminated, but when his car was checked, most of the brake fluid was missing."

Ian shook his head and wondered how much more ridiculous this could all get. "George, this whole scenario is a million miles away from my real world of art. I was once told, by a much wiser man than me, to never, ever, get involved with either the Mafia… or the police. In just a few weeks, I've not only managed to unintentionally tread on the toes of the police, but found myself entangled with a criminal organisation that might just be as villainous as the Mafia! How stupid is that!?"

George sipped the last of his beer. He could understand Ian's exasperation, but decided not to remind him that it was all due to his own determination to get his revenge on Northgate.

"A few months ago," continued Ian, "I was looking for a new challenge, but ended up putting both my own life, and that of my family's, at risk… all because I wanted to get my reprisal with Northgate. George… I've learned a very big lesson…"

George stood up and interrupted. "Before you tell me what monumental conclusion you've come to, Ian, let me get you another pint. You look, and sound, as though you definitely need one."

Look out for volume 7 in the Ian Caxton Thriller series.
Due to be published in 2026

DISCOVER THE FIRST FIVE VOLUMES OF
THE IAN CAXTON THRILLER SERIES.

'THE OPPORTUNITY'

Ian Caxton is a senior manager at Sotheby's. After successful career moves to Sotheby's branches in New York and Hong Kong, Ian is now based in London and earmarked for the top position. However, following a chance meeting with Andrei, a very rich Russian art dealer based in Monaco, Ian suddenly reassesses all his plans and ambitions. Even his marriage is under threat. The Opportunity charts the tumultuous life and career of Ian Caxton as he navigates the underbelly of the art world, one of serious wealth, heart-stopping adventure and a dark side. The big question is, will Ian take The Opportunity? And if he does, what will the consequences be, not only for him, but also for his wife and colleagues?

'THE CHALLENGE'

The art world is full of pitfalls, mysteries and risk. It is a place where paintings can be bought and sold for millions of pounds. Fortunes can be made... and lost! For those whose ambition is to accumulate wealth beyond their wildest dreams, expert knowledge, confidence, bravery and deep pockets are certainly needed! Ian Caxton is being tested by fake paintings, a financial gamble on the artwork of a black slave, his wife's life-changing news and a series of mysterious emails that suggest he's being watched. More dramatic events, mental conflicts and soul searching decisions. How will Ian cope with all these extra demands?

This is the big question, that is The Challenge.

'THE DECISION'

A worrying letter from a dead colleague, a Gainsborough painting downgraded by the experts, a new partnership opportunity, an unexpected statement from his boss and his wife's announcement of her new ambitions. These are just some of the new challenges we see Ian Caxton having to grapple with this time. The answers and consequences of which lead ultimately to his bold life-changing decision!

In Antigua, Oscar joins up with a new business colleague, but soon discovers a world of fraud, deception and murder. Penny experiences unforeseen changes to her life and Viktor is informed of an amazing surprise.

Another page-turning tale of adventure, intrigue, greed and risk, where millions of pounds routinely change hands. Welcome to the exciting, mysterious and sinister happenings that continue to occur in the art world!

'THE GAMBLE'

Ian Caxton has committed to a major change in his career, but will the gamble prove to be a success? More challenges face Ian and his colleagues as they attempt to unravel new mysteries within the art world. Who painted the valuable pictures of 'Sir Edgar Brookfield' and 'Mademoiselle Chad' and which famous artist is hiding behind the name of 'Madeleine B'? Why does Ian think a prized picture on display at the Musée des Beaux-Arts d'Orléans is a fake!?

Who murdered Millie Hobbie and why is Ian's nemesis, Jonathan Northgate, back in his life?

Another gripping page-turning story of adventures, risks and rewards, where paintings once considered lost are now worth millions of pounds.

'THE RESULT'

When Ian Caxton is offered a 'gift' of a painting worth £25 million, he knows it comes with strings… and he'll also be breaking the law. The result could be a fortune… or a long term in prison.

Viktor sees a chance to help repatriate hidden paintings stolen by the Nazies during the Second World War, but could his honest intentions bring him into conflict with Ian?

Emma is close to unravelling the history of her 'Mademoiselle Chad' painting, worth an estimated £3 million. However, this value can only be realised if she can identify the owner prior to 1889.

Another absorbing page-turning tale involving more risks and rewards, but could 'The Result' be the moment when Ian's successes finally come to an end?